awaken

Graphia and the Graphia logo are trademarks of
Houghton Mifflin Harcourt Publishing Company.

For information about permission to reproduce selections from this book, write to
Permissions, Houghton Mifflin Harcourt Publishing Company,
215 Park Avenue South, New York, New York 10003.

www.hmhco.com

The text of this book is set in Garamond.

The Library of Congress has cataloged the hardcover edition as follows:
Kacvinsky, Katie.
Awaken/written by Katie Kacvinsky.
p.cm
Summary: In the year 2060, when people hardly ever leave the security of their houses and
instead do everything online, Madeline Freeman, the seventeen-year-old daughter of the man
who created the national digital school attended by all citizens, is wooed by a group of
radicals who are trying to get people to "unplug."
[1. Government, Resistance to—Fiction. 2. Science fiction.] I. Title.
PZ7.K116457Aw 2011
[Fic]—dc22
2010007330

ISBN: 978-0-547-37148-1 hardcover
ISBN: 978-0-547-72198-9 paperback

Manufactured in the United States of America
DOC 10 9 8 7 6 5 4

4500474512

For Adam
for everything

May 7, 2060

My mom gave me an old leather-bound journal for my seventeenth birthday. At first the blank pages surprised me, as if the story inside was lost or had slipped out. She explained sometimes the story is supposed to be missing because it's still waiting to be written. Leave it to my mom to give me something from the past to use in the future.

They don't make paper books anymore—it's illegal to chop down real trees. They still grow in some parts of the world, but I've never seen one. Most cities have switched to synthetic trees, and people prefer them to the living ones. Synthetic trees come shipped to your house in any size you want, so you don't have to wait fifteen years for them to grow. Now you shop online and choose your desired size and height, and in days you have a full-grown tree in your yard, cemented into the ground and supported with steel beams anchored into the base. Instant. Simple. No fuss.

Synthetic trees never die. They don't wither in the fall. You don't have a mess of leaves and needles to sweep up. They're fireproof. They don't cause allergies. And they're always perfectly green (constantlygreen .com has the best synthetic tree selection, according to my mom). The leaves can fade a little from the sun, but you just spray-paint them green again. During Halloween, people spray-paint the leaves on their trees yellow, orange, and red. It's the colors leaves used to turn before they fell to the ground. My mom said she can remember seeing the fall colors when she was young. She said it was the most beautiful time of the year. It's hard to imagine anything becoming beautiful as it dies. Then again, it's hard to imagine much that Mom insists used to "be."

When trees were dying off in fires and overharvested, books were the first to go. These days books are downloaded digitally and you can order any book you want to be uploaded into your Bookbag in seconds, which I convert onto my Zipfeed. It reads the words out loud to me on my computer. Simple. Convenient. I know how to read, of course. We learn it in Digital School 2. I still read my chat messages on my phone. But it was proven that audio learning is a faster way to retain information, according to some Ph.D. researchers who studied rats in a cage. By observing rats they figured out the best way for humans to learn. Some politician thought this theory sounded glamorous, so they changed a law that changed the world. That's why I listen to almost all of my books.

I didn't escape the chore of using my eyes to read. Mom still enforces it. She saved all her old novels and stores them in these wooden cabinets with glass doors called bookshelves. Every year she hands down a few of her favorites to me. I have a collection slowly building in my bedroom. I have to admit, I like the look of them. I also like to escape inside their world, tucked behind their colorful spines. It forces me to fully invest my mind into what I'm doing, not just my ears or my eyes. I think barricading them behind glass is a little obsessive, but Mom says the paper in books will yellow if they're exposed to air. Just like the leaves on the trees that couldn't survive in this world. Hey, if you can't acclimate, you disintegrate. I learned that in Digital School 3.

So, you can imagine my surprise when my mom gave me a blank book. I rarely see a book with print in it, and now a blank one— what a waste. No wonder we killed all the trees. And I'm supposed to write in this thing. Longhand. It's this form of writing using ink on paper. It's so slow! It makes me laugh watching people do it in old movies. It hasn't been used in twenty years. We learn it in school, but it's simulated on our flipscreens. Only specialty online stores sell ink pens, but leave it to my mom to invest in this historic item. "Madeline," she told me, "it's good for you to write down your thoughts. It's therapeutic because it forces you to slow down and think about life."

I feel guilty writing on this paper, staining something with words when maybe it's their emptiness, the fact that they're unscathed, that's more interesting than anything I have to say. My life is far from remarkable. Sadly, it's the other extreme. It is predictable. Controlled. Mandated. Paved out for me in a trail I'm forced to follow.

Why should I take the time to write down my thoughts when no one else can even read them? I'm used to millions of people having access to everything about me. I'm used to a fountain of feedback and comments trailing every entry I type, every thought I expose. That makes me feel justified. It shows that people genuinely care about me. It reminds me that I'm real and I exist. Why try to hide it all in a book? Besides, there are no secrets. Sooner or later, the truth always leaks out. That's one thing I've learned in this life.

CHAPTER one

I pulled a sweatshirt over my head, and just as I opened my bedroom door, I was distracted by a red light flashing on my computer. I was running late, but the glow of the light caught my attention and held me in place like a net. I programmed my screen to flash different colors depending on who was calling. I knew red could only mean one person. I sat down and tapped the light with my finger and a single white sentence materialized on the screen.

Are you going to be there tonight?

I read Justin's question and bit my lips together. My mind told me to say no. That answer would please my father. He trained me to squeeze my thoughts through a filter so my decisions came out acceptable and obedient. But lately it was making me feel weak, like my mind wasn't really mine anymore, just a program to manipulate. That's why this time, I was tempted to say yes.

I met Justin two months ago on TutorPage—it's a live chatroom for students to get help on homework assignments. We were both stuck on writing a thesis sentence for our literary analysis paper, a requirement in Digital School 4. Since the tutor was being swarmed with questions and Justin and I had the same problem, we figured

1

it out together. I remember him writing the oddest comment that day. He wrote, "Two brains are better than one." It was strange because you can go through all of DS-4 without even looking at another person, let alone working with someone. One of the perks to a digital life is it forces you to be independent.

Justin and I coordinated to study two days a week together and then he started sending me invites to face-to-face tutor sessions held in downtown Corvallis. When he assured me the groups were small, but could be helpful, I still dreaded the idea of meeting him in public. I'm used to the security of living behind my online profiles and the clip art advertisements I create to define me. I can be whoever I want to be in that world. I can be funny, deep, pensive, eccentric. I can be the best version of myself. Better yet, an exaggeration of the best version of myself. I can make all the right decisions. I can delete my flaws by pressing a button.

In the real world anything can happen. It's like stepping onto an icy surface—you have to adjust your footing or you'll slip and fall. Your movements become rigid and unsure because behind all the fancy gadgets and all that digital armor, you realize you're just flesh and bones.

I stared back at the screen where his words floated patiently and a strange feeling, like a shot of adrenaline, pushed through my blood. I knew I had to meet him tonight. Intuition works closely alongside fate, like they're business partners working together to alter the course of your life.

I spoke my answer out loud and my voice was automatically converted into a digital message.

I decided *maybe* was the best response, just in case I lost my nerve. I hit send and a second later he responded.

Life is too short to say maybe.

I narrowed my eyes at the screen. Why was he pushing this? Why couldn't he let me be noncommittal and leave me alone about it?

Why are you going out of your way to meet me? I asked.

Why are you going out of your way to avoid it?

I've been grounded for a while. I hesitated before I hit send. I'd never opened up to Justin about my personal life. We always kept our relationship safe—bobbing just on the surface.

A while? As in a few weeks? he asked.

I laughed, but it came out sounding flat and humorless. Try two and a half years, I thought. I decided he didn't need to know this detail. It's easy to delete the truth when you live behind your own permanent censor.

Something like that, I said.

What did you do?

I have a rebellious streak.

That's a little vague, he said.

I frowned at the screen. *I'm not going to dish out my life story to an online stranger.*

Then I think it's about time we meet, he said.

I bit my nails when this sentence appeared. I focused on the words. They sounded so simple. But just when I believed something was simple, there was always more lurking underneath.

I'll be there, I said, and hit send before I could change my mind.

I hopped out of the chair, grabbed my soccer cleats, and ran downstairs to the kitchen. Dad glanced at me from the table where he was reading the news on our wall screen. My mom sat next to him, reading a magazine—she insists on having the hard copy, printed on plastic paper. She's the only person I know who complains that computer screens hurt her eyes.

Dad examined the shoes I was holding with disapproval.

"I thought your season was over," he said.

I felt my hands tighten around the shoes and I kept my eyes focused steadily on his. We had the same large, penetrating eyes, the color of swirling gray clouds with flecks of green floating near the pupils. When my dad was angry, his eyes turned as dark as storm clouds just before they erupt into a downpour. He could use his eyes to intimidate, to persuade, or to demand respect. I hadn't mastered those traits; my eyes only seemed to give me away.

"The league goes year-round," Mom pointed out to him.

He leaned back in his chair and crossed his arms over his chest.

"Did we talk about you playing soccer year-round, Maddie? I thought you were just playing fall and winter leagues."

I kept my eyes locked on his. He tried too often to make me duck under his discipline. Baley, our chocolate Lab, wagged her tail next to me and I bent down to scratch her ears.

"The spring league just started," I said. "It's only once a week. I didn't think it was a big deal."

"It's a little expensive," he said.

I tried not to roll my eyes since I knew my dad made more money than ten families would know what to do with, being the director of Digital School, Inc. The curriculum, medium, and content of what I learned—and where and when I learned it—was overseen and instituted by the signature of my father's hand. It was also his power and connections that got me in trouble two and a half years ago and created the constant rift of distrust in our relationship. Half of the time he didn't seem like a father to me, more like security enforcement.

"She's seventeen, Kevin," Mom said. "Didn't we agree to let her socialize more often?" I stared between them and tightened my lips. I hated it when they talked about me like I wasn't standing in the same room, like I'm a piece of clay they have to mold in order to hold a shape.

"I guess you're right," he finally agreed.

I nodded once and thanked him. I raced out the front door and ran down the sidewalk to try and catch the train. The air was warm and the sun was finally making its spring entrance, after a long winter of hibernation. Rays of light peered through the branches above me and painted a splattering of bright and dull colors on the turf grass below. The tower of green leaves crinkled in the breeze as I passed. I met the train just as it pulled to a stop on Hamersley Street. I jumped on and scanned my fingerprint against a tiny screen as the doors beeped shut behind me.

Erin sat by the window in the back of the compartment. She was watching something on her phone and nodding her head to the music floating out of the speakers.

"Hey," I said, and plopped down in the seat next to her. I took my phone out of my pocket to check a message.

"You almost missed the train," she said without looking up. "That's not like you."

I was distracted by a digital advertisement playing on a screen inside the compartment. A middle-aged man dressed in khaki shorts and a white T-shirt promised me I could transform my entire lawn into a colorful flower garden in five easy steps. I watched him roll out a thick carpeting of plastic grass speckled with fake flowers and staple it into the ground.

"Why were you late?" Erin asked.

"My dad wanted to have a little chat," I said.

She smirked and pressed a few buttons on her keypad. "What now?"

I tapped my foot restlessly against the rubber floor mat. "Oh, he just needs reassurance he's in complete control of every facet of my life."

Erin creased her eyebrows and continued to type. "He doesn't trust you to play soccer?" she asked.

I shrugged. "It's unsupervised, it's liberating," I reminded her. "He hates that."

When the train slowed to our stop, we jumped off and crossed the sidewalk to the turf soccer fields. I heard whistling in the distance and Erin and I looked up to see a small school of black birds soaring overhead. Their small inky bodies formed a moving arrow in the sky, like a kite with no strings attached to reel it back down to the ground. Seeing birds in the city was rare, since all the trees and gardens were synthetic, but once in a while they passed through and I always took it as a sign that something exceptional was about to happen.

I looked down at the dark outline of a bird tattooed on the inside of my wrist, where the skin is delicate and the veins are thick. I ran my finger along its outstretched wings and smiled. Every time I looked at my tattoo I was reminded of the person I wanted to be. Someone that's free to move. Someone that's too spirited to be caged in.

Erin and I sat down on the grass to stretch. We were the only two players that showed up early for practice every week.

"So, are you meeting Justin tonight?" she asked me with a grin. I frowned to show her, for the tenth time, it was not a date.

"It's just a study group," I reminded her.

Her phone beeped and she started typing a message. "Do you know what he looks like?"

I shook my head and told her we both used face-free chatting. I never revealed my real picture online. Now that I thought about it, most of my contacts (or friends as some people refer to them) didn't even know what I looked like. They saw cartoons, photographs, and clip art images that illustrated the idea of me.

"We never get personal," I told her. "I don't know anything about him except he has trouble writing thesis statements and conclusion paragraphs. He doesn't even know my real name," I added with a grin.

Erin set her phone down and met my eyes for the first time today. "You created a fake profile for a tutor site? Why bother?"

I shrugged and stretched my legs. "I want privacy," I told her. "My dad's practically a celebrity, but I don't want people to assume just because I'm his daughter I agree with everything he's doing. Besides, I never expected to meet Justin in person. I figured we'd study for a few classes and be done."

She shook her head with amusement. "Does he even know you're a girl?" she asked.

I couldn't help but smile. "I guess we'll find out."

CHAPTER *two*

I found the classroom for the study group and almost stumbled through the door with surprise at seeing students already inside. I naively assumed Justin and I would be the lone attendees. The room itself looked more like a laboratory than a place to study writing. All the walls were stark white and bare, except for a long screen that hung on the front wall. White tables with beige speckling stretched from one side of the room to the other, and brown upholstered chairs were scattered behind them. The floor was a hard beige tile that squeaked against my shoes as I walked in, to my embarrassment. The room smelled like bleach and cleaning products, or maybe the space was used so infrequently, it just smelled brand-new. I sat down in the back corner of the room so I could watch people without drawing attention.

A girl with blond glittery hair turned back to look at me. I met her eyes and offered her a grin but she turned away without saying anything. A boy sat in the other back corner of the room, distracted by something he was watching on his flipscreen. I glanced at him, but he appeared set on ignoring me, so I assumed he wasn't

Justin. The tutor, who looked young, was fussing with the Electric-Board power cords at the front of the room.

Three girls walked in the door and I observed them with fascination. They dropped their flipscreen bags on the front table and said hi to the tutor. He glanced up and asked them how their papers were coming along. Apparently they had done this before. I twisted a strand of hair around my finger anxiously as I noted how much more time these girls put into their appearance than I did. They wore dark makeup, their heavy eye shadow and black eyeliner visible from where I was sitting. They each had glitter highlights, the latest hairstyle trend that all the celebrities were sporting. My mom thought it looked trashy, so I wasn't allowed to get them, but I thought it looked stupid anyway. Why would I want my head to look like a sparkling disco ball? One of the girls had silver hair with gold glitter highlights. Her head was impossible to ignore—it lit up the room like a comet. I also noticed their bright, colorful scarves that matched their coats, their leather wrist warmers, and their shiny flipscreen covers. I looked down at my outfit. I wore my usual jeans and a boring, long-sleeved brown shirt. I didn't mean to look so drab; I just wasn't used to making a public appearance. I did manage to brush my blond straight hair so it fell long and in one even length past my shoulders, almost to my elbows. I looked invisible next to these girls but I've learned there's safety in blending in.

The tutor, who introduced himself as Mike Fisher, announced we'd be starting in a few minutes. I took out my flipscreen and opened it with a sigh. Where was Justin? This was his idea, and now he doesn't show? I frowned and watched the three girls in front of me giggle over something on their phone screens. One of them glanced over her shoulder and caught my eye. She looked me up and down and smirked at my style, or lack thereof. I rolled my eyes and when I heard footsteps, I glanced up. A boy walked in the door—well, hardly a boy since he looked more like a college student. The three girls' heads also shot up, I noticed, and their chatter abruptly stopped.

His tall, athletic frame nearly filled up the doorway. He walked in the room with a spring in his step, as if his body contained an overabundance of energy.

"Justin," the tallest, prettiest one said. I felt my stomach kick at the sound of his name and instinctively set my hands on top of it, wondering what just happened.

"You can sit with us," she said, and motioned to an empty chair next to her. I watched their interaction and was impressed she could be so outspoken. Looking at him only made me want to hide underneath the table. I was expecting he'd be some cyber nerd with challenged writing skills. Not a female lust magnet.

"I'm meeting somebody, but thanks," Justin said. Her face fell for a moment but when he smiled at her, his dimples set deep in his face, she beamed back.

My stomach did another flip and I winced at the sensation. It felt like Justin's presence stole the oxygen in the room. I tend to shrink when people look at me, as if my shoulders are sensitive to stares, but he was oblivious to the attention he was generating. He had on a dark baseball cap, pulled low over his forehead, but I could see tufts of dark brown hair spilling out around the edges. He wore faded jeans and a dark gray T-shirt. It made me feel a little better. Those girls might look like peacocks next to me, but from his apparel he didn't seem to care about fashion either.

He looked around the room and his gaze quickly passed over me. I wasn't surprised. In my brown shirt I looked camouflaged with the other chairs. I watched him and observed his expression change. He slowly looked at each face sitting there as if he thought he was in the wrong room. He waved at the other girl sitting by herself and addressed the guy in the back of the room opposite me as Matt. Then he looked at me, this time full in the face. I felt myself blush, but his look wasn't flirtatious. It was unbelieving, as if I shouldn't be sitting there. I bit my bottom lip and my eyes fell down to my flipscreen.

I kept my eyes on my screen until I heard the chair move next to me and was aware of him sliding into the seat. When I looked over at him, I was met with dark brown eyes that stared straight into mine.

"Hi," I mumbled. It was the standard social greeting so why was he looking at me like I was nuts?

"Alex?" he asked me with disbelief.

"It's Madeline, actually. Alex is just one of my profile names."

He leaned back against the chair and studied me. My eyes flickered to the three girls in the front of the room, blatantly staring at us with their mouths open.

"Madeline," he said finally. I felt my stomach contract again and tried to ignore it. He took his baseball cap off and ran his fingers through a heap of brown messy hair.

"Sorry I'm late. Traffic."

All I could do was stare at him. I felt my face heat up, infuriated he could see it. Meeting people in person makes you vulnerable, which my dad always preaches is a weakness.

"How did you know it was me?" I asked. His eyes took a turn around the room.

"I've seen them all before," he said. "The real world's getting pretty small. I think we're an endangered species." He looked back at me and there was a small grin on his lips, which forced me to stare at them too long.

I jumped when Mike interrupted us to scan our fingerprints. I brushed mine against the small, portable screen he carried, about the size of a cell phone. Justin quickly scanned his finger and turned his attention back to me.

"Just out of curiosity, why do you go by Alex in your profile?"

I lifted my shoulders and kept my eyes on my flipscreen. "I hardly ever use my real name. I like to keep my identity private."

"Why?" he asked me. It was a simple question, but it felt like an attack.

"Does it really matter?" I asked and my voice came out flat. Out of the hundreds of thousands of people I'd met online, I could count on one hand how many I'd met in person. I could make friends around the world without stepping out my front door. But people stretched themselves so thin, they started to lose shape. Online we were all equal. Social status wasn't important. Money and looks and jobs and clothes almost become obsolete. So who cares what my real name is? It's just a label, like a particular brand of person. Who cares who sits behind it when we only meet in waves of space?

Justin pursed his lips together as he thought about my question. "I was expecting a guy, that's all," he said finally.

I noticed his empty hands. "Where's your flipscreen?"

He tapped his index finger against his temple. "It's all in here."

"How are you supposed to do your homework?" I asked with a frown.

He pointed at my computer. "Call me crazy, but I find those things more distracting than helpful. Don't get me wrong, they have their benefits, but if you turned it off once in a while your heart wouldn't stop beating. The world wouldn't cease to exist."

"But *you* would cease to exist," I pointed out, and he answered me with a look that was so intense it made my heart skip.

"Is that really what you think?" he asked.

"I'm not saying I agree with it," I said. "It's just how life is."

He pulled a small notebook and pen out from his back pocket. He uncapped the pen with his teeth and jotted something down on the thin, plastic-based paper. I stared at his hand with fascination. I thought only my ancient-minded mother attempted longhand.

He glanced back at me. "I know. I get a lot of crap, okay?"

"I just didn't think anyone wrote longhand anymore," I said. "Except for my mom, who I swear time-travels back to 2010 every other day to pick up lifestyle habits to live by."

He creased his eyebrows and stared back at me for what I felt like was too long. "This is going to be fun" is all he said.

I frowned at his comment, but before I could ask what he meant, Mike began the study session. Justin distracted every brain cell I had, but I was determined not to let him see that. I raised my hand to ask one of the questions I had highlighted from the assignment.

Before Mike called on me, he smiled and asked me what my name was. I lowered my hand slowly and looked around the classroom, taken aback by this. A stranger had never come right out and asked me my name before. It was invading. He didn't need to know my name. This was just a tutor session. I chewed on my fingernail as I contemplated how to respond. I felt eyes turn to look at me, one set of eyes in particular.

"Why do you want to know my name?" I asked, defensively. Mike smiled, which irritated me even more. Was he enjoying making a spectacle out of me?

"It helps if I can say your name when I call on you, that's all," he pointed out. "It's more personal than saying 'Hey you.'"

"Oh," I said, as I made sense of this obvious logic. It *was* personal, which I wasn't used to.

"Sorry," I said. "My name's Madeline." It felt strange to hear my name out loud. My voice echoed off the walls as if I were speaking into a microphone. I waited for him to glare at me but he just nodded with encouragement.

"Okay, Madeline," he said, and used the ElectricBoard to answer my question for the class. As he spoke, humiliation flooded through my chest for being so rude. I'm used to the luxury of feeling embarrassed in the privacy of my own home. I wanted to explain myself, to remind everybody this was my first public study group, that I wasn't used to being around people. I turned my head to see Justin watching me.

"What?"

"Is this really the first study group you've ever been to?" he asked, keeping his voice low.

"I've been to a lot of study groups," I said.

"Okay, the first real one? Nondigital?"

I nodded and his eyes fell into an unbelieving stare, like I was lying. As if he already knew me that well.

"My parents limit where I can go online," I said quickly. "A lot of sites are blocked from my computer so I had no way to find these groups."

"That's right," he said with a nod. "You're grounded."

"That's right," I added, and gritted my teeth. "Now that we've announced I'm a juvenile delinquent to the entire room, can we please change the subject?"

I turned away but I could still feel his eyes on me as if they weighed down the air between us.

"We have a lot of work to do," he said.

I shot him a confused stare. What does he mean, *we*? The tutor started lecturing again, before I could ask him.

Through the rest of the study group I observed Justin out of the corner of my eye. I noticed a few odd things about him. First, he couldn't sit still. He was either tapping his foot, or drumming his fingertips on the table, or chewing on his pen or his nails. If he wasn't fidgeting, he was doodling in his notebook, as if the information being discussed was below him. He raised his hand once to help explain a question even the tutor was having problems articulating. If he was so smart, what was he doing here?

"You're using the semicolon wrong," he said once, and I shrunk away from him. First, he leaned in way too close to tell me that and I could feel his breath stir my hair. Second, why was he looking over my shoulder? Who was the tutor here?

"I see you bite your nails too," he said another time, and I sat on my hands and tightened my lips.

"So what?" I asked.

"Don't get so defensive. It's not a crime."

"According to my mom it is," I said. I pulled my hands out and frowned at my ragged nail beds. "She tries to force-feed me gum when I do it, but I can't chew gum."

"What?" he asked.

"It's weird. I swallow it right away. This one day, I swallowed four pieces of gum in a single afternoon. I thought I was going to be the first person to die from gum buildup clogging my stomach cavity." I shut my mouth before another word could escape. Why couldn't I be online right now? Definitely would have deleted that one.

Justin stared at me and raised a single eyebrow. I felt my face blush and looked down at my flipscreen to avoid his eyes.

"I think that's the most random thing I've ever heard," he finally said, and his lips turned up at the corners. As if his grin was contagious, I smiled back at him, a genuine smile that I don't think I've worn in months. In that instant I felt something inside of me shift, as though a hollow shell in my chest had cracked open and something warm flooded in. I glanced over at the three girls sitting in front of us. Maybe random is more alluring than glitter this season.

While Mike made his way around the room to answer individual questions, I called Justin out on his own quirky behavior, as he had yet to do a second of work. I leaned toward him, a wave of confidence coming over me.

"So, why are you really here?" I whispered. "You're not paying any attention to this."

He hesitated for a moment and then leaned toward me and fixed his eyes on mine. I could smell the cotton of his T-shirt, or maybe it was his skin, but it was sweet and strong and I inhaled a deep breath. I forgot people carry a scent, an energy that a computer can't transmit.

"I finished this assignment already," he said. "I don't come here for help. I could lead this if I wanted."

"Then why do you come here?" I whispered back.

Justin looked at me as if the answer was obvious. "To be around people. It's one of the only ways I can."

I creased my eyebrows at him and had to make an effort to whisper. "What? Are you nuts?"

He leaned closer. "I think people are nuts to shut themselves inside all day long. We're cutting ourselves off from each other and it's only going to get worse."

I felt goose bumps rise up on my arms. I grinned at him.

"And you think going to study groups and doodling in your notebook is going to change things?"

Justin smiled back, a plotting smile that held uncountable meanings.

"I have a plan," he said.

CHAPTER three

As Mike wrapped up the study session, I turned off my flipscreen and packed it in my bag. Justin slid his notebook back in his pocket and waited for the other students to clear out. The three girls in the front row walked to the door and the tall, confident one looked back at Justin and waved while her friends glared at me, stupefied.

I wouldn't be invited to join Team Sparkle anytime soon. Bummer.

Justin nodded back at the girls, still making no effort to leave. The last two students filed out and I finally stood up and pulled my bag strap over my shoulder.

"It's been interesting," I said. Justin stood up and pushed his chair back. He towered over me and I felt stunted by his height.

"Not a total loss?" he asked me.

I fidgeted with my bag strap. "I did finish the assignment," I offered, as I tried to downplay the ridiculous crush that was forming and how clearly it must be written on my face.

We walked outside in silence and the brisk night air was a relief compared to the stagnant, sterile air in the office building. I wasn't sure how to do the whole "Nice to meet you, keep in touch" kind of thing. Do we shake hands? Bump fists? Do one of those awkward side hugs? Instead of waiting to make a fool out of myself, I took a step toward the train stop but I felt a tug on my sleeve.

"I can give you a ride home," he said.

Justin pointed over his shoulder at a dark sports car and I blinked hard as if I was seeing things.

I stared up at the night sky. "Could this day be any more bizarre?" I asked.

"You've never been in a car?"

"You're looking at me like *I'm* strange. They're practically outlawed."

There's no need for cars these days with all the Amtraks, Zip-Shuttles, light rails, and subways available. They're permitted on some of the existing freeways and residential streets, but I can go days without seeing one. Even my dad thinks owning a car is out of the question; besides, anything that evokes a sense of freedom is banned from our property. Cars should only be used for emergency or law enforcement.

Justin pulled his baseball cap low over his head and studied me, his eyes shaded under the rim. "I guess this is a lot of new experiences in one day. I don't want to overwhelm you," he said, but there was an edge in his voice, like he was daring me.

I walked around the car, parked like an obedient animal waiting to be unleashed, and studied the side body, the tires with their silver sparkling chrome, the sleek glass windows. It was tempting. I ran my hand along the smooth surface of the roof.

"Why do you have a car?" I asked.

He shrugged. "It's a long story."

I crossed my arms over my chest. "I have time."

He gave me a long stare and I returned it. He opened up the passenger door.

"Your parents are probably expecting you home," he stated. Before I could argue, Mike called out to us. He waved from the bottom of the steps and jogged across the street.

"You own a Mustang?" he asked when he met us. He rubbed his hand along the sleek rooftop with fascination, just as I had done. He and Justin started talking makes and models and years and they lost me at "eight-cylinder engine." After a thorough discussion of turbochargers, Mike turned and handed me a business card.

"I wanted to give you this," he said. "Chat me anytime if you have questions." I thanked him and tucked the card in my jeans pocket. He turned and headed down the street and Justin motioned for me to get in.

When I slid inside, the first thing I noticed was the smell, a mixture of leather, plastic, and metal filled the air as if the car had been assembled recently and all its components were still airing out. I ran my hand along the tan leather seat. Justin started the car by pressing a button next to the steering wheel and I jumped in my seat when rap music pounded through the speakers.

"Sorry," he said, and turned down the stereo. "Fasten up, all right?" He pointed over my shoulder to where the seat belt was. I stiffened as his eyes, his lips, his profile, came so close to my own.

He pulled away from the curb and I watched one of his hands turn the steering wheel while the other one shifted gears. I was jealous of the freedom he had at his fingertips. Everything I had ever ridden in was controlled by tracks, contained, predictable. Zip-Shuttles ran off of electric waves and always stayed in their designated lanes. They ran about every five minutes and you could get personal ZipShuttles anytime you wanted. Businesses, like grocery stores and the post office, used them for all of their deliveries. It was so convenient I never imagined traveling another way.

I told Justin where I lived and he shifted gears and kept his eyes on the road.

"So, why did you really invite me to this tutor session?" I asked him.

"I wanted to meet you in person," he said, and his eyes met mine in the darkness of the car. He turned back to look at the road and I studied his profile while I had the chance. I noticed a small dent in the bridge of his nose and the way his jaw curved and framed his face and lips that made my chest heat up every time I let my eyes linger on them. I turned away so I could think clearly.

"What did you mean when you said '*We* have a lot of work to do'?" I asked him.

He shifted gears and we picked up speed. Justin focused straight ahead and I saw his mouth tighten, either out of confusion or hesitation. I decided to elaborate before he could play dumb.

"During the tutor session, when I didn't want to say my name, you said '*We* have a lot of work to do.' Who's *we*?"

"You like to start out complicated," he said.

"What did you think I was going to ask you? What your favorite color is?"

"It's pink," he said with a small grin. He looked over at me and I rolled my eyes. "Okay," he said. "*We* refers to my friends and me." He paused as if he was editing his answer, being careful not to expose too much. "Let's just say, we don't like the way society's headed and we're trying to rub off on people. Motivate a change."

"What do you want to change, exactly?"

He paused before he answered, his eyes on the road. "Basic life as we know it," he said. "Culture, government, the environment, education. Sitting at home all day in front of an electric device mistaking yourself into thinking you're living and experiencing. You think those are really friends you're making?"

I looked out the window and fought the urge to smile. I wanted to say I agreed with him, that deep down I always felt like DS had gone too far, that it was isolating people. But Justin could express his opinions with no consequences, whereas my past mistakes trained me to behave.

"Are you telling me I haven't lived?" I asked. "That's pretty harsh."

"No, it's not," he said, and shifted gears again. "How often have you left your house this week?"

"What does that matter? Just because I stay inside doesn't mean I haven't experienced anything. It's the way people live now."

"Does that mean it's right?" he argued. "To be controlled and spoon-fed knowledge and experiences other people have decided is necessary for you? Computers have turned life into a digital world and people are so wrapped up by the convenience of it all that they don't care they're as plugged in as machines."

A line of ZipShuttles whirred past us and a gust of wind shook the car. "Maybe more people agree with you than you think," I said.

"A lot of people *agree* with me. It's easy to have an opinion. But change only comes when you put your ideas into action." His dark eyes met mine. "Don't you think?"

"Okay, next question. How old are you?"

The corner of his lips turned up.

"You don't look like a teenager," I added.

"What makes you say that?"

"You carry yourself differently. Are you still in DS four?"

He laughed and I watched him closely. His face tightened as he thought about how to answer this. He glanced at the rearview mirror and shook his head.

"No, I'm not in DS four."

"What about college? That takes another two or three years of DS, sometimes longer—"

"I never went."

I creased my eyebrows. That was ridiculous. Digital college was free—I'd never met a person that passed it up. Justin pushed the boundaries of conventional, which, I had to admit, only made him more intriguing.

"Why didn't you go?"

"Let's just say there's only so much of life that can be taught by pushing a bunch of buttons and looking at a screen." He took a fast turn around the corner and I could feel the car accelerate.

"You haven't answered my question."

"First, I have one for you." His eyes focused on the rearview mirror. "Call me paranoid, but do you think we're being followed?"

I turned around to see headlights in the distance.

"This car has been on my tail since we left downtown," he said.

"Unbelievable," I said, and sighed loudly. "He's tracked me before." Justin raised his eyebrows at my casual tone.

"Who's tracked you?"

"My father," I said plainly. "He must have planted a bug on me before I left the house."

"So, this is common for you?" he asked. He shifted gears and I could hear the engine groan when we accelerated.

I watched the car in my sideview mirror. "It's a little control game he likes to play with me."

"This car's going to follow us all the way back to your house?" Justin asked me. His voice sounded more annoyed than shocked.

"Unless you think you can lose him," I joked. He looked over at me and his eyes lit up. A wide smile broke out on his face.

He suddenly turned a sharp corner and we were met by the bright headlights of a train in our path. Justin switched lanes and zigzagged around a caravan of ZipShuttles. He shifted gears and my body flew back against the seat as we gained speed. I glanced over my shoulder to see headlights close behind us. When I looked back at the road, two blinding train headlights headed straight for us and a horn blared so loud it made the car shake. I squeezed my eyes shut and felt my body jerk as Justin swerved out of the lane, dodging the train at the last second. I tried to catch my breath. "We're driving on a main train route," I pointed out.

"Trust me, I know what I'm doing," he said, his voice steady. "Except it's going to be hard to lose this guy if you think you're bugged."

I nodded and grabbed the flipscreen out of my bag like he just gave me an order. I turned it on and tried to type but the car was swerving so much I could barely keep my fingers on the keys.

"What are you doing?" he asked over the noise of a train shooting past us.

I pointed at the screen like it was obvious. "Trying to find the bug," I said.

He drove onto an emergency vehicle lane and red and blue lights snapped on. A piercing siren blared to warn pedestrians to get out of the way. Blinking lights rotated dizzyingly and my heart raced as we flew past groups of people, frozen in place and staring with shock at a car using the emergency lane like a highway.

"Why does your dad track you?" Justin demanded over the wail of the sirens.

"We have a trust issue," I shouted back, as if every father/daughter relationship involves spies and tracking devices. When I found the site I was looking for, I ran a search to detect the signal. My computer scanned the space of Justin's car and in a few seconds, a signal was located. I wrinkled my eyebrows at the screen to discover the bug was in . . . my hair?

I ran my fingers through my hair, which fell long and straight. There was nothing in it. Then it all came together, why Mike ran out to talk to us tonight and why he slid his hand along the roof of the car.

"Huh," I muttered to myself. I opened the window and stretched my arm over the roof until I felt the bug latched to the cold, metal surface. Justin watched me as I pulled my hand back and held out a thin, magnetic chip, about the size of a quarter.

"I think this bug needs to catch a train headed straight for Canada," I said, picturing the heated look on my father's face when he discovered I was fleeing the country. Justin smirked and guessed my thoughts.

"That might not help your trust issues," he pointed out as we swerved down the road. The car bounced and dipped between train tracks and I held on to the dashboard to steady myself. I looked back and the car behind us was still gaining ground. Justin pointed to a grab handle above my window.

"Hold on to that," he said quickly. I grabbed the handle and braced myself. He swerved over two lanes, nearly sideswiping a ZipShuttle. The other car followed and was right behind us again. He whipped the steering wheel and we spun off the road, the tires screeching and kicking up dust, just as a train flew by, blocking off the other car. He hit the brakes and the car squealed to a stop at the edge of the railway. Justin's arm was stretched out in front of me to hold me back in case I flew forward. He dropped his arm and just as I was about to take a breath of relief, another train sped toward us. I squeezed my eyes shut and swore under my breath. Justin accelerated over the curb onto the turf, speeding over the plastic grass landscape, barely missing the train as it pummeled by. The sports car jostled over bumps in the ground and we swerved around a scattering of plastic trees and shrubs.

"This is the scenic portion of the drive," he said, and I laughed out loud, finally opening my eyes.

"It's thoughtful of you."

We drove over the turf until we reached the next intersection and turned toward a tunnel heading downtown to the international station. I looked over my shoulder, but I didn't see headlights behind us. We entered the tunnel—lit above and around us with colorful advertisements moving on digital screens. It felt like we were flying through a cocoon of lights.

"I'm twenty," Justin said.

"What?" I shouted over the noise of traffic. I winced when a train blew past us, only inches from the side of the car. The tunnel opened up to expose a valley below, lit up with a thousand city lights. We turned a corner and sped down the hill, alongside the international train tracks.

"You asked me how old I was," he repeated. "I'm twenty."

I smiled and wondered what my dad would do if he knew I was in a car with a twenty-year-old DS dropout.

A train slowed down next to us with yellow lights illuminating the words *British Columbia* on its side. I threw the chip out the window and its magnetic surface stuck to the side.

We turned off the train route and headed back onto the residential streets. As we were getting close to my house, I stared out the window, wondering what to say to Justin. How do you thank someone for giving you a ride home and apologize for the inconvenient, near-death car chase? I glanced at him out of the corner of my eye but he just focused on the road, his jaw tight and his face thoughtful. We turned onto my street and I asked him to pull over.

"This is fine," I said.

"Which house is yours?"

"It's right up the street." I pointed to my house in the distance, which was hard to miss since it took up most of the block. "I'll get out here."

Justin pulled to the side of the road and when the car was still, he turned and stared at me. Everything was suddenly quiet and the space inside the car was too small. I felt trapped, like too much energy was circulating between us. My heart was still hammering against my ribs. Justin dropped his hands from the steering wheel. He looked surprisingly calm considering the last twenty minutes.

"Where did you learn to drive like that?" I asked.

"Where did you learn how to trace a bug that fast?" he asked me.

I shrugged. I had forgotten all about that. "It's easy."

"Easy?" He waited for me to explain. I raised my hands up in the air like it was no big deal.

"Those tags run on the electromagnetic spectrum—they use radio frequencies. So I found a program that can detect low or medium frequencies and I scanned a five-foot area. It picked up the signal."

His eyebrows flattened with disbelief. "And that's everyday knowledge to you?"

I smiled as his question sunk in. "Wow," I said. I slapped my hand over my forehead and leaned back in the seat. "I'm such a dork."

He didn't say anything. He didn't smile. His dark eyes stayed on mine, wide and surprised and it finally hit me what he was thinking. What kind of normal person is bugged and followed for going to a study group? What kind of teenage girl knows how to detect a tracker? He must think I'm either clinically insane or an escaped convict. I pulled my bag off the floor and tried to pretend like this wasn't the most humiliating moment of my life.

"Sorry," I mumbled.

"What are you sorry for?" he asked.

I hung my head. "Look, my life, like you might have noticed, is a little dysfunctional. So I won't feel bad if I don't hear from you again," I said, and avoided his eyes as I opened the car door. "Thanks for the ride." I slammed the door shut before he could respond. A couple seconds later I heard his car accelerate past me, but I refused to look up. I walked over the turf grass toward the front door and longed to hide inside the safe walls of my digital world where I could always appear perfect.

When I walked in the door, Baley bounded into the foyer to meet me. I squatted down and she threw her paws on my shoulders and slobbered my neck with kisses. At least someone loved me unconditionally. I heard my dad yell my name from down the hall and my face fell. His voice echoed against the high white walls and along the cold laminate floor. I followed his voice to his office, with Baley trailing behind me. He looked up from his computer when I walked in and motioned for me to sit down. I slumped into the brown leather chair across from his desk and awaited my interrogation. I glanced around the room; every inch of wall space was cluttered with certificates, plaques, and awards. Something came in the mail weekly to commemorate my dad on his honorable academic achievements and efforts to improve the education system. He moved his flipscreen aside and looked at me with a heavy stare. The glare of distrust in his eyes made my heart shrink in my chest.

"How was the study group?" he asked.

I babbled an automated reply he would accept. The tutor was great . . . he answered all my questions . . . I finished the assignment. The only thing that made my dad react is when I told him I was surprised by the attendance.

"What do you mean by that?" he asked.

"I was surprised with the turnout. There were—"

"Six other students there," he finished for me. "Seven people including Mike Fisher, the teacher. He told me you were sitting with a boy you seemed to know pretty well."

I stared back at him and my eyes narrowed. Of course he could check the attendance online. Of course he knew every tutor in the city, in the country for that matter. But that isn't what hurt the most.

"You didn't trust me."

My dad looked down at his hands. He interlocked his long, pale fingers.

"Madeline, I'm trying."

I shook my head with defiance. "You're *trying?* Is that what you call using Mike to plant a bug on me? Was he the same guy following us, or did you hire the police to do that?"

A mocking smile filled his face. "I see you caught on to that. And I'm happy you changed your mind about going to Canada." His eyes softened and he took a deep breath. "I'm sorry, but someone needs to look out for you."

I had to clench my teeth to keep from arguing. I pressed my fingers into the armrests until they made indentions in the leather.

"Your mother is the one that convinced me to let you go tonight. So you can thank her. I'm more concerned about this boy you met, Justin Solvi? How do you know him?"

I imagined he had already searched every file available on Justin's background.

"I met him at an online tutor session. It's no big deal."

His eyes were unconvinced and his silence meant he wanted a further explanation.

"I took a lot of writing courses this year and you know it's not my best subject. So, Justin recommended I go to a study group downtown. That's it."

As my father studied my appearance, I was grateful for the first time tonight that I looked so drab. I obviously didn't go out of my way to impress anyone. And I was telling the truth. Even if my dad read every online chat between us, which he probably had, Justin and I had only been studying acquaintances. I didn't have to admit he was also the most beautiful person I'd ever been in contact with.

My dad leaned forward in his chair and watched me carefully.

"I don't think you should see him again," he said, in a tone that meant this wasn't open for debate. "He isn't a good influence."

I glared back at him. "It was just a study session," I said. "And believe me, I doubt I'll ever hear from him again." My dad's shoulders finally settled and he leaned back in his chair.

"As far as I can see you're telling the truth."

My eyes pleaded with him. "Dad, we can't keep doing this. You need to forgive me."

He shook his head and stared down at his hands.

"It's going to take time," he said, and his eyes met mine. "You broke the law, Maddie. You stole from me and sold my computer files to a group of digital school protesters," he said, as if he had to remind me why I was on probation.

I groaned up at the ceiling. "I didn't sell anything. They offered me money but I didn't take it."

"I don't care about the money. It's your character that worries me."

"*My* character? Do you know what you've created?" I sat up in my chair and met his eyes. "You've turned my life into a computer program. People aren't robots; we're not a bunch of machines for you to operate."

He shook his head. "Go to your room, Madeline."

He always did this. As soon as I was brave enough to voice my thoughts, he always silenced me.

"You're not saving lives, Dad. You can't save lives when no one's really living anymore."

My dad stood up. "That's enough. I said go to your room."

I jumped up and stomped out of the office. I pounded up the stairs and it took every ounce of restraint I had to keep from slamming my bedroom door shut. I dropped onto my bed and pointed my finger at the wall stereo. The sensor recognized my fingerprint and I scrolled down a list of songs until I found the playlist I wanted. I closed my eyes and took a deep breath as acoustic music filled the room. The guitar chords slowly defused the memory of my dad's eyes, his ridicule and doubt. I let myself escape from my dismal world into a lighter one.

I grabbed my brush pen off the nightstand and turned on the ceiling canvas above my bed. The laser from the end of my brush pen painted the blank screen with color. I drew a picture of the birds I saw earlier in the day; I wanted to hold on to the image of the arrow they made in the sky. I drew words above the picture, words that were echoing through my mind like a prayer: *Please Don't Be Short-term to Me.* Then I realized I wasn't thinking about the birds.

I stared at the words and my mind traveled to Justin. I wondered where he was, what he was doing. Did he live alone? Did he have roommates? Did he have a girlfriend? I dropped my pen and grabbed a pillow to smother over my face.

Stupid, stupid Madeline. He's way out of your league.

CHAPTER four

Even though digital school is year-round, it's still customary to take weekends off. Saturday morning I lazily watched the weather channel on our kitchen wall screen and ate my routine breakfast of a protein bar and vita-float.

"Do you have any plans tonight?" Mom asked when she walked into the room.

I popped a piece of the granola bar in my mouth. "There's a book talk in New York I might go to. Or, a friend of mine's a film editor in Australia and his movie debuts tonight, so I might catch that." I swallowed the bar down with a mouthful of the orange float and felt Baley's wet nose nudge my leg. She sat at attention next to the table, her eyes fixed on my breakfast.

Mom poured a cup of coffee and sat down next to me at the table.

"You kids have so many options these days. Don't you ever feel overwhelmed in that cyberworld?" I didn't answer her because this wasn't a question. It was more like an opinion she felt obligated to voice on a daily basis. Sometimes I wondered how she and my dad could stand being in the same room together, let alone

31

be married. While my dad was trying to digitalize all of civilization, my mom was equally determined to humanize it.

"Your father had to go out of town this morning," she said.

My head automatically perked up at this news. When Dad left town it was as if a strangling collar was unfastened from my neck.

She noticed my reaction and frowned. "He's your father, Madeline, not your prison guard." She shook her head and told me she couldn't help overhearing our conversation last night.

"It wasn't a conversation," I said with a scowl. "Conversations are two-sided, which Dad doesn't seem to understand."

The only person who had ever been on my side was my mom. She believed digital school had gone too far. That it was an institution. But she also loved my dad and respected his vision to make the world a safer place.

"I wish he could let it go," I said. "I'm never going to steal from him again. I promise."

She nodded. "I know."

My mom and I had gone over my Rebellion a thousand times. When I was fifteen years old, I met of group of people online who were planning a protest against digital school. They wanted the confidential coordinates for all the radio towers in the country used to distribute the digital school signal. These files were only accessible to a handful of people, my father, obviously, being one of them.

I used the computer in his office to hack into his government folders. I still don't know what motivated me to go behind his back. Maybe I was just being rebellious; maybe it was a challenge to see if I could actually access his confidential files. Or maybe, in my gut, I felt like I was missing out on something. I knew there was more to life than a pixelated curtain. There was a wide, expansive world all around me and I was confined to live inside such a narrow one. And I wanted to break free.

I sent the protesters the information, thinking they would use it to contact students and parents to spread a message about fighting digital school. Instead, they used it in an attempt to destroy the radio towers and sabotage the entire digital system. They were caught after blowing up a tower outside of Portland, which provided DS to the entire state of Oregon. Before the protesters could be stopped, coordinates were leaked out and two more towers were bombed in California.

Shortly after the bombings, police tracked the leak to my father's computer. He was investigated for treason and could have gone to jail for what I did. It just so happened that the man in charge of the jurisdiction for the case was Damon Thompson, who is conveniently my dad's best friend. I immediately confessed and they agreed privately on my sentence—three years of probation—lasting until I was eighteen. If I stayed clean until then, my record would be cleared and my father and I would both be free from the repercussions of my Rebellion.

In the meantime, everything I do is censored. Every person I talk to online is tapped, all my websites are monitored. Even my cell phone lines are screened. My dad receives daily reports of every website I use, every person I talk to. It's understood by me, Damon, and my parents that if I ever violate probation, I'll go straight to a detention center for crimes committed against digital school.

My mom's more lenient with me, because she thinks my rebellious side is partly her fault. She's always encouraged me to see the world beyond a screen, the world unplugged, as she likes to call it.

She pressed her hand over mine. "Your father just wants you to realize that no amount of power is worth having when it means hurting the people you love."

I looked at her and raised my eyebrows. "Maybe you should tell him to take his own advice," I said.

My phone rang, interrupting us, and I looked down at the screen to see it was a private number. I answered the call and my heart went into palpitations at the sound of Justin's voice.

"Hey, can you meet up today?" he asked. I couldn't believe it. I spent the entire week accepting the fact I'd never hear from him again. I even deleted his name from my chat list to ease the rejection.

I opened my mouth to answer him but no words came out. I was still in shock that he found my number since I never gave it to him. It wasn't listed either—my dad took care of that one.

"Madeline?" he asked.

I nodded as if he could see me.

"This is Justin," he said.

"Okay," I mumbled.

"Okay, as in yes?" His voice was fast and it had an edge to it, like he was daring me to do something.

"How did you get this number?"

He exhaled a long breath. "Honestly, it wasn't easy. I had to have a friend of mine hack into some server to get it."

I pulled the phone away from my ear and stared at it. For a split second I believed him. But he had to be joking. Before I could ask, he spoke up.

"What are you doing later?" he asked, getting back to the point. I glanced at my mom and she watched me with curiosity. I figured there was no harm in chatting with him online.

"No plans."

"Can we meet at two?"

"I'll be around," I said, and tried to sound indifferent.

Justin hung up without another word. I set my phone down and tried not to smile. I had to restrain myself from jumping out of my seat and pumping the air with my fists.

"Madeline, you're glowing," Mom said.

I stared down at my lap. "No, I'm not."

"Look at you—you're pink all over."

"It must be the vitamins kicking in," I said, and slurped up the last sip of my float.

Her eyes were bright. "Who was that?"

"Justin, the guy from my study group." Her face instantly fell, as if I just referred to Justin as the neighborhood drug dealer.

"Oh, that boy" was all she said.

"First of all," I said, and pointed a finger in the air, "I wouldn't call him a boy. Second of all, Dad doesn't know him, even though he may think he does. And he's not interested in me. It's a purely academic relationship."

My mom rolled her eyes. "Purely academic on a Saturday afternoon, I'm sure."

I looked at the clock and dreaded the impossible idea of preoccupying myself for four hours. I went upstairs, cleaned my room, reorganized my closet, and folded laundry. With still an hour to spare, I changed into a T-shirt and tennis shoes to run in the basement. My parents bought me a running machine for my fifteenth birthday. I'd prefer to jog outside, but it was almost impossible in the city, with trains and shuttles slowing you down at each corner. I run for an hour every day—it's like an addiction. The movement reminds my blood to flow and my lungs to expand. I like the rhythm—the fluid motion it gives me without interruption. It makes me feel like I can outrun my problems, as if they're chasing me. Sometimes I pretend I'm running away.

I took Baley downstairs with me so she could exercise on our PetSpet; it's a running machine for dogs. I switched on the machine for Baley and she trotted along the rotating belt.

I stepped onto the virtual trail, turned on the power, and the belt sped up under my feet and a screen snapped on around me. I scanned through the trail options until I found the ocean scene. It was my favorite run. I turned the speed up and cranked the volume until the sound of the waves beating down on the sand drowned out my thoughts. A cool breeze brushed my skin and I could hear birds far off in the distance.

An hour later, flushed from my workout, I ran upstairs and sat in front of my computer. Baley followed me into the room and lay down next to my feet. I glanced at the clock and my stomach rolled in circles when I saw it was 1:50. I quickly signed in to the profile page Justin contacted me on. I checked my mail; I had over a hundred new messages since I checked it this morning. A dozen new clubs to join, twenty free offers, thirty comments, twenty chat invites, twenty new contacts my computer thought I would get along with. Zero messages from the one person I was craving to talk to. Figures.

I chatted up a few people while I waited for him to log on. A little after 2:00, I heard a low growl rumbling from Baley's throat. Her ears perked up and she bolted for my bedroom window.

"What is it?" I asked her.

"Madeline," my mom yelled from downstairs, "someone's walking up our driveway." There was fear in her voice, as if someone was trying to break into our house. My mouth fell open. Justin was coming over? Nobody ever stops by anymore. Is he demented?

I combed my fingers through my hair, only to remind myself I was still in sweaty workout clothes. Rings of sweat outlined my armpits, and my blue cotton shorts were frayed along the hems. I glared down at my shorts and running shoes, wondering if I could look any more unattractive.

The doorbell rang and Baley went ballistic. She sprinted out of my room, her high-pitched yelps echoing off the walls. I jumped up, practically tripping over my desk chair. I met my mom halfway down the staircase. She looked at the front door like a territorial animal watching a predator in the distance.

"Who is it?" she yelled over Baley's howling. I tried to calm everyone down.

"It's okay, it's Justin."

"Who?" Mom asked.

"Justin!" I shouted. I hurried to the door and curled my fingers around Baley's mouth to quiet her down to a persistent whine. I opened the front door to meet Justin's concerned face.

"Everything okay in there?" he asked.

Baley pawed at the screen and I pulled her back, my patience fading. My mom stood close to my side, her hand pressed against her chest like she was trying to suppress a mild heart attack.

"What are you doing here?" I demanded. "I didn't invite you to come *over*."

"I'm picking up on that," he said. We stared at each other for a few seconds but neither of us made a move. "Since I'm here, are you going to invite me in?"

"No," I said. A flicker of amusement passed over his eyes and my mom quickly stepped in once she caught his tall, stunning appearance in the doorway.

"Maddie, that's no way to welcome a guest," she said with a criticizing stare. "I'm sorry," Mom said, turning to Justin. "We're not used to the doorbell ringing." She nudged me out of the way and opened the door. I held my glare as if he'd just barged into a female locker room.

Justin walked through the door and his soft gray fleece brushed my arm as he passed. I tried to look annoyed, not enamored, by his presence. His dark hair was windblown and it strayed in all directions. His skin was smoother than I remembered, or maybe he'd shaved. He introduced himself to my mom and stretched out a long arm. She shook his hand with a huge smile. I rolled my eyes. My mom turned to mush around good-looking men.

"What ever happened to chatspace?" I asked him.

He stood close enough for me to touch him and the proximity made me lightheaded.

"Why talk online when you can meet in person?" He bent down to pet Baley. I let go of her collar, and she reacted to his attention by offering him a face wash. I stared down at her with a frown. Where was loyalty when you needed it?

"Is it so strange to stop by?" he asked. His eyes fell to my shorts for a few seconds.

"Yes, actually, it is. I'm not really dressed for company unless you came over to train for a marathon." I stretched my arms out, showing off my athletic gear while my mom informed him I was training for my second DS marathon. Justin stood up and raised his eyebrows like he was impressed, which I just found embarrassing. I hated being the center of attention.

"Good to know," he said, like he was filing this information away.

I put my hands on my hips. "What do you want to do?" I asked him.

"Do you drink coffee?" he asked.

I stared at him, confused. "You came all the way over here for coffee?" I asked, and glanced toward the kitchen. "I guess we can make some."

Justin returned my confused stare and shook his head. "No, I mean do you want to *go out* for coffee?"

"Go out?" I looked at my mom for approval and she took her eyes off Justin long enough to nod at me.

"I need to shower first," I told him.

He shrugged and stuck his hands in his pockets. "I can wait."

My mom was only too happy to keep him company. She treated him like long-lost family and wrapped her arm around his, guiding him to the kitchen. I ran upstairs and took a shower in record speed. I lathered my skin with lotion my mom bought me that smelled sweet and floral. I hardly ever used it but for some reason, now felt like the right time. I threw on a pair of jeans and a blue long-sleeved shirt and pulled a comb through my hair until it was straight and smooth. I grabbed a green jacket and quickly glanced in the mirror only to see a flushed, exhilarated face. For a moment I didn't even recognize myself. The girl staring back at me looked more alive than I'd ever seen before. My eyes were bright and my skin was glowing.

I hurried downstairs to find Justin at the kitchen table, still petting Baley and looking relaxed, as if we'd spent dozens of Saturdays this way. He looked over at me when I walked in.

"Maddie," my mom said, "did you know Justin works for Pacific Electric Company? He even owns a car, for emergency calls around the state." She grinned back at him. "Very impressive."

I gave Justin a skeptical look and he returned it with a careful smile.

"No, we never talked about that," I said. He stood up and asked if I was ready to go. I nodded and said goodbye to my mom, who was grinning widely from entertaining our first houseguest in years.

We walked out into the cool spring air. Small puddles gathered on the sidewalk and a light mist fell beneath a foggy sky. I fell into step beside Justin and zipped my coat up against the drizzling rain. He walked fast and had long strides, but so did I, so I matched his pace. The plastic leaves rustled.

I informed Justin this was my first real coffee shop experience. He frowned. "Are you serious?" he asked.

"You can make coffee at home," I said defensively. "What's the point of going out for it?"

"I don't know, to be social?"

"I interact with people," I pointed out, annoyed that he was criticizing my social life, which was normal as far as I was concerned.

We hopped on the south train line and when we sat down, I contemplated the word *social.* I met my contacts at virtual coffee shops all the time and we chatted for hours. I was in two coffee shop book clubs. Most of the programs came with prearranged questions that we answered back and forth, so there were never any awkward silences. Wall screens projected a 3-D image, so it looked like people were sitting in the same room as me. I could hear their voices. Wasn't that socializing?

Justin drilled me with questions about my parents during the train ride. He wanted to know how long they had been married, if I got along with them, what my brother was like, if we had always lived in Corvallis. He seemed intrigued by my life, but I felt like my responses were so ordinary. My older brother, Joe, worked at a computer software company in Los Angeles. He left home when he was eighteen to start an internship while he took college engineering courses. I hardly ever saw him. My parents had been married twenty-five years and gave me anything I could ever want. We had a fenced-in yard, a dog, a three-story home with gray siding, and a solar-panel roof. A snapshot of the perfect life.

"Do you live with your parents?" I asked. Justin shook his head and I mentally sorted out a heap of questions I had building. I sat back in the train seat and studied him like he was something abstract I was trying to critique, like if I studied him long enough I'd see something most people overlooked.

"Do you have roommates?" I asked.

"No," he answered, a little too quickly. He stood up as the train slowed to our stop and I felt a small smile creep onto my face. He could fire personal questions at me, but when they were turned back on him, he closed up. We jumped down from the steps but before we went inside the coffee shop, he turned to look at me.

"Madeline, I want you to meet a few of my friends before I leave town."

The way he said it hinted it wouldn't be a short trip.

"Are you leaving for work?" I asked.

He took a deep breath and hesitated. "You could say that."

"Where are you going?" I pressed.

He stopped outside the coffee shop entrance and I almost ran into him since my mind was still contemplating what he wasn't saying. A chime jingled when the front door opened and an older couple walked down the stairs with coffee cups in their hands. Justin moved over to let them pass and had to grab me as well, since my feet were stuck to the ground as I analyzed the flicker of reluctance I saw in his eyes.

"Can we talk about this later?" he asked.

"Why can't you answer a simple question?"

He frowned at my stubbornness. "It isn't simple."

"It isn't simple to tell me where you're going? And I know you don't work for an electric company. That's almost funny."

His eyes softened a little. He looked amused by my persistence, as if he wasn't used to being questioned by people. "I don't exactly live here," he finally said.

I waited a few seconds for him to continue but I could see I'd have to pull the words out of him.

"Where do you live?"

"Everywhere," he said, and looked away. "And nowhere."

Two girls passed us and climbed the stairs to the entrance. I glanced over at them just as one girl gave Justin a double take, but he didn't notice the girls. When I looked back at him, his eyes were studying me.

"You know, you're not the only one with a dysfunctional life," he said. There was a hint of a smile on his face but it didn't reach his eyes.

I looked inside the coffee shop window. "Who are you introducing me to?" I asked.

He listed off a handful of names. Jake who he stayed with when he was in town, Riley, his cousin Pat, his friends Scott and Molly. "Clare might be here. She's really cool. I think you'll like her."

I felt a tinge of jealousy spring up at the added mention of Clare being really cool and wanted to kick myself the moment I felt it. I followed him inside a café crammed full of people. A line curved around the front counter, and groups of people sat at high tables, on leather couches, and on stools around the coffee bar. Some people stood and mingled in groups. It was overwhelming to see and feel the presence of so many people packed together. I instinctively moved closer to Justin's side. He grabbed my arm and pulled me through a group of teenagers standing in a circle. I rigidly stepped around them, trying not to touch people, which was almost impossible.

"Is it always this busy?" I asked him, shouting over the noise. He nodded.

"It's the only coffee shop in town," he said. While we passed people I noticed how everyone seemed to recognize Justin. He stopped several times to shake hands and meet a high-five sailing through the air. Someone shouted to him over the crowd and I turned and recognized the barista, who gave him a swooping wave. She was the same girl from my tutor session that had kindly offered him a seat. Justin was right, the real world was pretty small. I watched him smile easily at her and I wished he'd acknowledge me like that. He usually looked at me like I was nuts or frustrating, or both.

Background music filtered through the air from ceiling speakers, but you could barely hear it over the buzz of conversation.

The noise, the people, the body heat, made my heart speed up. I was tempted to grab Justin's hand, afraid if I lost him I'd get swallowed in the crowd.

I stared at the landscape of people. "I can see why you like it here," I told him. He leaned down so he could hear me and his hair fell over his forehead, which I noticed, and his lips came dangerously close to my touch radar, which I really noticed.

Almost everyone we passed was talking and laughing, but a few people studied or stared into flipscreens. Some people wore MindReaders.

I nudged Justin's arm. "What do you think of those?" I asked, and nodded at someone wearing a MindReader. He looked over and shrugged.

"Is it really necessary to wear a headband that translates your thoughts onto a screen?" he asked.

"It's convenient."

"Yeah, because having to use your voice to communicate is such a nuisance."

He scanned the room looking for his friends and was sidetracked when he ran into two guys sitting at a table we passed. One was tall and skinny and looked about Justin's age. He had a short crew cut and dark-rimmed glasses. The other man was older; he looked about my father's age and had a thick, dark goatee peppered with gray.

"Justin, good to see you," the younger guy said. He glanced up at me with interest. Justin introduced me to Spencer and his dad, Ray.

"You look familiar," Spencer said. "Have I seen you before?"

"I doubt it," I said.

He leaned forward. "Wait, I've seen you on the news." I shrugged. My mom, dad, and I had been photographed for the news at benefits and public appearances, but no one had ever recognized me before.

Justin nodded. "She's Madeline Freeman," he said. I watched the smiles fade on both of the men's faces. Spencer regarded me coolly and I felt my defenses kick in.

"Well, the heiress of digital school herself," he said flatly.

I held his eyes. "I don't really go by that title," I pointed out.

Ray narrowed his eyes at Justin. "This is an interesting move," he said. Silence stretched out as Ray and Justin studied each other. "I hope you know what you're doing," he added.

Justin surprised me when he lifted his hand and curled his fingers protectively over my shoulder. He told Spencer and Ray he'd be in touch and then dropped his hand to my sleeve and pulled me through the crowd. The slight pressure of his fingers was making my skin burn. It baffled me that the smallest touch from him could alter how fast or slow the blood traveled in my veins and the speed my lungs expanded and contracted.

"Sorry about that," he ducked down to say to me. "They're a little anti–digital school."

I felt my stomach ball up with nerves. What was I doing here? I was standing in the middle of a group of DS protesters, me, the daughter of the enemy. Were all his friends going to treat me like I was an infection?

His eyes met mine and he could see the doubt behind them. "Don't worry, my friends are cool. They want to meet you," he assured me.

Another group of people stopped Justin to talk to him and I stared at a wall displaying shelves of bright, colorful coffee mugs on sale. They were all different sizes and mismatched and original. I stared at them and thought about our kitchen at home where everything matched and had its designated place and all our mugs were white and sterile and plain. I heard once that the things you own define you and I didn't want to be seen that way. I reached my hand out to touch one of the shiny, smooth cups. I wanted to own something that didn't fit in. I wanted something in my life that looked misplaced. It was such a strange feeling, because I'd never craved anything like that before.

I turned to find Justin watching me stand there, transfixed by a display of coffee mugs.

"You okay?" he asked with the trace of a grin.

I dropped my hand from the shiny red mug. "Yeah," I said. "Just thinking."

I followed him into a side room and he nodded to a group of people sitting in the corner. Occupying two tables and a couch were his friends, all eyeing me with interest. I walked toward them and felt like there was a spotlight trailing above my head the entire way.

Justin began the introductions. Jake and Riley sat at one table, Clare and Pat at another, and they all offered me laid-back grins. They dressed as casually as me, Jake in a stocking hat and Riley in a baseball cap and T-shirt. Clare had on a red pea coat and a turquoise flipscreen bag rested on the ground by her feet. She sipped a cup of coffee and her bright blue eyes welcomed me.

I met Scott and Molly, who sat on the plush brown couch in the corner, their fingers interlocked in one another's. Scott nodded at me. He wore glasses with yellow-tinted lenses, one of the latest trends. His hair was black and so thick it looked like fur. Molly eyed me skeptically and offered a grin that didn't reach her eyes.

Justin headed back to the line to get our coffees and Clare pulled up a chair so I could sit next to her. She smiled as I sat down.

"It's so great to meet you," she said.

I blinked back at her without knowing how to respond. I'd never been introduced to this many people all at once and they all watched me as if I was on display.

"Really?" is all I could manage.

"Yeah," she said. "Justin's always building our social circle."

Pat smirked next to her and I glanced over at him. I could see a resemblance to Justin. Pat had the same dimples and mouth as Justin. He also looked tall, his head rising well above ours even though we were sitting down. His eyes were lighter than Justin's, a bright hazel.

Clare asked me what classes I was taking and I was impressed how easy it was for her to start a conversation with a stranger. We discussed digital school while Jake, Riley, and Pat chimed in to make sarcastic comments, mostly directed at Clare. I'd never seen a group of people be at such ease around each other and I felt a pang of jealousy. Not a single one of them was on their phone or staring into a flipscreen. They were listening. Their eyes were absorbing everything. I was starting to understand what Justin meant about being social. The difference between his world and mine was intimacy. Here was a group of people entertained by just being in the presence of each other, not needing their interactions to be orchestrated by an electronic device. This was genuine, like art being created before my eyes. I was seduced and I hadn't even noticed when Justin set my coffee down.

I listened while Pat teased Clare about wanting to get a permanent tattoo. Their easy banter entertained me more than any movie I'd ever watched because this was real, unscripted life happening before my eyes.

"Clare, that fad passed, what, forty years ago?" Pat said.

"That's what people did before semi-tatts came around," Riley added.

"I want a permanent one," she insisted.

"That's stupid," Pat argued. "Your skin will stretch and it will look like graffiti in ten years."

"I don't think my skin will stretch that much in ten years, Pat. I'm over my growth spurt."

Pat raised his eyebrows. "What growth spurt?"

Clare rolled her eyes and looked back at me.

"Oh, the joy of hanging out with good friends."

I felt like I had to defend Clare, as if we were already friends.

"I can see why she wants a permanent one," I said, speaking to all three of them for the first time. Everyone stopped talking and turned to stare at me. Even Scott and Molly. I felt like I was on center stage again. I sensed the gaze of one pair of eyes in particular. Justin was standing against the wall, close to Scott's side. Why did everything I say seem somehow important to these people? I looked between Pat and Clare and shrugged.

"Permanent tattoos are more meaningful. It's more of a commitment," I said.

"I don't see it," Riley said.

"The idea that one thing that will define you, forever, is pretty amazing," I said. "It makes you choose it more carefully."

Pat grinned at me. "Okay, where is your tattoo?"

I instinctively started biting my nails while everyone continued to stare at me.

"What makes you think I have one?" I asked.

"Please tell me it's not on your lower back," Pat added.

"Oh, who doesn't love the tramp stamp?" Jake said.

"Or a butterfly on your foot," Riley chimed in. "That's an original one." I glanced around and felt anger climb up my spine since they were ganging up on me, but I realized by their smiles they were teasing. I pulled back the sleeve of my jacket. Riley, Jake, Pat, and Clare leaned in to study the bird on my wrist.

They all agreed it was a good choice, and Pat surprised me. He reached out and traced his index finger along the outline of the wings. No one had ever touched my tattoo but me. His touch was warm and I could feel my skin heating up underneath it. He smiled at me and took his hand away.

"Cool" is all he said.

Clare leaned in and told me we should hang out sometime.

"I study here all the time," she said, "if you ever want to meet up."

"Yeah," I said, and rubbed my thumb against the rim of the coffee cup. "I don't get out much" is all I said. I didn't know where to begin, how to explain I've been grounded for most of my adolescence.

"Nobody does these days," she said. "That's what needs to change," she told me. I looked at her and something sneaky glowed behind her eyes. She knew something I didn't—something that fit into why I was here today and why Justin was pursuing me.

"What are you doing for Memorial Day?" she asked as we exchanged phone numbers. I sighed, reminded of the event that would take place in two weeks. Every Memorial Day a formal fundraiser, the National Education Benefit, was held downtown. My father was always the guest of honor, as it was a charity event hosted by Digital School, Inc. My parents dragged me to it each spring and I was reminded, every year, of my father's obsessive cult following and how impossible the idea to change his rigid education system would be. During the event there's a five-course dinner followed by a virtual shopping spree and a digital dance contest. The state's wealthiest and most notable highbrow elites are invited (or those willing to pay $1,000 a plate to get on the guest list).

"I have to go to the National Education Benefit," I said.

Clare's eyes narrowed for a moment. "Oh, I've heard about that." She offered a sympathetic frown. "At least it's for charity," she said.

Riley coughed at this and I glanced at him, my intuition flickering. His eyes looked mocking for the briefest moment.

"Maybe you can meet us out afterwards?" she asked.

I nodded but knew it would never happen. The benefit lasted all night and my parents would be busy trying to set me up with

Paul Thompson, the son of their best friends. We dined together every year at the fundraiser and our parents encouraged our relationship to blossom *every* year. I studied Clare, and something in her playful smile gave me hope this year might be different.

I glanced quickly over at Justin and he was leaning down, talking to Scott. Scott nodded and his eyes immediately went to mine. I looked away. My gut told me there was more going on than a casual introduction to his friends. It felt closer to an initiation than a coffee date.

CHAPTER five

Justin and I left the coffee shop and climbed onto the north-bound train. We both took a seat next to the window. He stretched out his long legs across the aisle.

"So, what do you do when you're not in school?" he asked. I blinked back at him.

"You mean for fun?" He nodded and I started listing the social sites I hang out on—TeenZone, Mentropolis, BookTalk, and MovieMainstream.

He interrupted me.

"No, I mean, what do you do when you're not online?"

I narrowed my eyes at him and felt like he was attacking me. But his eyes weren't judgmental. He just looked curious.

"There aren't a whole lot of options," I pointed out. He nodded and waited for me to continue. I told him I worked out.

"On your running machine?" he asked. "That doesn't count, it's still a screen."

"I play soccer," I stated.

He nodded. "Okay, I'll give you that."

I racked my brain to try and think of anything else. I told him I drew on my ceiling canvas.

"Still doesn't count. It's plugged in, right?"

He was grinning and for once I was too annoyed to let his smile tie my stomach into knots. I glared back at him.

"Sorry," he said. "It's just my favorite question to ask people. Because it proves a point. Most people, no matter what they do, are always plugged in. That's the problem."

"What do you do for fun?" I asked. "Interrogate innocent people?"

He ran his hands through his hair to try and calm it down but it just made it stick up even more, like his hair had the same independent energy he did.

"You're looking at it," he said.

I glanced around the compartment. "You ride trains around?"

He nodded and told me he doesn't have time these days, but when he was younger, he spent entire days taking trains wherever they went.

"Haven't you ever jumped on a train for the fun of it?" he asked.

"No," I answered. He stared at me like I was crazy and I returned the look. "You know, you're the anomaly right now. I'm the normal digitalized citizen."

His eyes narrowed like he didn't believe me. Like he could see inside of me. "What's the fun in always knowing where things will take you?"

I frowned at his question. I always knew where my life was headed. Life has a way of mapping itself out for you and that's what you follow.

"What's the fun in getting lost?" I asked. I didn't expect Justin to answer me, but he started rambling. He told me you see the most when you're not looking for anything in particular. He told me when you look too hard for something, you get nearsighted because you only see what you want to see.

"It's like looking through a microscope your whole life," he said. "You miss the whole picture. Sometimes you need to get lost in order to discover anything."

I stared at Justin as he was rattling this off, like it was just everyday words to him. But I wanted to record his words. I wanted to write them on my ceiling canvas and wake up to them every day. Because suddenly I realized everything he was saying were words I'd been waiting to hear.

I looked out the window and the sidewalk blurred past as the train sped north along Third Street, stopping periodically to let people on and off. A metal jungle of office buildings passed us by. I stared up at the giant businesses blocking out the sky. I thought about the people who worked inside of them, people who woke up to computers, worked all day behind them, and came home at the end of the day to their flipscreens or wall screens to live vicariously through a life that was more entertaining than their own. That's what our culture had become, bodies moving mindlessly between digital worlds.

We passed miles of apartment buildings, and the train stopped in front of the Willamette River Park, the largest public park in town. I looked out at a green expanse that seemed misplaced between the sky-rises. Huge plastic trees swayed back and forth. They were beautiful and so real that if you didn't know they were fake you would never doubt it; their form and movement were natural in the wind. It was like most of digital life: it wasn't exactly real but it was such a perfect resemblance people never questioned it.

"You know," Justin said, and nodded toward the window. "You can see all of this online. But that's cheating. No computer program can compare to the physical experience. It's like learning how to play a virtual sports game. You're not really playing anything, against anyone. You're just a spectator. People are becoming spectators of their own lives instead of living them. But the best part is *getting in the game*. That's when it's all worth it." He looked around the inside of the train and then leaned closer to me. "And I love observing people. There aren't many opportunities to do it these days, but trains are one of them."

I glanced at the two other people in our compartment. One man, in his late thirties or early forties, drooped low in his seat at the back of the car. Two large suitcases sat on either side of him. He looked tired and weathered and his glossy eyes stared straight ahead of him. An older man, his face covered in a thick gray beard that fell to his chest, sat at the front of the car. He was mumbling to himself and swaying from side to side like he was following some rhythm no one else could hear.

Justin kept his voice low. "I like trying to figure people out. You know, where they're going, what they're thinking." He nodded at the man with the suitcases. "Like that guy. What do you think his story is?"

I studied his bags on the floor. "It looks like he's traveling," I said without giving it much thought. Justin shook his head.

"I don't think so," he whispered. "Look at the shirt hanging out of his bag. He packed in a hurry. Something impulsive, like he just got in a fight with his girlfriend, grabbed everything he owned, and moved out."

I looked back at the man and saw anger behind the tired gaze of his eyes. He didn't look physically tired, more emotionally drained. "Maybe she was cheating on him."

Justin nodded. "Definitely something heated."

He glanced at the other man in front of the car. "Then, we have chatty Kathy over there," he said. I raised my eyebrows at the old man who was still jabbering on to himself. "What's going on with him?" he asked.

I rolled my eyes. "He's talking to himself. My vote is he's crazy."

He thought about this. "Maybe he's normal and we're the crazy ones. Maybe everyone should talk to themselves. Maybe we're all just afraid of what we'd say."

"Yeah, right," I said. But Justin's words lingered in my mind like they were on repeat. People were programmed to live inside accepted roles. I wondered what life would be like if we always spoke our minds without having to fear the consequences.

The train stopped on Hamersley and we both stepped off and headed down the sidewalk. The daylight was fading and I noticed a change in the air, or maybe the change was internal. In the hours I'd spent with Justin it felt like a tight, confining layer of skin had lifted free. It was a subtle transition, a shift that happened effortlessly, like when the rain stops falling and the clouds silently open up to let the sun run out and play.

"Thanks for introducing me to your friends," I said.

"It wasn't too terrifying?" he asked.

I shrugged. "I see what you mean, about being social," I admitted. I chose my next words carefully because I wasn't used to opening up about my honest feelings.

"Sometimes, online, I feel like we're not really people. We're more like characters." I felt him studying me while I said this. "It's like living inside a reality show all the time. We edit out the scenes so we can appear a certain way. It makes me wonder if I really know anybody."

Justin nodded but he didn't say anything.

"When am I going to hear from you again?" I asked as we turned onto my street.

"That's why I wanted you to meet those guys. They'll be in touch."

I glanced at him. "What if I want to talk to *you*?" I couldn't explain how or why but I felt closer to Justin than to some of my online contacts I'd known for years. He was one of those people who charged the air with an energy you wanted to absorb. Like if you were in his presence long enough, he could rub off on you. And I realized now that being in the raw presence of someone makes you connect on a level that words can never reach.

He stopped walking and turned to look at me. His expression darkened in a way I sometimes saw my father's features change when he wanted to hide his emotions, when he felt like his words could hurt. A trickle of disappointment rose in my chest.

"There's something you need to understand right away," he said, slowly articulating each word. "My life, what I do, is really unpredictable. I'm never anywhere for any length of time.

"You can trust me. I'll always be honest with you. But it's really hard for me to be there for people. It's just the way my life works. The sooner you understand that about me, the better. I contact people when I have a reason to. But that's it."

I felt my own face mirror the intensity in his eyes. I wanted to depend on Justin more than anyone. I needed to.

"But what if I need to get ahold of you?" I asked again.

He shrugged. "You can call Clare," he offered.

"That not what I asked."

Justin's lips tightened and he started walking again. "I have a lot going on in my life, Maddie. More than you can comprehend." He spoke the last sentence slowly.

"Who doesn't?"

"Don't compare me to the majority. It's not the same."

I stared at him. "If your time is so precious, why are you investing it in me? You've been trying to drag me to that study group for weeks, for a class you're not even taking. Why?"

He hesitated for a moment but appeared satisfied with an answer. "Because we all want to get to know you."

Our feet brushed the turf in the front yard and Justin and I both stopped to study my house. For the first time, I was embarrassed to live in a mansion. The design is classic: a three-story colonial home covered in dark gray siding, with black shutters outlining each window. It's easily the largest house in the neighborhood, with six bedrooms and four private balconies. In a house as large as ours, the three of us can live inside all day without even running into each other. Sadly, we're comfortable that way.

I looked back at Justin.

"I get the feeling there's something you're not telling me," I said. He stared back at me and his eyes were dark.

"Maybe there's something you're not telling me."

We stood there, facing each other with our arms crossed over our chests. His eyes pulled at mine and I couldn't look away. But I couldn't tell him the truth. I wasn't allowed to tell anyone what I did when I was fifteen. It was part of my probation terms. My father and I spent months covering my trail to make sure the media never found out the truth, or he could have lost his job. My past was the one thing I needed to keep secret and the one thing Justin seemed determined to pull out of me.

"There's nothing to tell," I said. "I'm like every other kid in this country. I go to digital school so I can eventually go to digital college and someday lead a happy, digital life."

Justin shook his head. "I'm not talking about everyone. I'm talking about you. And I'm getting the impression that's not what you want at all."

"I'm fine with it."

His eyes narrowed with disbelief. "Then why are you grounded? Why does your dad plant bugs on you?"

I opened my mouth to argue but I didn't know how to lie to him. Or maybe, for the first time, I didn't *want* to lie. His eyes locked on mine but before either of us could say anything the front door opened and my mom's head peered outside.

"Madeline, your father's on his way home from the airport." She glanced between us and Justin nodded, taking the hint. His eyes met mine for a brief moment and he told me he'd be in touch. I took a deep breath and headed up the stairs to the front door, silently thanking my mom for her perfect timing.

May 19, 2060

Here's the breakdown of a day in my life: My computer wakes me up every morning. You can program whatever morning greeting you want—mine plays a song it thinks I would like. It never shuts off—it just sleeps when I sleep. We have eight computers in our house: one in the kitchen, living room, basement, and dining room. Another is in my dad's office and he and my mom both have computers in their bedroom, wired to separate wall screens. My dad even has a wall screen in his shower so he can watch the news in the morning. The noise never shuts off.

My mornings begin with class. I attend DS classes for six hours a day and only take a break during lunch for a protein fruit drink and either a Fibermix sandwich or a VeggieTray salad. The same meal every day. Healthy. Convenient. Fast.

Based on grades, it appears school comes naturally to me. I don't even check my scores anymore at the end of the term, but Dad prints them out and calls me into his office to show me the straight As. I used to assume these grades were what everyone achieved, until I got older and took advanced computer classes and realized I'm in the top 97 percentile of my peers. The top 10 percent of DS students are offered *the most competitive internships and highest college-placement classes. The top 5 percent are usually scouted by the major digital universities. I guess being in the top 3 percent is especially unusual but it really doesn't faze me. My dad is pleased to define me with an arbitrary letter based on statistical averages, but I think labeling someone's intelligence with a letter grade isn't a sign of their ability. Earning an A in digital school is more than being smart. It means being obedient. Doing what you're told. Selling out to the system. I show up to class and follow the leader. I earn an A for regurgitating other people's thoughts, not by forming my own.*

When I'm not taking classes, I spend my free time on social sites with all my contacts. My favorite site used to be DS4Dropouts, made up of teenage kids sick of living their lives behind their computer screens. I made most of my contacts through that site, but after my Rebellion, my dad blocked those sites and friends from my computer. But being compliant doesn't suit me for very long—it's like an outfit that I grow out of so fast, I never feel comfortable living inside of it.

Justin's helping me understand why I rebelled against DS when I was younger. It's limiting people. We'll never realize our potential if we always live inside the boundaries of what we fear. Teaching society to be afraid and stay tucked safely behind their locked doors is not the answer to human problems. It only conceals the problem, like a bandage. It doesn't fix it. Giving the problem open air and room to breathe, to mix with other elements, is what helps it heal.

Justin is also reminding me life shouldn't be a law that a few people impose down on you, it should be what people collectively decide is best and grow from there. Digital school should be a choice, not a mandate. We should have alternatives: real schools, digital schools, private schools, small schools, public schools, home schools, alternative schools, schools in airplanes, schools on the sea, I don't care.

I'll never go to the extremes I went to when I was fifteen to change the system. It almost destroyed my family, and I will never willingly cause that pain again. But I know there are quiet ways to rebel. There are tiny seeds to plant. Even small voices can ripple change along.

My father's ideas are becoming my gauge for what not to do. How not to live. What he believes, I suspect. Whatever rule he applies, I quietly write on the top of my list to fight. That is our relationship. Ironically, he inspires me more than anyone because he shows me what I don't want and sometimes that's the only way to discover the things you do want.

I have more online contacts than I can count. I make about one hundred connections a day. I have access to millions of people. I used to think that I had friends in these numbers. But these virtual friends are like stars stretched out in the sky. They're out there, they exist, and I can imagine what they're like, but we'll never meet. We all just co-exist in this vast universe with a length of space between us. For a long time I thought that could be enough for me and I've been programmed to believe people do better alone and apart; DS always preaches that. Distance is healthy; solitude breeds peace. But in the past few weeks, after meeting Justin, I'm reminded of how I used to feel. Of how wrong that mentality is. There's a reason why stars can only exist in the sky—they're just rockets of light traveling through space, so it feels right to admire their form from a distance. People, solid and living and breathing together in the same world, are not meant to be surrounded by that much darkness.

CHAPTER Six

"Hurry up, Madeline!" I heard Mom yell from downstairs. I looked over at Baley, who lay sprawled on my bed, her head resting between her front paws.

"What I wouldn't give to be you right now," I said to her as I dreaded the evening ahead, the annual National Education Benefit. Baley blinked back at me and wagged her tail. I took one last look in the full-length mirror. The worst part about attending the benefit was the formality of the event. Dresses show too much skin for my comfort and heels are the most painful idea of footwear ever invented. Shoes are meant to protect your feet from conditions, not make the conditions worse. My toes already felt squished. I studied myself in the mirror and tried to be optimistic. My green dress, I had to admit, fit well, and the color complemented my eyes. Mom picked out the halter-top design and it clung to my hips, flaring just slightly at my knees. I teased my hair up into a twist, following directions from an online stylist. I put makeup on for the first time in months and my eyes looked magnified, highlighted in black eyeliner and mascara. I walked down the stairs, careful not to twist my ankle in my heels. My mom gasped when she saw me.

"Madeline!" she cried. "You look beautiful."

"I feel like a green bean," I said, because it was easier to make fun of myself than take a compliment.

She beamed and told me to turn around. "That dress fits you perfectly."

I ran my hands over my hips and smiled. "Thanks for picking it out."

"You mean you like it?" she asked hopefully.

"I'd rather be in jeans."

She shook her head. "Maddie, you're a woman," she informed me, as if I was confused on this detail. "It's okay to let people see that once in a while."

I nodded and told her she looked stunning, in an elegant black gown that fell nearly to her feet.

My dad walked into the room in his tuxedo and I glanced at him for a moment with awe. When he wasn't trying to conquer the education system and control my life, when he was caught in moments of just being an ordinary person, he could be breathtaking. His tall, steady presence usually commanded attention. But sometimes, when he wasn't trying to run the world, his eyes lightened and his handsome features relaxed. He looked like a real person, even vulnerable. This only happened when he was truly happy, like tonight, in the privacy of our house as he smiled proudly at his two girls.

We stepped outside and walked to the end of the driveway, where a private ZipLimo was waiting with a security guard at the door. My father always traveled with at least one security guard to his public events, due to all the media buzz his presence generated. When we got inside, the door buzzed closed and my dad's phone rang.

While he was distracted with his call, my mom wrapped her arm around my shoulder.

"You're going to torture Paul tonight with the way you look."

I rolled my eyes. "Paul is so boring."

She sighed at my attitude. "Give him a chance, Maddie. You barely know him."

"You can't get to know him. That would require him having a personality, which he doesn't."

"You shouldn't be so critical of people. He's smart and he's good-looking. And he's tall," she added, which was one point I couldn't argue.

"His personality downplays his looks."

She watched me and lowered her voice to make sure my dad couldn't hear us.

"Have you heard from Justin?" she asked.

I shook my head. "Nope, not since he stopped by," I said with indifference as I picked a ball of fleece off my coat. I spent the first week after having coffee with Justin and his friends expectantly checking my phone, my e-mails, my profiles, my study group chat sites, only to be continually disappointed. The more sites I checked, the more profiles I logged on to, the more times I felt rejected. So, in an effort to save my pummeled self-esteem, I avoided the chatspace he normally found me on.

I tried not to miss him, which just made me miss him more. Without him, part of me went numb. Like I wasn't quite awake in his absence. In my mind, Justin was as temporary as the birds that passed through my life for a brief, exhilarating moment, but continued on because their survival depends on constant movement. My brain had decided to let go of my crush. Now I just had to convince my heart to follow.

"I bet he'd love to see you tonight," Mom said.

"I don't think he does formal events." *Especially ones that support digital school,* I wanted to add.

She admitted she told Dad about my date with Justin. I leaned back on the seat and shook my head.

"It wasn't a date. Would you stop trying to make this a bigger deal than it is?" It was depressing enough that Justin wasn't interested in me. Did I have to spell it out for my mother?

"Well, your father wasn't happy to hear about it," she said under her breath.

I looked out at the dark night sky, broken up between clusters of frozen lights.

"I think I'm old enough to start making decisions for myself," I said.

Our ZipLimo came to a smooth stop in front of the Stratford House, a historic hotel and conference center on the west side of Corvallis. The hotel was a spacious white mansion, with tall Doric columns framing the two-story oak doors; all of the ground-level windows were decorative stained glass. The white marble steps leading up to the doors were dressed in red carpet and roped off in gold ribbon to honor the guests. A concierge greeted us as the doors of our ZipLimo slid open.

"Good evening, Mr. Freeman," he said, recognizing my dad as he stepped out of the car behind the security guard. News cameras were waiting behind the gold ribbon barricade and photographers snapped pictures frantically when they recognized my dad. Reporters fired questions as we stepped onto the velvet carpet in front of the hotel. I squinted as lights flashed and blazed in our direction.

Dad wrapped one of his arms around my mom's waist and he locked his other arm tightly inside mine. We stood and smiled as flashes showered us in a strobe light.

"People are rioting in New Jersey, Kevin. Do you think DS could lose its nationwide support?" one reporter yelled out.

My dad's calm smile never faltered. His hard eyes lost any of the childish light I saw earlier.

"Digital school is stronger than ever," my dad said. "The program is right and it's working." He emphasized the words *right* and *working,* as if his statement was a scientific fact, not an opinion, and his confidence quieted the reporter.

Another reporter took the floor. "A study at DS Berkeley claims eighty-five percent of sixteen-year-olds want the choice of whether to attend digital school. What do you think about that, Mr. Freeman?"

"Every child deserves a safe, free, and quality education. That is what we provide," my dad stated. "When they are eighteen years old, or have met all the graduation requirements, they will be emotionally and mentally ready to opt out of DS. Until then, I will deprive no child of an education."

I listened to my dad with fascination. His answers were always formulaic. He didn't pause to think about the questions, he only listened for key words and plugged in the calculated response he'd scripted for these kinds of events, like an automated recording. Fast. Emotionless. Efficient.

The three of us stood outside for another hour, allowing photographers to snap our pictures and the media to either praise or criticize my father, a scene I had grown accustomed to whenever I was in public with him. When we finally made it inside the labyrinthine lobby, Mom checked our coats and I walked into the huge dining hall, set with over a hundred round tables. Golden chandeliers hung from the ceiling and sprinkled dim yellow lighting around the room. I always loved the grand chandeliers, their long and slender gold arms holding balls of light. We found our table at the head of the room, where it was every year, near the stage where my dad would give his annual speech to highlight another successful year in DS and promise another one yet to come.

Paul and his sister Becky were already sitting at our table. Becky was typing on her phone and Paul yawned as he picked at some cheese and crackers on his plate. I sat down next to him and felt him gaping at me.

"Madeline," he said. I offered Paul a forced smile and told him it was good to see him. He ran his eyes down my dress. "You look really pretty," he said. I winced and thanked him with a smile that felt more like a grimace. His sister glanced up from her phone long enough to catch my reaction.

"That color looks really good on you," he added. I felt my face flush.

"Paul, you might want to wipe that drool off your chin," Becky said, and gave me a sympathetic frown. Paul's parents sat down across from us at the table and my parents sat on the other side of me. I could feel Paul still staring dumbly at me out of the corner of my eye. I sighed to think that the tiniest glimpse from Justin set my heart completely out of rhythm while a glance from Paul made me cringe.

"How's school going, Madeline?" Paul's mom, Meredith Thompson, asked. I was about to answer her when my dad interrupted.

"She's in the ninety-seventh percentile of her class," he said. "Right now she's trying to sift through all the college offers out east."

"Very impressive," Paul's dad, Damon, said. "It helps that she has two role models to look up to." I nodded politely at Damon, who was the city sheriff, my dad's best friend, and my probation officer. He offered to do the latter as a favor to my dad.

A waiter in a black tuxedo set down salads and bread at our table.

Meredith put her hand on Paul's arm. "Paul began his police academy credits last month. He's already shadowing Damon."

Paul grinned in my direction to make sure I was absorbing Meredith's news. I held back a deep sigh. No wonder my dad was encouraging Paul to date me. Just one more set of eyes to keep me in check. I glanced around the room and noticed how quiet the atmosphere was. I watched groups of people, eight per table, picking at their food in silence. Every year I felt like the effort of face-to-face socializing was becoming more awkward for people. I looked over at Becky, who was messaging her contacts. I observed a handful of people at every table peering into their own hand-held, portable lives. It's ironic, I thought, here is life passing, like clouds drifting over the sky, yet they don't see what's right in front of them. They believe there is something more substantial going on in that little screen in their hands.

I looked down at my plate. It wasn't that I felt better than these people. Just out of place.

A voice boomed over the speaker system and I jumped in my seat. On the main stage in front of our table, an older man with a thick head of gray hair combed smoothly back on his head held a microphone and addressed the audience.

"Good evening, everyone, and welcome to the fifteenth annual National Education Benefit."

An energetic applause rang out and I tapped my fingers together.

"To commence this honorary night, please welcome the designer of DS himself, Kevin Freeman."

The applause escalated and soon everyone in the room was on their feet as my dad marched to the podium through a flash of lights. I set my napkin on the table and rose to join the crowd. He shook hands with the announcer and stood, proud as an eagle perched on the highest branch of the tallest tree. He beamed out at his ecstatic supporters.

"Thank you." The crowd slowly settled back down in their

seats. I folded my hands in my lap and stared at my father, preparing myself for the startling statistics he threw out every year to fire up the crowd. When the cheering quieted down my dad continued.

"There's much to celebrate. Please, raise your glasses and toast to the most successful educational program ever initiated in the history of this great country."

The room erupted in whistles and shouts of agreement as everyone raised their glasses in the air. I looked around and felt a chill run through my body to witness so many powerful people who adored my father.

"Digital school is a success," he yelled, and people hollered and cheered in agreement. I exhaled sharply and straightened up in my seat. Did they have to cheer after every sentence?

"Teenage violence is at an all-time low."

Cheers rang out again.

"Teenage shootings and deaths have fallen sixty-seven percent since 2048, when this program was initiated." The audience interrupted my dad with a celebratory roar.

"Teenage recreational drug use has fallen sixty-six percent." Again, he paused for the applause.

"Since the implementation of this program, teenage suicide has fallen forty-five percent. Teenage pregnancy has fallen a staggering ninety-one percent!"

The crowd stood on their feet again and cheered with jubilation. I stood up as well and observed the room and the man standing on the stage in front of me. My dad soaked up the adoration like a sponge before he continued.

"One hundred percent of the children and young adults in this country receive a free education with the free resources necessary to make their lives and this world a better place. Every child and young adult in this country has access to a safe, challenging, secure educational program that is the finest this world has ever offered and will ever offer. American students currently test the highest in the world. This program is working and it will continue to work. Digital school has made education what it's intended to be and America has never been safer for our children."

The standing ovation after his speech took several minutes to dissolve and my dad was swept away by the press to give interviews.

I drummed my fingers on the table, too keyed up to eat my dinner, and looked over at Becky, who was still absorbed in her phone.

"Isn't this party exciting enough for you?" I joked.

She gave me a sly grin. "My friend's at a table on the other side of the room and we're rating who the hot guys are in here." My eyes took a turn around the room and I frowned at the sea of older couples. What hot guys were there to rate?

"What are you up to tomorrow?" Paul suddenly asked. I blinked in surprise and stared into his blue, confident eyes. I studied Paul's face—his smooth, flawless skin and high cheekbones. His thick blond hair was spiked at the top of his head. He was attractive, there was no doubt about it. Then why did I find him so irritating? Was it only because he was safe and predictable? Was it because he was the one boy I could date with my father's approval? What was the challenge in that?

"I have a paper to write," I told him.

"I thought we could go on a chatwalk." He said it as more of a statement than a question.

I chewed on my bottom lip and tried to think of an excuse.

"I just got a program to hike Mount McKinley. Are you up for that?" he asked with a grin, as if his adventurous spontaneity would leave me speechless. I played with the napkin on my lap and stalled.

"It's hard for me to chat at such high altitudes," I finally said.

He laughed at me. "Okay, we could stay closer to sea level. How about a walk along the beach?"

I picked up a piece of bread and chewed a corner of it as I thought this through, trying to find a nice way to say no. In all the years I'd known him, even chatted with him online, he'd never asked me out. I decided to answer him with the one response I knew he'd never expect.

"We could just take a shuttle to the beach and actually walk."

Paul stared at me like I had just suggested dropping out of DS and joining the circus.

"Why would we do that?"

I smiled and shrugged my shoulders.

"It's always raining at the beach," he pointed out. "And it's freezing."

I stared back at his bewildered expression. "Can't you handle a little rain?"

Paul sat up straighter in his seat and lifted his chin. "Of course I can handle it. I just don't think you would like it."

I smiled. "Right, of course."

Paul wrinkled his forehead as he tried to read me. I glanced around the room again and had the feeling that someone other than Paul was watching me. I looked over at my dad instinctively, but he was still buried in a mob of reporters. Then I saw him, standing next to Riley and Jake in the back corner of the room. I felt the air stop in my lungs halfway through a breath. Justin met my eyes and offered me a subtle smile, a smile more cautious than friendly, more intense than lighthearted. I felt like I was melting into my chair. In the two weeks since I'd seen him, I'd forgotten the way his presence was like high-voltage electricity coursing through the room. My mother leaned toward me.

"He's been watching you all night," she whispered between her teeth so Paul couldn't hear her.

I was finally able to drop my eyes. "Why didn't you tell me he was here?"

"Because I wanted you to be able to think straight, Maddie," she said. "That young man has a strange effect on you and your father would have noticed something was up."

Becky caught on to our whispering and looked over to see who we were talking about. She gawked when she realized it was Justin and set her phone down for the first time all night.

"You know him? We just voted him unanimously the hottest guy here."

I grinned at Becky and couldn't help but nod in agreement. In his dark slacks, black dress shirt, and suit jacket, Justin looked like the model celebrity invited to boost the benefit's media coverage.

"Would you both stop staring?" I pleaded, and forced myself to avoid his eyes, eyes that tugged at me with a magnetic force. What was he doing here? Why didn't he warn me he was coming?

Paul looked across the room and smirked. "You know those guys?" he said condescendingly.

"I might."

"You don't want to get mixed up with that crowd," he said. "Especially Justin. His parents were arrested, on more than one occasion."

My mouth dropped open so fast you could practically hear it. "What?"

My mother watched me carefully. I looked at her and stole another glance at Justin. He was facing his friends now, still across the room from us.

"Cool," Becky said, and gushed in his direction.

"Breaking the law is hardly cool, Becky. Grow up," Paul scolded.

"What did they do?" I asked, still looking at Justin. As if he could feel my stare across the room, he turned and his dark eyes met mine again. I quickly looked away.

"I don't know for sure. I think they led a few riots in D.C., back when DS was going national. They served a couple years in prison."

I looked back at Justin. He was talking to Jake and they were both laughing. I never would have guessed he came from a family with that kind of background. And I thought I had a sketchy past.

"Is he dangerous?" Becky asked. She sounded more hopeful than afraid.

Paul shrugged. "People are less concerned with him. I heard he emancipated himself from his parents when he was younger. I think he grew up in a foster home or something. So, I guess if his parents didn't learn, at least he did." Paul's wide eyes met mine. "But he's got a lot of baggage. I don't know how much I'd trust a guy like that."

Interesting, I thought. Justin insisted the one thing I could do was trust him.

I stole one more glance at Justin and found him watching me. He lifted his head and motioned for me to come over.

I picked the napkin off my lap and set it on the table.

My mother looked at me. "Are you sure that's such a good idea?"

"What, to miss the virtual shopping spree?"

She grabbed my hand and her eyes turned serious. "To mingle with that boy. You know it upsets your father."

"He might not mind if he could learn to give people a chance."

"I trust you," she said. "You know *I* do. But I'd get back here before he notices you're gone."

I nodded and looked over at my dad, who was still surrounded by a herd of photographers and reporters. I knew it would be at least another hour before he was done with interviews. I stood up and ignored the disapproval on Paul's face. I walked the length of the room and felt Justin's eyes on me the entire time, which made me feel self-conscious with each step. I tried to act like walking in heels didn't require all my concentration not to trip.

"What are you doing here?" I asked as soon as I was in earshot.

He took a sip from his glass and set it down on the table behind him. "It's nice to see you too," he said.

"I doubt you were invited," I said, and stuck my hand on my hip to pretend I wasn't ecstatic to see him.

He shook his head. "I just love hearing your dad's riveting annual statistics," he told me.

"They are inspiring," I agreed.

"I'm in town for a few days." He looked over my shoulder. Even in my heels he was a head taller than me. "Say hi to Paul Thompson for me," he added.

"Garrlgh," I gagged. The corner of his lips curled up.

"What was that?"

"That was vomit creeping up the back of my mouth when you mentioned Paul's name."

Justin's mouth widened into a full smile and he told me I should speak my mind more often. "You're pretty funny when you do," he said.

I soaked up his face and his eyes like someone soaks up rays of sun after days of rain and cloud cover. I felt starved of him. I glanced back over at my dinner table.

"Paul did invite me on a chatwalk next weekend," I said.

He raised his eyebrows. "I've heard about those. Make sure you right-click on all the billboards you pass. You can win prizes."

I rolled my eyes at his mocking face. If I didn't feel so out of Justin's league, I'd swear he was acting jealous.

"Is that why you're here? To give me a hard time for being forced to endure bad company at a boring formal event?"

He looked across the room and his dark eyes reflected the glow from the chandeliers. His gaze stopped on my dad and his face tightened for an instant.

"I like to be reminded what I'm up against." He looked back at me. "I actually came to get you. Don't you want to get out of here for a while?" Before I could answer him the lights flickered and wide screens on every side of the room rolled down from the ceiling with an electric hum. An automated female voice encouraged everyone to pick up their handsets from the tables (which the wait staff set down after plates were cleared) to join the video shopping spree. The voice reminded us that all money used to purchase items during the shopping spree would be donated to charity. It was strange how much the modern digital screens juxtaposed against the ornate chandeliers and the waiters in old-fashioned tuxedos. It was like two different worlds colliding and people were caught somewhere in between.

"At least it's for a good cause," Justin whispered. I felt myself shudder, either from his voice so close to my ear or the feeling that I needed to escape.

"Didn't you say something about getting out of here?" I asked him and met his eyes. He nodded. "Then what are we waiting for?" I asked. He told me to wait a second and turned to say something to Jake and Riley. I pulled out my phone and voice-messaged my mom as the shopping spree began. I promised her I'd be back to watch the dance competition. I knew my dad would be occupied until then.

"Shouldn't you grab a jacket?" Justin asked me. I shook my head and told him I was fine. I took a final look around the room full of people comfortable now, staring at the warm, glowing digital screen and not at each other, entertained by a virtual shopping spree competition. I followed Justin through the lobby and he held the towering door open for me. I walked through it, into the dark night to meet a world so different from the one I'd always known. As the solid doors closed tightly behind me I didn't feel scared or anxious or worried. Everything settled inside of me, like pieces falling into place.

CHAPTER seven

We walked down the white marble steps of the Stratford House and I breathed my first full breath in hours. The red carpet was empty of media and spectators. I felt like I was standing on a stage after a rehearsal, like tonight was all a show, full of actors performing their roles.

Justin stood on the sidewalk waiting for me while Jake and Riley gained distance ahead of us. I squinted down the street, which looked dark and silent next to the lit-up Stratford House.

"We're walking?" I asked with surprise. I took a few steps toward him.

"It's only a couple blocks." He glanced down at my feet. "Those couldn't be comfortable," he said to my pointy-toed heels.

I stared back at him. It wasn't my shoes I was worried about. The problem was that other than the Stratford House, there wasn't another light on down either side of the street.

"Come on," he said. "No hesitating when you're with me."

He walked close to my side and his presence made my heart pound. I asked him where he was taking me.

"Maddie," he said slowly, as if he was overthinking his words, editing out some and inserting others. "You trust me, don't you?"

I watched him, puzzled, like he had overheard the conversation I had with Paul.

"Of course I do," I said. We continued to walk and turned the corner down a narrow side street. There was a slight mist falling from the sky, so fine it was like walking through a thin cloud.

"What were you and Thompson discussing?" he asked. I sighed, not wanting to mentally go back to the benefit.

"He gave me something to think about."

A small grin played on his lips. "What's that?"

"Let's just say I have a few more questions for you."

Justin suddenly grabbed my arm and we stopped in the middle of the dark, quiet street. I felt my skin tingle where his fingers held on. Sometimes when I was around Justin I couldn't think. All I was capable of was how I felt. It was like sensory overload.

"I have a favor to ask," he said, his eyes fixed on me. He let go of my arm and lifted up his hands and moved them as if conducting his words. "Tonight, I want you to try and forget who you are and who I am and live in the moment. Try not to *think* at all. Just let go."

I stared at him, confused by his words, and nodded. Riley and Jake called our names and I turned to see them standing in front of a deserted building.

"What is this?"

He turned and yelled we'd meet them inside. He looked back at me and grinned with his usual daring eyes.

"You said you'd be open-minded," he said.

I studied the silent, three-story brick building. The white paint along the door was warped and the wood looked like it was rotting. The two windows on the ground level were boarded up.

"You're taking me inside an abandoned building? This is what you guys do for fun on a Friday night?"

"There's this whole other world going on around us," he said, "but most people pretend it isn't there. So we keep it underground. You just need to trust me."

"If it's so safe why is it hidden?" I asked.

"Because most people don't know how to let go. People have closed their minds. They've forgotten how to use their senses, so they feel threatened by people who do."

I nodded because I agreed.

"People like to keep things they don't understand in the dark. It's easier that way. But if you want, I can show you how to find these places," he said.

I looked at the building and back at Justin. "I'm intrigued."

"Come on, life passes you by when you stand around talking about it."

I followed him up the walkway and he opened the door to a long stairwell lit dimly with one overhead light. It smelled musty with age. There was no railing so I automatically wove my arm around Justin's for support. I felt the muscles in his arm tense, but just as quickly he understood and let me lean on him for balance. The stairway led down to another double set of closed doors. I could hear music faintly seeping through the walls. I turned and looked at Justin when we reached the bottom.

"It's a club?" I asked, and he smiled.

"Not so scary, is it?"

He opened the door for me and when I got inside, the energy in the room hit me like a gust of wind. The sight stunned me first because it was the polar opposite from where we had been; the room was full of people, mostly young, sitting around tables, on sofas and barstools, just laughing, talking, *being*. There were no televisions, no computers, no screens, flipscreens, or earpods. I saw real life happening before my eyes.

The sound hit me next. A small stage occupied the far corner of the room and a woman with streaks of gray in her hair sang into a microphone. Her eyes were closed and she moved her hips slowly to the music. She threw her head back and belted lyrics with such a deep, sultry voice I could feel it touch my skin. Three men surrounded her on the stage. A guitar player stood next to her, his face half covered under a brown cap, and his foot tapped to the rhythm. A drummer was perched on her other side, his face hidden behind a thick beard and sunglasses. He smiled out at the crowd. A bass player stood next to the drummer, his head nodding along to the beat.

The sound pulled me closer to the stage. I had heard music all my life. Listened to it, absorbed it. But I'd never seen it so close to me. Performed. Created. I stood, frozen in place as I watched the fingertips of the guitar player wriggle up and down the strings. I could almost feel the chords myself, thick and coarse, running underneath my own fingers. People passed back and forth in front of me and I realized they were moving with the music. Dancing. Their arms were wrapped around each other. Their hands traced each other's hands and waists. I watched with a dull ache growing in my chest. I wanted to be out there, with them. I wanted someone to show me how to move like that. The music encircled my mind like a spell. I felt a hand on my back that snapped me out of my trance.

"What do you think?" Justin leaned his head down to mine so I could hear him over the music and I met his eyes. I wanted him to reach out to me with his other hand. I wanted him to trace his fingers along my waist. Instead, he pulled his hand away and a cautious look came over his face, as if he read something in my eyes.

"It can be a little overwhelming at first," he said.

I looked back out at the dance floor. "It's fantastic. How long has this place been here?"

He shrugged. "Since forever. You can't stop people from being human. We're creative, we're social. People are like water. If you try to contain them, they find a way to break free."

I stared adoringly at the woman singing.

"She's beautiful," I said. She wasn't beautiful in the standard definition of the word. She was overweight and her face was aging and lined with wrinkles. She had dark, sun-kissed freckles on her cheeks. It was the passion in her voice that made her beautiful and the sensual way her body moved with the music.

Someone shouted Justin's name and he turned but I barely noticed him walk away. The beat started to pick up and the drums pulsated through the room like a wild heartbeat. I inched my way deeper into the crowd to get to the band. I felt hot, sweaty skin brush against mine. I watched the singer's chest rise and fall and the muscles in her neck flex with each word she sang. My feet started to move and my shoulders swayed without my trying to make them. It was as if I lost myself, or maybe I was starting to meet a part of myself for the first time. I felt someone's fingers tap my arm and I looked over as Clare wrapped her warm hand around mine.

"Hey," she yelled, and her eyes fell to my dress. "Look at you!" she said. I knew I was overdressed for the club but her smile made me feel welcome. She squeezed my hand and pulled me deeper into the crowd to join her friends. We danced in a loose circle and I watched Clare move effortlessly to the music. Her arms floated in the air as if invisible hands guided them. I watched the people around me and tried to mimic their movements, but I didn't want to follow anybody so I closed my eyes and focused on the beat. When I stopped thinking, my body started to move on its own. My hair escaped the hold of its twist and I shook it back and forth to free it from the confining pins. It dangled in soft curls past my shoulders and down my back. For the first time in my life, I just let myself go. The music lifted my arms and guided my body. Something inside of me shifted again, as if an invisible hand was pushing and pulling my insides around, stirring me.

How long had I been dancing? How many times had the music stopped, only to start again? I felt sweat on my cheeks and forehead and drips roll down the back of my neck. Clare fanned herself with her hand and yelled in my ear.

"I think I need to sit this one out," she said.

I nodded and followed her to the bar and ordered two bottled waters. Clare pressed the cold bottle to her sweaty forehead.

"This much sweat is not sexy," she said with a frown. I grabbed her hand and we pushed through the rest of the crowd. Her hand felt so soft and warm inside mine. I never noticed how incredible skin felt—how velvety. We headed out the double doors and up the stairs. Once we got outside, the cool, quiet night air blew against our steaming skin. I let go of her hand and stretched my neck toward the sky as I gulped in the fragrance of the mist.

"You don't look too freaked out by all this," Clare said after she took a long gulp of water.

I opened my eyes and looked over to find her studying me. "What do you mean?"

"Well, you've been exposed to a lot lately. You seemed cool at the coffee shop, but you never know how people are going to react to being unplugged."

I looked carefully at Clare. "Can you relate to all this?"

She smiled. "Not exactly, but if it wasn't for people like Justin and Pat, I'd probably be a hermit. They make me get out more. But I am in DS, so I have to use computers once in a while. Justin makes sure to give me crap for it whenever he's in town."

"How long have you known Justin?" I tried to keep my voice casual, like he didn't consume most of my thought process.

Clare took another swig of water. "Since I was eight or nine. I met him through Jake. All those guys are amazing, even Scott and Molly—they're a little on the aloof side, but underneath, their hearts are in the right place."

"I'm still wondering what I'm doing here exactly," I said.

Clare creased her forehead at my comment. "What do you mean? At this club?"

I waved my hand in the air. "At this club, at the coffee shop two weeks ago. Everything. Why did Justin pluck me out of all the people on the Web? You don't meet someone every day that's set on changing your life."

Clare watched me with a worried expression. "He hasn't explained anything to you?"

I thought about this. "Well, he goes off about changing the world and fighting the system. But why's he opening up to me? I'm going to college after I finish DS four. I'm already applying to schools for computer law. What difference am I going to make?"

Clare gave me a knowing smile. "You mean, you've never thought about trying to change DS?"

I stared back at her and for the briefest moment considered telling her the truth. But I couldn't risk it. I had shut that part of my life away and sealed it in the back of my mind in such a thick wrapping, I had convinced myself that girl in the past wasn't even me.

"I used to," I said. "But I straightened out. I'm ready to go to college. That's what I want." I heard myself force the words as if I was trying to convince us both.

"I think you need to talk to Justin about it," she said. "I can guarantee he's singled you out for a reason. He doesn't waste his time on people. I know that much about him. His time's way too valuable."

Her blue eyes studied me for a few seconds and she laughed to herself.

"What?" I asked her.

She shook her head. "It's just entertaining watching him around you."

"What's that supposed to mean?"

She continued to smile and her face turned thoughtful. "I haven't seen him react to anyone the way he does with you. It's like you make him nervous."

I shook my head. "I highly doubt that."

Clare shrugged. "I don't know. Justin never pays too much attention to one person. It's like people all blend into him. But he notices you."

"Probably because he thinks I'm insane," I said. Just as I said this, the front door opened and Justin walked through with long strides. When he saw the two of us he sucked in a deep breath.

"There you are," he said, looking at me with relief, but his eyes were hard. "I've been looking everywhere for you." I glanced at Clare and she raised her eyebrows for a split second.

"I'm fine. Where did you think I was?"

"I don't know. I thought something freaked you out and you ran off."

I crossed my arms at this. "I may have led a sheltered life, but it would take a little more than live music to freak me out."

Clare excused herself to go inside. The door closed behind her and when I took a step to follow her, Justin blocked me.

"You promised your mom you wouldn't be gone long," he reminded me.

"She'll get over it," I said, and tried to push past him but he wouldn't budge.

His eyes were serious. "You can come back here another time."

I frowned and matched his stubborn expression. "No. I'm staying." I didn't care. I felt like I had found a piece of myself tonight, and had such a short time to be with it.

"I'll call my mom right now. I'll tell her I'm not feeling good and I'm going home."

"You think your dad will buy that?"

"I don't care. I want to stay. This is where I belong, not back there." His face tightened and his eyes pleaded with me.

"Madeline," he said, and sighed with frustration. He took a step toward me, his dark eyes demanding. "I love this wave of confidence you've got going, but right now your parents don't trust me. You're not going to be rebellious on my time. Do you ever want to be allowed in the same room with me again?"

These words made me hesitate, and his eyes flickered when he realized what my weak spot was.

"You need to go back there for me. Right now you live under their roof, under your father's rules. You have to care, for now." I clenched my teeth to keep from arguing, but I knew Justin was right.

I turned without another word and headed back toward the hotel, hugging my arms over my chest to shield the chilly breeze. I pictured my father in the dining hall, still being idolized like a hero. I was angrier toward him than I thought I was capable of and it scared me. Mist fell heavily in the air now, so thick I felt like I was swimming through it. A shiver crept over my skin and I felt something brush my arm. Justin reached his suit jacket out to me, which I took without looking at him and pulled my arms through the warm, silky fabric. I could feel him glancing at me while we walked; I could always sense his gaze, as though his eyes physically touched me. I balled my hands into fists and pressed them hard against my ribs.

When we finally met the white pillars of the hotel entrance, I threw open the door. Justin followed me and I stopped abruptly at the edge of the main dining hall. The digital dance competition was under way. Black dance pads were sprawled around the floor of the giant room and virtual ballroom dance halls were projected on wall screens. People bounced on their electric pads to move with the gorgeous digital dancer on the screen in front of them. Everyone's eyes were on their pixelated version of life. Ballroom music infused the room, but it didn't reach anyone. People were too busy being superior versions of themselves. On the digital screen they were beautiful, young, skinny, and talented, dancing with someone equaling their perfection.

I watched people smile and laugh as their digital bodies moved gracefully with another stranger. I looked over at my parents. My dad danced on the screen with an elegant blond woman in a white gown and my mom laughed and clapped to encourage him. I stared at the scene and felt a cold knot forming in my chest. People were dancing with air, with empty space, didn't they see that? Here was a room full of married couples ignoring the person they loved and choosing to be sensual with a fabricated form of reality.

A wave of nausea came over me as I stood there, overstimulated for the second time tonight. What a forced lifestyle our technology, our inventions imposed on our lives when we tried to live synonymously with computers; when we stepped inside their world, we left the natural one behind.

I felt my legs start to buckle.

"I need to get out of here," I heard myself say in a strangled voice, like I wanted someone to wake me up out of a nightmare.

I leaned on Justin and he helped me to a bench against the wall in the lobby. I was waiting for him to force me back into the room, to tell me he knew what was best for me. People always loved to tell me that.

He surprised me when he opened my purse and took my phone out. He handed it to me and told me to message my mom.

"Tell her you're going home," he said. "I'll drop you off."

I stared down at the phone. "I don't want to go home." I looked up at him and pleaded with my eyes. I didn't want to be alone.

"Will you stay with me?" I asked. It was strange saying the words because it wasn't strange. I was starting to believe Justin knew me better than anyone, even my own parents. He didn't try to see what he hoped was there. He just saw me. And slowly, I was starting to throw back that thick curtain that censored myself from the rest of the world. He told me that he wouldn't be a good friend for me, so why did I feel like he was the best one I had?

He nodded and motioned for me to follow him.

"Come on," he said. "I think I know what will help."

CHAPTER *eight*

I followed him outside to his car parked down the block. We were both silent while we drove down the desolate streets, and I concentrated on the soft sprinkle of rain hitting the windshield. My thoughts were shooting and firing in my mind so quickly it felt like there was a war going on in my head. I watched the windshield wipers swipe the glass clean and for a moment the world was clear again, but in the next second it muddled in a blur, like eyes brimming with tears. We pulled up to the side of an apartment building. The bottom floor had three large windows and they were all showered with light. There were no signs outside to advertise what the space was, but Justin pulled the front door open and we were greeted with a chime.

We walked inside a restaurant that was long and narrow, the walls painted a dark blueberry color. A white counter stretched along one side of the café and red leather upholstered booths lined the other. Behind the counter was a coffee machine and stacks of cups and plates. There was a glass cooler filled with pies and desserts. A young couple sat at one of the tables, artsy-looking types with scarves and slouching knit hats, leaning into each other and whispering. A man in a wool jacket and jeans sat on a stool at the counter and I noticed he was reading a paper book, like my mom gave me. It smelled like coffee inside and something so sweet it was making my mouth water. A woman sauntered over to greet us, wearing an old waitress uniform I used to see in movies—a white dress that buttoned up the front with pink trim at the collar.

"Justin," she said in a voice that sounded worn and scratchy. She had tan skin and teeth that looked stained from drinking too much coffee, but her smile was warm. Her pink lipstick matched the trim of her dress.

"Good to see you," she said. Justin ducked down to hug her. She had to stand on her toes to reach him.

She turned to study me. "Who's this?"

"Madeline," I told her, and found that saying my name wasn't so strange. It actually felt nice to hear it.

"Irene," she said with a nod, and we followed her to a booth next to one of the windows. She asked Justin if he'd be having his regular. He nodded and ordered two cups of coffee.

It was warm inside, so I took Justin's coat off and laid it on the booth cushion next to me. I gathered my skirt together and sat down, surprised that I didn't feel embarrassed to be so overdressed. I looked around the small space and it was exactly what I was craving. Quiet. Relaxed. Soft lighting. No digital screens or advertisements. The only background noise, other than voices, was some music filtering through a speaker by the register. It sounded like jazz.

Justin told me they didn't have menus. They only served home-made desserts and coffee.

"How do they stay in business?" I asked.

"People don't run these kinds of places to make a profit. Irene's had this place as long as I can remember. She does it because she likes being around people."

"What did you order?" I asked.

"You'll see," he told me. "Believe me, it will change your world."

I stared back at him, at his messy hair, sprinkled with mist. I wanted to tell him I didn't need dessert for him to change my world. His presence did that already.

Irene came back with two cups of coffee and a tin full of cream. She set them down, followed by a single plate, taken up by a giant slice of triple-layer chocolate cake. Between each layer and slathered on top was a heap of whipped chocolate frosting. I licked my lips at the sight of it and looked up at Justin.

"Feeling better yet?" he asked with a small grin.

Instead of answering him, I grabbed my fork and dug in. The fluffy chocolate melted in my mouth and I washed it down with hot coffee. I decided this was the best medicine for a mood shift money could buy. Present company included.

I glanced up to find Justin watching me, but his eyes were distracted. He reached his hand across the table and just as he did this I noticed my hair was dangling over my shoulder and brushing the rim of my coffee cup. I moved to sweep it away just as Justin was about to do the same thing and I ended up grabbing his fingers in mine for an awkward second. He quickly pulled his hand away as if my skin stung his hand.

"Sorry," he said. "Your hair was getting in your coffee."

I pushed my hair behind my back and mumbled thanks. I could feel a blush setting in. I took another bite of chocolate cake, careful to stay on my side of the slice.

"It's a little depressing to know this always existed and I just discovered it," I told him while I savored a bite of frosting.

"At least you discovered it."

I took a drink of the hot coffee and looked out the window, at the rain hitting the glass like fingers lightly tapping. "It makes me feel sorry for my parents."

Justin shook his head. "Don't. They wouldn't respond to it like you do. They'd feel just as uncomfortable in this world as you feel in theirs."

I told Justin that my mom wouldn't.

He licked the frosting off the back of his fork and asked me what I meant. I had to force myself to focus.

"My mom and dad are polar opposites," I explained. "My mom practically encourages me to fight DS, but then my dad freaks out if I even question it. It's like they're playing tug of war with my mind. I don't know who to listen to half the time."

He shrugged. "You don't have to choose sides," he said. "Make up your own mind and believe that."

We finished the cake but there were a few crumbs scattered on the plate that I dabbed up with my finger. I swept up the last smear of frosting because it was too good to waste.

I told Justin my mom stopped making homemade food when I was little. Now you can order all your meals premade and prepackaged and they come shipped to your house every week. I described our kitchen, how our refrigerator was neatly organized with bags of chopped fruit and vegetables, trays of salads, and bottles of floats and fruit drinks. Our freezer was stocked with labeled casseroles, pastas, pizzas, and soups ready to heat up. Our cabinets were full of air-tight sandwiches, snack bars, and vitamins.

Irene stopped to refill our coffees and clear the empty plate.

"I can officially say it now," I said. "I've been deprived."

"That's what I don't get," Justin said. "People look at eating like it's an inconvenience. Like our lives are too busy and important to bother with feeding ourselves. But we're human. Our bodies were designed to enjoy food." He set down his coffee mug and fixed his eyes on me. "Did you know there are over ten thousand taste buds on your tongue? Ten thousand. And taste is the *weakest* of our five senses."

I pushed my tongue against the back of my teeth as he said this. I could still taste the chocolate.

"And our hands," he continued. He reached across the table and grabbed one of my hands in his larger one. I stared down at our hands and felt my skin heat up under his touch.

He flipped my hand over gently so my palm was facing up. I wondered where he was going with this, but I could tell from the look on his face he wasn't flirting. His eyes were serious. He was proving a point.

He rubbed his fingertips over mine and slowly added pressure. "Our fingers have thousands of nerve endings. They're one of the most sensitive parts of our bodies. And what do we do with them all day? What do we touch?"

I thought my heart was going to explode it was beating so fast. I looked back at him and managed to shrug my shoulders.

"We push buttons," he said. "That's it. We click and press buttons. And that's supposed to be satisfying? Aren't we designed for something a little more authentic than that?"

He pressed his fingers against mine before he pulled his hand back. I looked down at my hand and tried to bend my fingers. Every nerve ending was standing on edge like they were all reaching out, craving more. I took a deep breath and cleared my throat.

"You said earlier you had a few questions for me," he told me. His eyes were dark on mine. His hands were off of the table, probably a good thing or I might have grabbed for his fingers again.

"Tell me about your parents," I said.

I noticed his mouth tighten. "What do you want to know?"

"Do you live with them?" I asked. He shook his head.

"I'm never settled anywhere very long. When I'm in Corvallis I stay with Jake's family."

"How long has that been going on?" I asked.

I could hear his foot tapping underneath the table. "A while. My parents were relocated," he offered. His voice was steady. Unreadable. He said the word *relocated* like it was a business decision.

"Did they move?" I expected Justin to hesitate, but he answered immediately, as if he saw the question coming.

"No, they were arrested. And they're never allowed back in the state." Justin paused as if he was considering whether to keep going. His eyes took a turn around the room before they met mine again. "They live in California now, along the coast. There's a growing community there, of people that are abandoning some of the modern ways of life and are adopting older traditions like growing their own food and living with technology, not through it. They're trying to form face-to-face classes again."

I had heard of the place he was referring to. My father mentioned it sourly in conversation—a pocket of people who "fought" the system were relocated to a community in California. There were dozens of names for it, Trashtown, UC Slums, Berkinstocks, but some people referred to it as Eden. I also knew it wasn't open to the general public and it wasn't a place you would choose to visit. You were usually banished to the area.

"What happened?"

He grinned and I saw something in his eyes, something I saw in my dad's eyes sometimes when he bragged about my grades or how hard my mom worked at charity events. Pride.

"They tried to shake things up," he said.

I waited for him to continue.

"They helped lead the Digital Riot about twelve years ago. Then they fought the ID Scan laws. You remember, right? Hundreds of people were killed in D.C. for storming the Capitol."

I remembered, even though I was little. That year the government was trying to mandate a law that every person in the country be paired with an ID bar code that would be imbedded in their skin. The number would be used for all transactions, purchases,

IDs, and to register on any websites. It would replace licenses, pass-ports, social security numbers, birth certificates, student IDs—the system would make a person's identity no longer an address or picture or even a name.

What really crossed the line for protesters is when the govern-ment pointed out the advantages for parents to have the code implanted in their children's skin. Not only was it a way to have information accessible at any time, it was also a tracking device. Parents could always find their child by tracking them online like a radar. But, as protesters argued, so could the government, so could anyone. It was one more way to lose our freedom. Rioters stormed D.C. to fight the issue and hundreds were killed in the stampede when a bomb erupted in the middle of the mob.

"Your parents helped organize that?"

He nodded. "And luckily their effort paid off, since it never became a law. It took that many lives to prove a point."

I asked Justin where he was living during all of this.

"All over," he said, "but I spent most of the time crashing at Jake's. His parents are my godparents. I've lived with the Solvis off and on my whole life. Sort of like joint custody."

I frowned at this. "It must have been hard to grow up hardly ever seeing your parents."

He shook his head. "It wasn't," he said with sincerity in his voice. "I'm prouder of them than anyone. I wouldn't have wanted it any other way."

"You say that now, but did you feel that way when you were young? When it was the holidays or your birthday and they were in jail?"

He smiled slightly. "I've been brought up to always put other people before myself. You can make a lot more of a dif-ference when you focus your energy on other people instead of yourself."

I tucked a loose strand of hair behind my ear. "How long were your parents in jail?"

"The first time? About two years."

I gave him an apologetic nod but it only made his eyes harden.

"My parents are the bravest people I've ever known," he said. "They've taught me everything I believe in. So many people are full of talk, Maddie. But nothing happens unless someone steps up and takes action. That's what my parents taught me."

"Do you ever see them?"

He nodded. "I visit when I can."

"So, where do you call home?" All my life, all I've known is my home. Four walls and a ceiling and this island of security.

He tapped his fingers on the table and told me he never thought about this. "Some people say home is where you come from. But I think it's a place you need to find, like it's scattered and you pick pieces of it up along the way."

I shook my head.

"What?" Justin watched me with interest.

"I've just never thought of a lifestyle like that."

He lifted his shoulder. "You were brought up to think love and family is about protection. Like you need to hold people close in order to care about them. But that's just living inside a bubble. It's control. I was brought up to think love is trusting people enough to let them go. Like you can expand your family and your feelings and carry them anywhere."

I let his words soak through my pores and into my brain, where I wanted to store them away in a compartment where they would always be safe, so I could go back for them whenever I wanted.

"You never thought your parents were being selfish?" I asked.

He wrinkled his forehead. "For what?"

"For putting rioting before being good parents to you?"

"They have been wonderful parents to me."

I disagreed. "Really? Where are they? Banished? How often do you see them?" I couldn't fight the animosity rising in my chest. I didn't care if his parents cured cancer and secured world peace. They still should have been more involved in his life.

Justin took a deep breath and slowed down his words. "It's because of the selflessness of people like my parents that we're sitting here right now without a radar machine picking up on a bar code embedded in our skin." He paused and leaned closer to me. "It's because people like my parents put their words into action that we saw those musicians tonight, that this world has any happiness left in it. And if it means a little sacrifice, that I can only see them a few times a year, I think that's fair. They want a better life for me, and they're fighting for it. I think that's the greatest thing a parent can do."

I looked down and folded my hands in my lap. "I'm sorry," I said. "I know it's none of my business. But you're the most amazing person I've ever met and it's just sad that your parents don't get to see that."

Justin sat up straighter, clearly surprised by this. I felt my face heat up. Where is the delete button when you need it?

I stared down at my lap, trying to think of some way to change the subject.

"There's one more thing you should know," Justin said. "About five years ago my parents were involved with a group of protesters that were trying to locate the DS radio towers."

My fingers tightened around each other and I refused to meet his gaze. I knew exactly what he was talking about.

"What happened?" I bluffed.

I could feel him studying me. "Their plan was to disrupt the signal for one hour and broadcast a national public announcement about fighting digital school. But my parents were tracked and arrested before it was ever organized. Then a year later, another group of rioters got the information, except their mission was a little less subtle. They bombed a tower in Portland that shut down the DS signal for the entire state."

I nodded slowly and he continued.

"It took so long to get the signal back, people were considering forming face-to-face schools again. It was the strongest impact anyone's had on trying to fight DS since it was started."

Of course I remembered. For two weeks, the entire state lost access to DS. Meanwhile, my life had nearly ended and my father was being investigated by the FBI for being a possible terrorist.

Justin stared at me before he spoke as if he thought I might add something. I asked the one question that would erase any doubt.

"What are your parents' names?"

"Thomas and Elaine Sabel."

I tried to hide the shock on my face as I recognized the names of his parents. They had come up in more than one occasion in my household, referred to by my father as radicals. It was Justin's parents that, numerous times, tried to destroy everything my father built.

"You don't share the same last name?" I asked, and could hear my voice strained.

"No, they changed my last name when I was young. For my protection."

I nodded and kept my eyes on the table. "I should probably get home," I said. Before he could respond, I grabbed his coat and scooted out of the booth. He stood up and left money on the table and waved to Irene before we left.

I was quiet on the ride home, still trying to absorb everything I had learned. When we pulled up to my house, the rain was pelting the windshield. I found the door handle and opened it.

"I'll be around for a few days, so I'll be in touch," Justin told me. I nodded and got out of the car, feeling lightheaded from the intensity of our conversation. Justin drove off and I turned back to watch the taillights of his car disappear down the road and out of sight. I took my heels off in the driveway and stretched my feet on the cold, wet cement. I was beginning to piece together why Justin singled me out but I still didn't understand what he wanted and why he waited two and a half years to find me.

CHAPTER nine

The next night, my mom and I sat in the living room in front of our digital fireplace and watched a game show on TV. It's an interactive show, where anyone watching can guess the trivia questions and submit their answers online. People play it all over the world and anyone with a webcam has the chance to appear on the show. Tonight my mom and I weren't playing; we just watched other contestants.

I threw some buttery popcorn in my mouth and curled up on the couch with Baley at my feet. My dad was out of town and it felt easier to breathe in his absence. I heard a slow rumble in Baley's throat. Mom and I exchanged surprised glances when we heard a car pull up outside.

I sat up and stared out the window, shocked.

"You didn't tell me he was coming over," Mom said.

I gave her a bewildered look. "I didn't know. Apparently he doesn't even call anymore."

My mom and I both stood up when the doorbell rang.

"That boy gets stranger every day. What was he even doing at the benefit last night? It cost one thousand dollars to get in."

98

I walked over to the front door and opened it. Justin strode in quickly and carried an impatient energy into the room.

My mom invited him to watch *Money Talks* with us, but he shook his head and told her he was just stopping by. His anxious eyes met mine.

"You want to come with me?" he asked. I looked at my mom for permission and she nodded slowly but her eyes were careful, as if to remind me of what my father would think.

"Let's go," I said, and grabbed a hooded sweatshirt out of the hall closet.

"When would you like her home?" he asked my mom. She studied the two of us standing next to each other while she thought this over.

"Maddie, I'll let you be the judge of that. But if you're going to be too late, call and let me know."

I followed Justin outside to his car and he opened the passenger door for me, as usual. I hopped in and fastened my seat belt.

He slid into his seat and started the car. I turned up the stereo, and the loud bass made the seats vibrate. I nodded my head to the music and drummed my hands on my knees. Independence was like a drug and it was making me high.

I looked over at Justin and he was watching me, almost comically. I turned the music down.

"Are we going to a club?" I asked. He shook his head. "More homemade chocolate cake?"

"Not exactly," he said.

"How long are you in town for?" I asked.

He pulled out of the driveway and was playing with a car dial. "It's not really set. My schedule's unpredictable these days."

He glanced at me. "You looked really nice last night, by the way. I forgot to tell you that."

I felt my face heat up at the compliment. My mind quickly

began to analyze what "really nice" meant. Cute? Extremely cute? Hot? Attractive, but only in a friend sort of way? I frowned at the last thought.

"I'm bad with those kinds of things," he added.

I looked over at him with disbelief because I couldn't fathom anything he was bad at. "What things?"

"You know, compliments." He took his eyes off the road for a second to look back at me. "Girls like compliments, don't they?"

I felt my blush deepen and had a sudden urge to pull my hood over my face and hide behind it. "I think everyone does if it's sincere. Not just girls."

"Yeah," Justin said, and scratched the back of his head. "Well I'm pretty clueless in that department."

I stared ahead and wondered where this conversation was going. Was Justin trying to open up about his dating life? He completely baffled me.

We turned onto a highway ramp headed for the coast and I asked him where we were going.

"Do you want to see what I do?" he asked. His eyes were dark and held a daring edge.

I wanted nothing more. "I might be mildly interested."

"You know you can trust me, right?" I groaned as the question escaped his lips.

"Justin, yes, we've had this discussion. I trust you."

He turned back to watch the road and nodded, satisfied with this.

"That's all I need to know."

"What are we doing, exactly?"

"We're intercepting." He explained that one way to fight DS was to stop the government from sending students to detention centers.

"It's ridiculous," he said. "They're arresting people just for try-ing to drop out of DS, or for forming too many face-to-face study groups and sports teams. The government sends them away to get straightened out before they become a threat. They're usually fight-ing DS one way or another, so, if we intercept them, they're happy to join our side. It's how we recruit most of our supporters."

"Why don't you just contact them after they're released from detention centers? It'd be a lot less dangerous."

Justin looked at me like I was crazy. "Because they crack. That's what detention centers do. They hold you until they break you. We don't know much about what goes on inside of them. People come out pretty screwed up."

We exited off the highway toward a town called Toledo, only a few miles from the coast. Justin slowed down as we turned onto a residential road. I glanced down the street at a modest-looking neighborhood. Two-story homes were spaced equally apart and windows were lit up inside with the shades closed. He pulled the car over to the curb and turned the engine off. Silence filled the darkness between us. His smooth voice cut through the air and enveloped me.

"When I train people I never tell them what to expect. I let them experience it all firsthand. I think it's pointless to try and tell you what's ahead because nothing ever happens the way you think it will."

I stared back at him. "Train me for what?"

He ignored my question and handed me something. I took the narrow cylinder in my hand and studied it. Justin flipped open the console between us and punched in a code.

"I need you to agree to something. Tonight, you need to do exactly what I say, when I say it. And you need to stay right by my side. Those are my two rules."

I nodded.

He looked down at the console and after a few seconds pushed another series of buttons.

"Let's do this," he said. His eyes met mine for a brief instant until he was gone.

Every street and house light around us disappeared as if someone had stretched a canvas between my eyes and the rest of the world. Blackness reached out and swallowed me inside.

CHAPTER ten

I tried to scream but I felt a hand clasp my lips together. Justin's calm, low voice was close to my ear.

"Everything's fine. Get out of the car and stay by my side," he ordered. He opened his car door and I followed his lead. I stumbled blindly against the curb and fell into Justin's arms just as he came around the side of the car.

"Turn that on, Maddie," he said as he steadied me. I fumbled with the cylinder, trying to figure out what he meant. Justin shined his flashlight on mine to show me the switch. Light shot out of it and I gave a sigh of relief.

"Oh" was all I said. I'd never used a flashlight before. If the power went out at our house, which only happened once that I remembered, a generator in the basement kicked in and illuminated track lighting along the ceiling of every room.

"Now we walk. Let me do the talking."

Our flashlights cast a beam several yards in front of us. If I hadn't seen the row of homes stretched out on both sides of the street earlier, I would have never known they were there. I was acutely aware of sound since my vision was so impaired. A breeze whipped through the trees and dogs barked in the distance. I heard a front door open and a man called out to us. He held a flashlight as well and aimed it at the ground in front of him. He followed its path through the yard.

"Hey, do you know what's going on?" he yelled after us. Justin and I turned and waited for him. He hurried down the lawn and pointed his flashlight up and down the street.

"Looks like the power's out on the whole block," Justin said. I glanced at the man, middle-aged and wearing sweatpants and a bathrobe.

"I've never seen anything like this," he said. "My fuse box didn't even work." He took his phone out of his pocket. As he was dialing, other people came out of their homes. I noticed a few had flashlights, and one woman carried an old-fashioned camping lantern. Little balls of light flowed toward us as if the sky were falling in around us. Behind the streams of light were curious faces.

"Do you know what happened?" an older woman asked as she and her husband approached us.

The man in the bathrobe shook his head. "I'm calling the electric company right now," he said.

"Well," she said, chuckling, "it's nice to finally meet the neighbors. I've lived here fifteen years and I've never seen people out like this." She pulled her knitted shawl tighter around her shoulders. I watched the interaction with fascination. I hardly ever saw my neighbors. We knew their names, of course, the ones on either side of our house. We knew their occupations. We knew if they had pets, or kids, the common things. But we didn't know what they were like.

More families timidly approached, adults and kids, all asking what was happening.

"I think it's just a power outage. Probably an underground line blew a fuse. It's pretty common," Justin said, trying to keep people calm. He grabbed my arm and slowly led me away from the group while neighbors continued to introduce themselves and joke that it took something like this to finally force them outside. I glanced back at them over my shoulder and grinned at the sea of faces, huddled together and whispering as if they discovered something rare in the ray of their beams. As we walked down the street, we passed other groups of people. One porch had lanterns lit around the edges and people sat on the stairs, talking and laughing as if they were routinely out enjoying the night together. Justin tightened his grip on my arm and we picked up our pace. He checked his phone before he slipped it into his pocket.

"So, you're a runner, right?" he asked me.

I nodded and when we turned the corner, he let go of me.

"It's time to prove it," he said. He broke out into a sprint and I raced behind him, across the street and through an open yard. We came out onto another sidewalk, this one as dark as the last. I chased after him, down the wide open street and passed blocks of empty space, lit only by a cluster of flashlight beams shooting through the air like trails of comets. The crisp night air brushed my skin and filled my lungs. Running outside was different than running on a machine, where my steps just follow each other. Now my feet were pushing off something hard and solid, and it kicked up my speed. We turned and ran through an alley between two high office buildings. Justin halted to a stop so suddenly I almost ran into him. He aimed his flashlight at a Dumpster parked along the edge of the building. Hiding behind it was a young man, maybe fifteen. He squatted low to the ground. Justin shined the light on his face, white as a ghost.

"Let's go," he said, and the young man stood up without question. Justin grabbed his wrist and used something in his hand to deactivate a tracker bracelet the boy wore. He threw the bracelet in the Dumpster and turned to me.

"Turn that off," he said, nodding to my flashlight, and the three of us ran through the alley, our feet echoing around us and splashing through dirty puddles. My eyes had adjusted well enough to the darkness to see my way. I could hear sirens approaching in the distance. The boy was panting now and starting to slow down.

"We're almost there," Justin said over his shoulder to encourage him. The moon and the stars cast a soft light and guided us down the street and past hovering shadows of homes. We ran to the edge of another neighborhood where the freeway was blocked off by a metal fence, and Justin and the boy cleared it with one leap. I jumped up and managed to get one leg over the top. Justin grabbed my waist and pulled me over the rest of the way.

He set me down and we picked our way through a thick barrier of plastic bushes, and I gashed my leg against something sharp sticking out of the ground. I could feel warm blood slowly trickle down my leg but the adrenaline shut out any sense of pain. We jumped out onto the shoulder of the highway and headlights sped toward us. I stared with shock as a vehicle pulled up next to us. It was Justin's car and it was completely empty.

"Get in," he demanded. The young boy dove into the back seat and I dashed into the passenger side. Justin slammed his door shut just as two policemen sprinted out of the bushes we had run through just seconds before. They shot at the car, bullets ricocheting off the windows. I screamed and ducked down in my seat, squeezing my eyes shut and covering my face in my hands. I felt the car accelerate and heard Justin laugh next to me. I glanced up at him through the slit between my fingers.

"What's so funny?" I asked, my breath coming out in sharp gasps. Justin barely looked winded.

"Sorry, but it's the same thing every time, they just shoot those stupid guns at my car." He laughed again and I tried to find the humor in the situation. I slowly pulled my hands off my face and the boy in the back seat sat up as Justin shifted gears and the car sped down the highway. I pulled sticky strands of hair out of my face and felt drips of sweat rolling down my neck and chest.

Justin pressed another code into the keyboard. I understood what he was doing now. He somehow had the ability to shut down the electrical power grid in the neighborhood. Turning it off provided a diversion so the boy had a chance to escape.

"My car's bulletproof," he said. "All cars are these days— bulletproof, fireproof, but cops still shoot their guns because that's all they know how to do. I just think it's funny."

I looked back at the young boy and noticed flashing lights behind us.

Justin checked the rearview mirror but he looked more amused than concerned. The car accelerated and I sucked in a sharp breath when a sign came into view that said FREEWAY ENDING.

"Um." I pointed to the sign. Justin looked at me and grinned.

"This is when things start to get fun," he told me, as if the last half hour had been dull. "You don't get claustrophobic, do you?" he asked.

"I don't think so," I answered. I had no idea what he was talking about.

"How do you feel about water?"

"Water?"

Just as I said this, the highways converged into a two-lane road and signs warned that the beach was straight ahead. I clung to the grab handle above the window and braced myself when I realized we weren't slowing down. The car flew off the pavement and fell with a heavy thump on the sand and we all lurched forward in our seats. Thrashing ocean waves crashed straight ahead. The water looked gray in the headlights and the waves spiraled and churned like they were threatening to crush us.

Justin reached under the steering wheel and punched something with his hand. The car reacted by vibrating. In a few seconds, the wheels stopped tumbling over the sand and we started to glide. I screamed as our car hit the water, but we didn't sink—we skidded and rolled over the surface of the curling waves. The waves broke over the car with such a loud crash I swore the windshield was going to snap in half. I could hear the boy cheering in the back seat and Justin had a huge smile on his face, his dimples standing out. I squeezed my eyes shut. Maybe I lacked the necessary testosterone levels to be enjoying this.

The car rolled and dipped like we were on a roller-coaster ride as the waves threatened to flip us. I screamed again as we were tipped violently from one side to the next, like a ship caught in a storm, but we somehow managed to stay above the waves.

"How are we doing this?" I yelled.

"Hold on," he said. Justin kept his foot on the accelerator. I turned to see two pairs of headlights behind us. I watched with shock as the police cruisers skated onto the beach after us. I looked out the front window and the car was settling on smooth water, past the breaking waves. We were heading out to sea. The boy in the back seat spoke up.

"I've heard cars can do this," he said. "But I've only seen it in the movies."

Justin nodded. "I prefer driving on the ocean over the road any day. No stoplights." I tightened my lips together and glanced back at the cop cars, which looked farther behind now but were still chasing us.

I turned and blinked out the front window like I was trapped inside a dream. We were well beyond the beach now and the tide was calm. We slid along the surface of the ocean as smoothly as if the car was gliding on ice. The light from the moon and the stars made the water glisten a metallic yellow all around us. I couldn't see the coastline anymore and wondered how well engineered these cars were for water travel. I hadn't told Justin I couldn't swim.

A minute later he took his foot off the accelerator and we started to slow down. I looked over at him.

"What happens when we turn around? They'll be back there waiting for us," I pointed out, as if he didn't think that far ahead.

"I guess we'll just have to drive to Asia," he said. I opened my mouth to argue but instead my voice caught halfway up my throat.

We were sinking. Water slapped the side of my door and splashed against the windows. Panic flooded through my chest and squeezed my lungs until I couldn't breathe.

Justin gently caught my head between both of his hands.

"Maddie, look at me. This is supposed to happen. Just breathe."

Breathe, I thought, yes, breathe while I still can, before I drown.

"We're fine," he said. His face was only inches from mine and his eyes were sincere. "I know what I'm doing."

"We're sinking," I said. My breath came out in gasps. "We're sinking and I can't swim."

"You don't need to swim, this car works underwater."

The boy in the back seat cheered again and clapped his hands. Justin let go of my face and I watched with disbelief as the moon and the stars disappeared and we were enveloped inside a pitch-black ocean current. Everything was quiet. I waited for the car to explode, for the windows to leak, for the oxygen to run out. But nothing happened. Justin leaned forward and turned off the headlights. The engine made a knocking sound and he told me it was adjusting to the water.

"The engine," I whispered, "works underwater?"

We continued to sink slowly into darkness so black I couldn't see an inch in front of me. I listened to the water bubbling and gurgling around us as if we were floating in the stomach of a giant. I could hear Justin's breath, and the boy shift in the back seat. A faint siren passed overhead and a slow ripple lightly rocked the car back and forth.

Once the cops passed over us, Justin revved the engine. He snapped on the headlights and the interior lights turned on, casting an orange glow around us. I could only make out the shadow of Justin's eyes. I looked out at the water caught in the headlights, but couldn't see anything other than floating debris flying past us like snowflakes. I gulped and kept my eyes straight ahead.

"This is partly why I wanted you to come tonight. We don't do the ocean escapes nearly enough."

I wasn't sure if I should thank Justin or slap him.

The boy in the back seat leaned forward. "How long have cars been able to do this?" he asked.

"They still haven't perfected it," Justin said. "Not for very deep dives anyway."

I pressed my palm against the cold window.

"Is it safe?" I asked, and closed my eyes to prepare for the answer.

"More or less," Justin said.

"That's reassuring," I said.

"You can't go too deep, that's the only thing. The last car I did this with leaked." We moved through the water smoothly and gained speed. Justin sat back easily in his seat like he did this every day. I was sitting ramrod straight, my hands squeezing both of my knees.

"Are you still scared?" he asked with surprise in his voice.

"Scared?" I mocked. "Of being in a possibly not airtight vehicle in the middle of the Pacific and I can't swim?"

"I think it's awesome," the boy in the back seat chimed in.

"There's a blow-up raft in the trunk in case something happens," Justin said. I looked over at him and rolled my eyes. "Although," he continued, "we're deep enough now that if anything happened the car would implode from the pressure. So, we'd die instantly. If that makes you feel any better."

"Tons," I said.

"Do you ever see sharks out here?" the boy asked.

Justin shook his head. "They're practically extinct," he said.

I looked out into the dark abyss, debris still floating past us like confetti.

The tone of his voice dropped. "There hasn't been a shark sighting on the coast in almost ten years."

We were all silent as we watched the ocean water drift past us. I remembered seeing documentaries and pictures of what the oceans used to look like, swarming with colorful reef and fairy tale–looking creatures. A few small fish darted in front of us, their eyes curious and bright like glowing stars, reflected in the ray of the headlights. When the ocean floor came into view, it was littered with rocks and sand. There was hardly any vegetation growing; it looked as sandy and naked as a desert.

The wheels of the car met the sandy bottom and our windows slowly rose above the water level. I inhaled a deep breath of relief.

Justin broke the silence.

"I'm going to drop you off down the street, Mark. My friends will take care of you from there."

He looked at the boy over his shoulder and grinned. "By the way," he said. "Welcome to the real world."

CHAPTER *eleven*

We pulled in to the driveway next to a small, one-story home. I recognized Riley walking across the front lawn toward our car. He stood next to a young girl I didn't know.

We all got out of the car and Riley shook Mark's hand. I stood up and stretched my arms skyward to try to release the tension in my shoulders. Justin threw his car keys to Riley and he grinned at the young girl.

"Emily," he said to her, "I owe you one." Emily's frown turned into a smile from his attention.

"It's okay," she said. I walked over to join them.

"What do you mean 'you owe her one'?" I asked.

Justin's grin widened. "This interception was hers, she's on call tonight. But she let me have it."

I looked back at the car and considered the past two hours of my life. I felt my mouth tighten.

"You mean, you didn't have to do this? You just felt like it?" I asked with a glare.

Justin nodded. "I haven't done a water escape in years. Besides, I like to keep up the practice."

"How'd she do underwater?" Riley asked. Justin looked over at me.

"She freaked out a little at first but I think she came around," he said.

Riley smirked. "Dude, I meant the car?" Justin creased his eyebrows and glanced back at the car. I couldn't help but grin.

"Oh," he said. "Not bad, a little tough to navigate, though." I blinked at the car, still shocked I had ridden in it like a submarine.

"What happened?" Justin asked, pointing to the stain on my jeans. I looked down at the blood and felt the ache beginning to throb in my calf. I bent down and lifted up my jeans to expose a deep cut that ran up the side of my leg. The skin was swollen and still glistening with blood.

"Nice battle wound," Riley said. "Does it hurt?"

I shook my head. "Not too bad."

"You're going to feel it in a couple hours," Justin said. "Come on, let's clean you up before we go."

Riley drove the car into the garage while the rest of us walked inside. The house looked like it was decorated by an eighty-year-old woman with a flower fetish. All of the chairs and couches were upholstered with pastel floral designs. Paintings of flowers hung on the wall and a large rug displaying a giant sunflower was laid out at my feet.

Justin brought a first-aid kit over to the couch and told me to sit down. He squatted next to me and carefully rolled up my bloody pant leg. He eyed my calf and gave a short whistle.

"That's impressive," he said. I leaned over to see the dried blood, which covered a good part of my leg. Justin dabbed some disinfectant on a cotton ball. He met my eyes and rested a warm hand on my knee. "This might scar," he said. I shrugged down at him.

"I need a few scars. It'll toughen me up."

"I'm sorry," he said. "I didn't mean for you to get hurt."

He looked more concerned than he should be; it was a cut, not a bullet wound. "It's okay, it looks worse than it feels."

"This might sting a little," he said. I wasn't sure what I felt more, the heat from Justin's touch or the alcohol burning my skin. My body tensed from the sharp burn and I looked around the room to distract myself.

"This isn't the hideaway I expected," I noted of the atmosphere.

Justin smiled. "Yeah, most of the houses we use are donated by older people. They retire and volunteer their homes; we can't be too picky about the decor."

"Was her name Daisy by any chance?" I asked as I studied the daisy paintings on the wall.

Justin looked up and considered it for a moment. "I think it was Petunia." I laughed out loud at this and Justin applied another master dose of alcohol while I was distracted. The burning shot through my entire leg and I instinctively kicked out at him. He held my leg down and I watched the muscles in his arms contract.

"Sorry," I said, for almost kneeing him in the face.

"I should have warned you that one was coming." He took out a small tube and inserted the tip carefully between the gash in my skin.

"Is that skin glue?" I asked. My mom had some in her bathroom drawer at home, but I had never used it. He nodded.

"It works pretty well," he said. "It dissolves in your skin as the cut heals."

I watched with fascination as he lightly squeezed the cut together until the skin on my leg closed up and sealed itself shut. It was like magic.

He took a syringe out of the box and uncapped it with his teeth. He glanced at me for approval.

I looked at the needle and nodded for him to continue. I could hardly feel it pierce my skin.

"What was that?"

"Maybe the greatest invention ever created. It's like Advil, but five times as strong and it lasts for days."

Justin wrapped some gauze around my leg expertly and taped it up. He carefully, almost tenderly, pulled my jeans down over the gauze.

"You must do this a lot," I heard myself say. I was acutely aware of his hand still lingering on my leg. His face was only inches from mine. Our eyes held together a moment longer than necessary. He dropped his hand and stood up.

"You're good to go," he said, and handed me a ball of gauze. "I'd change that in the morning and try not to get it wet for a few days."

Riley, Emily, and Mark sat at the kitchen table studying a map of Washington. Justin walked over to them. "I need to get her home. Is there an extra pair of pants in the house?"

Riley looked over at my jeans.

"Her mom might get upset if I bring her daughter home soaked in blood," Justin pointed out. Riley told him the bedroom down the hall had clothes in the dresser.

I stood up and winced at the soreness in my leg. Justin watched me with a worried look and I assured him it was fine.

"It'll take some time for the drugs to kick in," he said. He walked down the hall and motioned for me to follow him. The bedroom light automatically snapped on when we walked in and he rummaged through an old dresser. He pulled out a pair of black sweatpants.

"Will these work?" he asked. I grabbed them out of his hand.

"As long as there aren't flowers on them," I said. I sat down on the bed and looked up at him.

"Who trained you to do all this?" I asked. He sat next to me and ran his hands through his hair. I tried to stay calm. I'd never been on a bed with a guy before, at least not with a guy I wanted

115

to kiss so bad it felt like my heart was having some kind of a seizure in my chest.

"No one trained me. I pretty much taught myself."

Finally, things were falling into place. Why Justin was seeking me out. What I was doing here tonight. "I get it," I say. "You're the one that trains."

"Right."

I leaned back on my hands and studied him. "And you recruit people?" I asked.

"Sometimes," he said.

"What's the name of your class? Anti-establishment 101?"

"Funny," he said. He leaned back on his hands, too, so his face was level with mine. I felt the soft blanket under my fingers and had an urge to lie all the way back on the bed. And pull him down with me.

"What does a person have to do to get in?" I asked. "Break the law?"

"A rebellious streak doesn't hurt," he said, and held my eyes. "And knowledge of underwater-driving vehicles is a bonus."

I glanced down at my leg and could already feel the pain beginning to fade. "Any pointers for me?"

His eyes stayed on mine. "On what?"

"On how to outsmart a probation officer? Hypothetically."

His lips curled up and he looked away for a moment.

"My best advice is to get to know your strengths. You can't always count on technology to save you. You need to know what you carry in here," he said, and he tapped his head. "And in here," he said, and tapped his chest. "The gadgets, the cars, those things are great. But first you have to be able to think on your feet. That's been our biggest advantage. We try to sever the connection between technology and people. Like tonight in Toledo. Turn the power off and people are too numb to react. That's when we make our move."

"Know my strengths," I thought out loud.

"Yours are pretty obvious," he continued, and I raised my eyebrows. "You're smart, that's your greatest advantage. And you're also a woman, another huge advantage."

I wrinkled my forehead. "How is being a woman going to help me get away from the cops?"

He grinned. "Guys are easy to distract," he said. "You're young, you're gorgeous—that's a huge power, if you know how to use it."

I felt my face heat up. Gorgeous? Did he actually say that?

Justin stood up and told me we should get going and shut the door behind him. I sighed and stretched my legs out in front of me, exhausted. I took my phone out of my pocket and saw it was almost midnight.

"Crap," I muttered out loud. I voice-messaged my mom, apologizing, and said I was on my way home. I slowly took off my shoes and jeans and studied the gauze wrapped clean and secure around my leg. My skin still prickled where Justin's hand had touched me and I couldn't tell if it was from the cut or from the memory of his fingers.

I was pathetic. Who gets aroused for getting first aid? He was being kind and responsible and I was being ridiculous. I pulled the soft black sweatpants over my legs and put my shoes and socks back on. I opened the door and walked down the hall to the main room to find Justin standing by the door waiting for me.

I said goodbye to Riley, Mark, and Emily and followed him into the cool night air. He unlocked the door of a blue sports car and I slid in. The medicine was taking effect and making me drowsy.

I yawned and rested my head against the back of the seat. His phone rang and he glanced down at the screen.

"I have to take this," he said. I nodded as he pressed an earpod into his ear. While Justin talked, I was content to listen to his voice and I found myself drifting off to sleep.

The next thing I knew someone was saying my name and I opened my groggy eyes to see the front of my house, the porch light on. I yawned again and heard Justin tell somebody he'd call them back. He took out his earpod and looked over at me.

"I'm heading out of town tomorrow," he said. "Have fun on your chatwalk this weekend," he added with a mocking grin.

I shuddered at the memory of the virtual walk Paul asked me to take. "That might have to fall through."

"You could fake a sprained index finger," he offered.

"Yeah," I said, "or a hand cramp."

Justin grinned and his eyes reflected the porch light. I stared back into them and I knew I was gaping but I couldn't look away. Silence stretched between us in the small space of the car and something electric charged the air.

His face turned serious. "The next time I'm in town, will you meet with my friends again? We have to talk to you about something."

I felt dazed but I couldn't tell if it was the medicine or sitting so close to him in the confined space. Close enough to hear him breathe and smell his skin.

"You know where to find me," I said. He finally let my eyes go. I opened the door and had to give my full concentration over to walking toward the front door. I didn't know what was coming over me. My body tingled and my stomach was tied in knots and my head was so light it felt like I was floating, back and forth, in a dark ocean current.

CHAPTER twelve

I slept in until almost noon the next day and woke up feeling like a truck had run me over. A rock song suddenly pumped through my wall speakers, the music tugging at me like hands trying to pull me out of bed. I trudged into the bathroom and took some pain reliever; the shot Justin gave me didn't live up to its pain-free promise. I washed my face and smoothed out my messy hair with a brush. After I dressed, making sure to put on baggy pants so they wouldn't rub against my leg, I tied my hair back in a ponytail and hobbled down the stairs for breakfast. I walked into the kitchen and jumped to see my dad's face staring back at me, his image projected on our wall screen. For a second I thought I was seeing a ghost.

"I was wondering if you'd ever get up," he said to me. My mom stood in the middle of the kitchen, obviously talking to him online.

"You scared me," I breathed. I passed my mom to get to the coffee machine and poured myself a cup, pumping cream and sugar inside.

"What else is new?" she asked him as she pointed out a breakfast bar and a bowl of vitamins set out on the table for me.

I sat down and picked at the protein bar. It was stale and tasted bland, but I never considered it until Justin pointed it out to me.

"There was a power outage last night in Toledo," my dad said with annoyance.

I quickly took another bite of the bar and raised my eyebrows in surprise.

"Is everything all right?" I asked with my mouth full.

"It only lasted twenty minutes." He smirked. "You'd think with all the advances in technology they could avoid things like this."

I nodded with agreement and hoped my acting was convincing. "How long will you be traveling?" I asked, and did my best not to sound hopeful.

"Probably another week," he said. He gave me a careful stare. I noticed dark circles under his eyes and wondered how many hours a week my father worked. The older I got, the more I noticed his job demanded him twenty-four hours a day.

He and Mom discussed a volunteer luncheon she promised to organize this week. He turned to me before they hung up and his identical eyes met mine.

"I love you, Maddie," he said. We always ended conversations this way. And I never thought much into it. They were just words, like a standard greeting. But now love was starting to mean more to me than a simple expression, than a routine. Maybe I was demanding more out of the word.

"Have a safe trip," I said. My dad nodded and his face disappeared from the screen. Even though his image was gone, I could still see those dark, untrusting eyes. I looked outside and low gray clouds swept by overhead. I felt lonely for my dad. I wondered if he, like Justin, let himself get close to anyone.

❂

I stayed in my room the rest of the week sulking. This life had always been my routine but now it felt like a cage. I had walked from a moving, living, breathing artificial world back into my digital real one but now it felt so backward. I sat at my computer and pressed buttons, but found myself staring at my fingertips, craving more.

My mind drifted away from school and papers and practical things I should be concentrating on. My brain decided irrational ideas were more important to consider, like how many girls Justin had trained. Probably hundreds. I imagined how many girls, like me, he was recruiting.

I wondered if there was a Justin Solvi fan site. Most likely. The thought made my heart sink. Every girl he meets has to fall in love with him. *But,* did he call those girls gorgeous? Did he take those girls out for cake and coffee? Was that a date? Oh, god. Obsessing over a boy is like throwing precious time into the garbage, and all I have to show for it is chewed-off fingernails, self-doubt, and emotional distress.

Saturday night, a week after I'd seen Justin, I sat at the window seat in my bedroom and stared outside. I studied the leaves intently, as if I could see all the answers to my questions perched on the branches if I looked hard enough. I spent too many days thinking, only to end up back where I started. Thoughts are circular, they don't take you anywhere. They don't have feet—they can't gain any ground. They can trap you if you don't eventually stand up and make a move.

I heard a knock at my door and sat up straighter.

"Maddie?"

"Yeah," I mumbled, still gazing out the window.

"Can I come in?"

My mom opened the door. I moved over on the seat to make room for her. She crossed the room to join me and carried two books.

"Here," she said, and sat down next to me. "I thought you could use these tonight."

I took the books and ran my finger along the spine of one, titled *Emma,* and opened it up. I inhaled the strong, rich scent of the aged paper and ink and flipped the soft paper through my fingers. This was the third Jane Austen book my mom had given me. I looked at the other book, small and thin, titled *The Little Prince.* I didn't recognize the French author.

She looked at the cover and smiled. "That was one of my favorites when I was your age." She laughed to herself. "You're probably going to think this is dumb, but I kept a reading journal all through school. Every year I wrote down my top ten favorite books. I even wrote reviews on them. Those are the books I've been handing down to you."

I looked at the bookcase in my room, a large, dark mahogany wooden unit with glass doors, and realized she was right. She gave me about ten books a year and each one felt like a friend to me, always there when I needed it to lift me up. My bookshelf was my favorite part of my room. It had a calming presence. Maybe there was something to be said about the feeling and presence of real books.

"That isn't dumb at all. It's your passion." I held the books tightly in my hands and thanked her. She creased her eyebrows and studied me like she was worried about something.

"What is it?" I asked.

"Your father loves you, Maddie. You believe that, don't you?"

Her words surprised me. I looked out the window and thought about the question. "He pretends to trust me but then he turns around and questions everything I do."

"You're too young to understand. Someday—"

"Mom," I interrupted, "you've been telling me that since I was five years old. And you know what, I grew up. Look at me. I'm an adult. If I had to go out into the world tomorrow and live on my own, I'd be okay. Making all my decisions for me on who I can be friends with and where I can go isn't love. It isn't helping me. It's limiting me."

My mom took a deep breath as she registered this.

"Pretty soon I *will* have to start making decisions for myself," I said. "So I'd appreciate it if you guys would start weaning me off of your control a little bit."

She shook her head. I knew she thought I was overreacting.

"I'm serious. Do you want me to call you when I'm thirty-five and ask you if I can watch an R-rated movie? Do you want me to be that needy? Because that's how Dad's trying to raise me."

Mom had such amazing patience with me. I always said too much around her and she always listened, never raising her voice, never contradicting me. She was the one person my dad listened to, the only person who could ever make him reconsider his ideas.

"It's partly my fault," she said. "I've been trying to give you more freedom and convince your father to let you socialize. But certain people aren't the best influence for you."

I knew exactly who she was referring to.

"I've seen the way you act around him," she said. "And it worries me a little bit. He brings out another side of you."

The best side of me, I wanted to say.

"We're just friends, it's not a big deal."

My mom looked at me, confused. "What do you mean? You're not dating Justin?"

I groaned at the ceiling and could feel my face turning red. "No, we're not dating. He isn't interested in me like that."

Mom looked away as I said this. "Hmm," she said thoughtfully. "That's not the impression I get."

I brushed my hand in the air as if I could swat her comment away.

"I really don't want to talk about this. The point I'm trying to make is if Dad really loved me, he would let the past go." I stammered over the last few words. "It's been over two years. He can trust me."

"Trust comes by earning it, not expecting it," she told me.

"So does love," I said. She studied my face and slowly nodded before she stood up.

I looked down at the two books on my window seat after she left. A car passed by outside and my ears perked up hopefully and my heartbeat doubled but the sound faded away. I flopped down on my bed and stared at the ceiling, counting all the things I wished I could change about my life. But I'm learning it's human nature to want the things you can't have. What changes is how you go about pursuing the things you want. When you're a little kid and you're told no, you scream and throw a temper tantrum. When you're a teenager and your parents tell you no, you're old enough to internalize your temper tantrum. But you're smarter and you're sneakier this time around. So you nod and act like you care when they say no, when they tell you who you can be friends with, when they say *they know what's best.*

But then you go behind their backs to do it anyway.

Because at some point, you need to start calling the shots. At some point, you have to start believing *you* know what's best. Or, I thought with a smile, you just stop asking for their permission in the first place.

❁

When I hopped on the train for soccer practice, I found Erin in her usual window seat at the back of the car. I sat down next to her, relieved to see someone in person again. I felt like my senses were waking up again and stretching out after being packed away for too long.

"What's new?" I asked her when I sat down. She was wearing a MindReader and staring at her flipscreen. She nodded in response and I raised an eyebrow. Another second went by.

"How's life?" she asked me. I watched her with interest. She rarely looked at me and it never really bothered me before. But I wanted her to look at me. I needed her to. I wanted to be seen and heard and appreciated. Isn't that what friendship was?

"Awful," I told her. She didn't hear me. She asked me what I've been up to.

"I blew my grandma's trust fund on gambling," I said.

She raised her eyebrows and nodded. I waited for her to look up, but she was engrossed in her computer. Her eyes stared straight ahead like she was hypnotized by the screen.

I studied her face and for the first time in my four years of knowing her, doubted if we were ever really friends. "Hey, Erin?" I waited for her eyes to meet mine but they never did. They hadn't since I got on the train.

"Yeah?" she asked. She leaned closer to me. I took a deep breath and kept my voice friendly.

"Can you turn that off for a second?" I asked, and pointed at her computer. She glanced up from the screen with surprise. At that same instant, her screen flashed and she touched the light to check a message. I clenched my teeth with annoyance.

"Don't you ever get sick of all this?" I asked. Erin slid her MindReader off her head and stared at me like she didn't know who I was.

"Sick of what?"

"All this . . . shit," I said, waving at her hands and ears and eyes, all plugged into some device as if her brain was a battery and couldn't be charged, couldn't think without all these programs and voices and messages doing it for her.

"Can't you just leave it alone once in a while?" I asked. "Why do you need to bring all this to soccer practice?" I felt bad for attacking her. I wished I had Justin's words, the patient way he could explain things to me, but I accepted years ago that patience is a genetic trait that was never passed down to me.

Erin's mouth dropped open and she looked down at the flipscreen in her lap. She stared dumbly back at me.

"I dare you to turn that off for an entire day," I said.

She blinked back at me. "Why?"

"Why not?" I challenged her.

"I want to be connected," she said.

"Who are you connected to?" I asked.

She wrinkled her eyebrows, clearly puzzled. "My friends, my clubs, my life."

"You don't think there's more to life than that little screen? Believe me, if you shut it off for a little while, you'll live. Just in a different way."

"Whoa, Maddie," she said. "Where is this coming from? I've always been like this. And, might I add, until recently your flipscreen could have been surgically attached to your hands."

I couldn't help but smile. Erin's eyes were on me, her attention was mine. This might be the longest uninterrupted conversation we'd ever had. I stared at her eyes and never realized how beautiful they were, a dark blue with rings of brown around the center. I never noticed her eyes before because she barely gave me the chance to look at them. I told her this out loud and her face reddened. She closed her flipscreen with an awkward smile on her face.

"Maddie, you're being weird." She looked at me skeptically. "Who have you been hanging out with?"

❁

When I got home from soccer practice my mom sent a voice message saying she met my dad for an interview downtown and they'd be home in a few hours.

I had a window of time. I knew what I needed to do. Who I needed to see. After I showered and dressed I pulled on my favorite brown army cap over my damp hair and headed downstairs. I stepped outside and the warm sunshine stroked my bare arms. I headed down the street and hopped on the train toward the coffee shop Justin took me to over a month ago. Just as I jumped down to the sidewalk, I noticed Clare walking down the steps of the café.

"Clare!" I yelled, and ran to catch her.

"Madeline," she said with a grin, and threw her arms around me. Her eyes were wide and shining and genuinely happy to see me. "What are you doing here?"

I glanced in the windows. "I need to talk to Justin. Have you heard from him?" I asked.

She nodded. "I'm actually on my way to see him."

"He's in town?" I asked with surprise. Something deflated inside of me, as if I expected to be the first person Justin would call. Like I was more than just a name on a long list of people he was recruiting.

"Why don't you come with me?" she offered. "I'm sure he wants to see you."

She told me they were at Scott's apartment and it was right down the street. She pointed out a gray sky-rise apartment around the block. Before I could say no, Clare wrapped her hand around my arm and pulled me along. We walked up the steps to the glass entry doors of the apartment. She pressed Scott's number and shortly after his voice spoke over the intercom.

"I see you brought a friend," he said flatly, and the metal door buzzed open.

"Maybe I shouldn't have come," I whispered as we walked up the stairs to the second floor.

Clare shook her head. "Scott has zero people skills," she said. "Try not to let him intimidate you." When we got to apartment 28, Clare knocked and a voice yelled for us to come in. I followed Clare inside. We entered a large, open living room and Scott's voice echoed off the bare walls.

"Well, speak of the devil."

Scott sat next to Molly in the middle of the room. I narrowed my eyes at the mocking grin on his face and goose bumps rose up on my arms. My intuition was right: he didn't want me here. I glanced around and saw the apartment was bare except for a tattered couch and folding chairs spread out haphazardly. Jake, Riley, and Pat sat in one corner and all nodded to me. The room was quiet, so quiet it screamed.

Clare introduced me to two other men sitting there, Spencer and his dad, Ray, the same ones I met at the coffee shop, and I nodded in their direction. The strongest energy in the room came from the far wall where Justin stood. He was watching me. He leaned against the wall with a baseball cap pulled low over his face and his arms were crossed over his chest. He looked about as happy to see me as Scott.

"Where'd you pick her up?" Scott asked Clare.

Clare sat down and glared back at him. "She was at the coffee shop so I invited her along. What's the big deal?"

There was another spell of silence that lasted too long. I stood at the edge of the room, close to the door, and thought about turning to go until Scott spoke up.

"You might as well be part of this."

"Why don't we finish that matter up later? I still need to talk to her," Justin interjected.

"She's a big girl, she can handle it." Scott looked back at me and I met his gaze.

"I can handle what?"

Scott smiled again. "Come on, Madeline, you've got to know why you're here."

Another heavy silence fell. I glanced around the room and cleared my throat.

"I'm assuming you're recruiting me, if that's what you mean," I spoke up.

Scott nodded slowly. "You know how helpful you could be to us."

I frowned at this. "Helpful? How exactly?"

He smirked. "You have connections we could only dream of acquiring. Right at your fingertips."

My jaw tightened. "What are you talking about?"

Scott gave an exasperated sigh and glared at Justin. "Haven't you told her anything? What the hell have you been doing this whole time?"

Justin returned Scott's question with a livid glare.

"Look, Madeline, I'll set it straight in two minutes." He shot Justin a look before he continued. "We've had our eye on you for years."

"You've had your eye on me?"

"Ever since Portland. You helped lead that sabotage. It was you that hacked into your dad's files and handed out the location of those towers. Only about five people in the entire country have access to that information."

I felt my breath start to come out shallow. Too many steady eyes were on me. There was no point in denying it now. In fact, it was almost a relief to let the truth go.

"How did you find out?" I asked.

Scott stood up and paced back and forth. "It wasn't easy. What were you, about fifteen when you pulled that off? After it happened, you created enough false computer trails to make the media give up investigating the case. So it never leaked out as to who actually released that information. It was brilliant, I have to admit."

"If it was so brilliant I wouldn't have gotten caught in the first place," I pointed out. I didn't want to be complimented on the greatest mistake of my life, one that I paid for every single day.

"Still, it couldn't have been easy to pull off. I assume there's some pretty high security set up on your father's computer. We've been trying to figure out who that hacker was for the past few years. You keep your identity pretty anonymous."

I forced my voice to be steady. "My dad's a political celebrity. I have to set up different identities if I want any privacy."

"Or maybe you just don't want to be associated with what he represents?"

I narrowed my eyes. "Maybe."

"Well," he said, "you made it a challenge to find you. Before you were caught, you were part of a lot of anti-DS groups. But then all of a sudden you disappeared."

I rolled my eyes. "Obviously. My dad blocked all those sites from my computer. He almost went to jail for my mistake," I added. "He would have been tried for treason."

"Oh," Scott said mockingly. "I'd hate to see your dad in jail." His face held a sarcastic smile that made my hands ball into fists. "Justin's been trying to track you down. A couple months ago we finally traced the traffic of your profiles back to Corvallis and realized the hacker came from inside the Freeman family itself." He chuckled to himself and looked at me with half-lidded eyes.

"What's the phrase?" he asked me. " 'Sweet irony'?"

"Why don't you get to the point?" I shot back.

He took his time. "We investigated you and your mom but we assumed it was your older brother that stole the files. Not that a girl couldn't pull that off, but we just didn't expect it since your brother's a computer engineer. Then we realized he lives in L.A., which is what confused us. So Justin made plans to meet you in person to figure out who was behind all this."

"Well, congratulations on cracking the case. Why don't you tell me what you want?" Scott smiled at my blunt attitude but his eyes were still hard.

"We need inside information that is only accessible on your father's mainframe computer, which you can obviously hack into. Justin thought if he got through to you, you'd eventually help us."

"What makes you think I can still access any of his files?"

"You got it once. I believe you could do it again, if it was important enough to you."

As I listened to Scott, realization began to sink in. Justin wasn't recruiting me to train me. He was using me to get to my father. They knew I aided in one rebellion and assumed I'd be easy to persuade again. It was easy enough for them; they didn't have to live with the consequences. And if they wanted to take down digital school, they were right. I was the perfect person to do the dirty work. I was the key they were looking for.

"Let me get this straight. You guys have all been pursuing me just to get to my dad?" I refused to meet Justin's gaze, but I could sense him watching me out of the corner of my eye. His body was rigid against the wall. It all made sense now. If Justin's time was so valuable, it would take a monumental reason for him to invest so much of it in a single person. Apparently, I was that monumental reason. I was his little business investment. And I dared myself to believe that finally someone cared about me, that these were my first, real friends. I swallowed and felt a cold chill run over my body.

Scott stopped pacing and faced me. "If we're serious about leading a reform to stop digital school that has some backbone behind it, we need your dad's connections. We need names and files and contact lists. He has the technology available to contact every member, student, and teacher of the digital school system simultaneously. It would be nice to obtain that listserv."

I glared back at him, since these were the same files I hacked into when I was fifteen. The same information that landed me with a lifestyle similar to house arrest.

The room was silent. You couldn't hear a breath or a movement, as if everyone was sitting on the edge of their seats, waiting for the verdict.

"We want you to join our side, for a cause we know you believe in," Scott said. "We're the good guys and you know it. We want people to have a choice and we're not going to back down, ever. But it would make our job a lot easier if you'd commit to helping us."

Justin's voice filled the air and it made me wince because it was cold and hard. "Maddie, we need your help. We've come a long way, but we hit a dead end. You're the catalyst we need to get this going," he said.

"That's right," I said, and narrowed my eyes at him. "I'm your little investment."

I looked down at the ground and shook my head. After the bombing, I witnessed the havoc my mistake had on my family. I knew it was too high of a price to pay.

I met Scott's eyes and crossed my arms over my chest. Every eye in the room was on me. "My dad still gives me lie detector tests," I said. I could hear my voice echoing off the walls. "Now it's only every six weeks. It was every day for three months, just to make sure I felt guilty for what I did. To make sure I wasn't working with any of the protesters again. I had to go through counseling for a year. If I screw up one more time, that's it. I'll get arrested. Asking me to go behind his back again is asking me to choose you over my family. I can't do that."

Clare broke in. "But they forgave you, Maddie. They can't stay mad at you forever. It might be hard at first, you might have to stay away for a while but they'll forgive you. They might even thank you someday," she pleaded with me.

I glared angrily at her. "I really doubt they will thank me for betraying them. I doubt my dad will *thank* me for trying to take down a system he's worked his entire life to build." I shook my head firmly. "I can't do it. I'll support you, I believe in what you're doing, you're right about that, but you're asking me to destroy my family."

Scott threw his hands down with impatience. "Then you're worthless to us."

"I'm worthless?"

"We have plenty of supporters. But we've hit a brick wall. The only way to break it down is to get into your father's files. That's the only reason Justin wasted his precious time to find you. Do you think he has time to go around and make friends? We work night and day at this job. We don't have time for friends. We're committed to this cause. So you're either in one hundred percent or you're out."

"Well I won't keep you in suspense. I'm out." I turned and felt my eyes burn as I slammed the door shut behind me. The stairs were difficult to see through a blur of tears but I took them two at a time. I stumbled out the front doors and when I got down to the sidewalk I heard a voice I simultaneously loathed and loved.

"Maddie?"

I ignored him and lengthened my strides but I could hear him catching up to me.

"Would you wait a minute?"

"You're a little late, Justin," I yelled over my shoulder. He grabbed my arm when he caught up and tried to turn me around, but I yanked it back and kept my eyes forward, concentrating on the train stop ahead of me.

"Look, I was going to tell you everything."

"Really? What were you going to say exactly?" I asked. My voice shook with humiliation and anger.

"I was waiting for the right way to bring all this up," he said. "I wanted you to trust me first, and that takes time to build. Would you look at me?" He grabbed my arm again and forced me to turn around.

"I'm sorry," he said.

"You're an asshole!" I yelled. He dropped his hand to his side and a brief flicker of amusement passed over his eyes. This just made me more infuriated. I stuck my hands on my hips and glowered at him.

"You were using me the whole time. And now, after you all *admit* you're using me, you have the nerve to ask me to betray the only people that love me in the entire world to help you lead a revolution?"

"Wait, I—"

"Then," I cut in, "after I agree to be your magic key to unlock my dad's treasure chest of stupid listservs, and probably get arrested and disowned by my family in the process, what are you going to do? Pat me on the back and say thanks? Give me a rebel of the year award to hang up in my jail cell? Call me crazy, but that doesn't sound appealing to me."

I took a deep breath. I just needed to calm down. In a way, it was a relief to finally know the truth. Maybe it would put an end to the stupid infatuation I had with him. At least I knew his motive for spending so much time with me. It never made sense why someone as amazing as Justin would give me so much attention. I turned and headed down the sidewalk and he followed me. I could feel his eyes on my back.

"I was never using you," he said.

"Leave me alone," I said, but he was next to me again.

"Would you just listen? Scott doesn't know how I feel."

I threw my hands up in the air. "Why weren't you honest with me the first night I met you at the tutor session? You're the one always telling me I should speak my mind."

A small grin played on his lips. "Look, if you want to know the truth, I was a little intimidated the night I met you."

I stopped and turned to stare at him.

"*You* were intimidated?"

Justin looked away as he started to explain.

"I researched everything you did when you were fifteen." He looked back at me with admiration. "My parents talked you up to be some kind of martyr. So, I guess you could say you've been an inspiration to me for a while."

I stared blankly back at him. It never occurred to me that what I did inspired people, or that people supported me. I'd only seen the negative effect it had.

"We've been watching your moves online the past few years. And like Scott said, you stayed pretty anonymous."

"You've been spying on me?"

"We had to make sure you were still"—he considered the right word for a moment—"impressionable. And we didn't know who you physically were." He grinned. "It took us almost three years to find you. We've never spent that kind of time trying to track down anyone. And you're right, I should have been honest with you the first day we met. But—"

He cut himself off and looked away. I watched his face change into an expression I'd never seen before. He almost looked embarrassed. Or nervous. He drummed his hands against his sides.

"You threw me off," he said finally.

I wrinkled my eyebrows in confusion. "How?"

He sighed, and whatever guard he was hanging on to crumbled and his shoulders sank a little bit. "The night I met you? I was looking for a guy. I thought you were your brother."

I couldn't help but smile. Was it that unbelievable to think a girl could be just as rebellious as a guy? That a girl could be just as technically savvy as the boys? Justin looked down at his feet.

"When I realized it was you—"

He began to trip over his words as he tried to explain. I'd never seen him so unsure of himself before. He pulled his hands over the rim of his hat. He looked back at me and I felt my stomach knot up.

"I don't spend much time around girls so it threw me off. I didn't know how to act with you. It doesn't help that you're—"

He trailed off again and it made me smile.

"What?" I asked.

He gave me a knowing look. "You're pretty easy on the eyes, Madeline. In case you didn't know."

I felt my face flush at his words and looked away. I still couldn't believe it. Justin Solvi was attracted to me. That didn't quite compare to the obsessive crush I had on him. I started walking again and he followed me to the train stop.

"I still don't understand why you didn't bring up Portland sooner."

"I did bring it up," he reminded me. "I talked about the bombings, I told you everything about my parents. I answered every question you asked me about my past. And I never talk to people about my family. I keep my personal life private. But I thought if I was honest with you, you'd open up to me. I didn't want to force it out of you. That's why I waited."

A ZipShuttle hissed past us and kicked up a gust of wind.

"I can't believe you were nervous to meet me," I said with a grin. "You're always the picture of cool and confident."

"It's a front. I've been working on it for years," Justin said. His eyes narrowed at me. "And you're pretty hard to read yourself."

I shrugged. "It's a front. I've been working on it for years."

He smiled. "You know, you and I aren't so different. Our backgrounds are pretty similar if you think about it. Fighting digital school, hiding our identities, screwed-up families."

I looked down the street and saw the train approaching.

"You save people every day," I told him. "I hacked into my dad's files because I was too young to know any better. We're not that similar."

"Don't downplay what you did. I help people every day. One at a time. Helping out a person here and there, what I do is great but practically a joke next to what you're capable of. I can build a snow fort. You can start an avalanche."

I closed my eyes and spoke slowly. "I'm not the same person I was back then. I was stupid and rebellious and confused."

"Is that what the therapists tried to convince you, what your dad tells you?"

I shook my head. "I'm not that girl anymore. I've grown up and I learned from that experience."

"Really?" he said, and took a step closer to me. "Then why did you even agree to meet me in person? Maybe one out of a thousand people would have agreed to do that. That's how scared most people are to leave their homes these days. Why did you throw your dad's tracker on a train going to Canada? Why did the education benefit make you physically sick? You *are* that girl, Maddie. You're just getting it beat out of you."

I stared back at him and felt goose bumps creep up my arms again. Sometimes talking to Justin was like having a mirror pulled in front of me so I could see myself for who I really was.

"Maybe you're right. But I won't hurt my parents again," I said. "It's not worth it. It will never be worth it to use people to get what you want. I learned that when I was fifteen."

"We're not asking you to pick us over them," Justin said quietly.

"But you are," I said. I sighed as the train slowed to stop in front of us. My mind was exhausted with arguing. "Listen, I know this is probably a typical day for you, but I'm ready to snap. So, can you give me some time to think about this?"

His features tightened but he nodded. I boarded the train and I didn't have to look out the window to know he was still standing there, watching me. But I forced my eyes ahead of me as the train pulled away. I let the train move me forward to somewhere safe, predictable, a place where I could call the shots and I could hold people away and where no one reminded me of who I was because no one really knew me. And sometimes, that kind of a life is the safest place to be.

June 14, 2060

I chatted Justin a few nights ago. I printed out our discussion because I miss his words. They remind me of who I want to be. Or maybe who I've been all along. I like the idea I can carry them with me.

BaleyF: *I miss our talks.*
MustangV-8: *Then let's talk.*
BaleyF: *Can I ask you something?*
MustangV-8: *Anything.*
BaleyF: *Why are you so anticomputers?*
MustangV-8: *It's not that I'm anticomputers. They have their advantages. But technology can be like a drug if you don't keep it in check. After a while it gets in your system and you're addicted. You get to a point where you can't live without it and that's when the drug controls you. We've become so dependent on computers we can't cut ourselves off.*
BaleyF: *What makes us so different from computers?*
MustangV-8: *Lots of things, thank God.*
BaleyF: *Like?*

MustangV-8:   *Our brains.*

BaleyF: *Computers have brains, sort of.*

MustangV-8:   *But they don't have a conscience. We can feel guilt, regret, remorse, sympathy, because we can think about our actions.*

BaleyF: *Computers think. They figure things out every day.*

MustangV-8:   *But do they feel anything? Do they get embarrassed, frustrated, excited?*

BaleyF: *I guess not.*

MustangV-8:   *It's our consciousness that sets us apart. That makes us human. That makes us artists and creators and destroyers. Lately, more destroyers than anything.*

BaleyF: *Do you think your parents are creators?*

MustangV-8:   *Some of the last of them, yes.*

BaleyF: *Then you must think my father's a destroyer.*

MustangV-8:   *I think your father has more depth than that. He also has a job to fulfill. But maybe we can work together to change his mind?*

BaleyF: *Maybe we're stuck with this life.*

MustangV-8:   *Why would you say that?*

BaleyF: *This is reality. It's permanent. Why fight it?*

MustangV-8:   *Because that's the point, nothing is ever permanent. We're just being brainwashed to think there isn't more out there. Here's the truth: your situation is never permanent. It's what you make it. Life isn't solid, it's fluid. It changes. You say we're stuck but that's a hopeless way to look at it. It's like saying we should give up.*

BaleyF: *Most people prefer to be guided. It saves a lot of energy to follow a path than carve out your own.*

MustangV-8: *That's what we need to fight. Life should be a risk. It's more than a straight line that you can see clearly from one point to the other. It dips and curves and you never know what's around the bend sometimes until you get there. That scares a lot of people. But that's the beauty of it.*

BaleyF: *I know, but everything is disoriented right now. It's like I'm seeing everything with new eyes, there's too much to take in all at once. You need to give me some time to adjust.*

MustangV-8: *Yeah. But sometimes the more disoriented you are, the more clearly you start to see.*

CHAPTER *thirteen*

A few weeks passed and boredom fell over me like a suffocating blanket. I couldn't lift it. I spent every day in my bedroom. Stifled. Enclosed. I looked up some of my online contacts that I'd neglected. But now our friendships seemed condensed and unrealistic, like a postcard picture of a place I'd never been to. I lost hours of time searching people's profiles, looking for more Justins and Clares. I heard once that you meet the same people over and over in life. But now, I didn't believe it. I'd lived seventeen years and had never met people like them. Some people try to tell you the things you want in life are out of your grasp, while others lift you up on their shoulders and help you reach them. I may not know a lot, but I prefer to fill my life with people who let me climb on top of their shoulders, not people who try to keep me planted on the ground.

I hung out at my usual social sites and went to movies with friends but I couldn't shake the idea that I wasn't *going* to a movie *with* anyone. I was just this girl, sitting behind a screen being tricked into thinking I was experiencing something. I face-chatted a few of my contacts but I wanted to reach through the screen and hold their hands and feel their presence. I wanted more than this hollow life.

My friends had become billboard advertisements of themselves. Is that all people were anymore? An advertisement of a person that catches our attention because we like the layout, the copy, the font? Had people become that easy to define? I used to think so. But now I realized all of my digital friendships hovered on the surface. There was never any depth. We didn't discuss ourselves because we didn't take the time to know ourselves. We were too busy being shown who we should be, what we should wear, what groups we should join. Who we should mimic. We didn't have time to form our own thoughts or opinions so we quoted others.

Before I met Justin I was starting to accept my life and where it was headed. Now I didn't know who I was; I didn't know what I wanted anymore. It felt like someone tipped me upside down, shook out my thoughts, my past, my goals, and turned me right side up again, only to start over.

My cell phone rang and I inhaled a breath of relief when I saw the name on the screen.

"Hey," Clare said.

"What are you doing?" I asked, and tapped my foot impatiently.

"Researching a paper I have to write about geothermal energy," she said. "Thrilling."

I nodded and stared at my flipscreen. "Sounds like it."

"I need a study break," she said.

I sat up straighter. "Want to do something?"

Clare laughed. Her laughter was light and contagious. It made me smile.

"Are you as stir-crazy as I am?" she asked.

"Want to find some music? We could go to that club, the one on the Westside?"

"I was just going to ask you the same thing," Clare said. "Meet me at the train stop on Hamersley and Fifth."

I turned my phone off and jumped to my feet as if the door of my locked cage suddenly sprang open. I looked down at my baggy jeans and sweatshirt and they were comfortable and known, but they didn't reflect my mood. Life can change drastically at night. So should clothes. I opened my closet and rummaged inside until I found a short black skirt with the price tags still attached. I pulled out a tight blue tank top I'd never worn and discovered a lonely pair of heels stashed deep in the back of my closet. I had to wipe a layer of dust off of them; they were probably a gift Mom gave me in hopes that I'd one day try to look feminine. I quickly changed and examined myself in the full-length mirror. My eyes went directly to the scar on my calf and my stomach did flips at the memory of the night it happened, of Justin's fingers touching my skin.

Before I wasted another minute fantasizing, I went into the bathroom. I figured, if I'm going all out, I might as well do something with my hair. I opened up a drawer below the sink and rummaged through its contents. I swore I owned some sort of hair-styling device. I finally settled on straightening gel and smoothed some of the sticky liquid through my hair. I combed it out and the gel gave it the exact effect I wanted. My long hair fell straight and severe over my shoulders and had a soft shine. I dabbed red lip-gloss on my lips and dusted dark eye shadow on my eyelids. I looked at my reflection in the mirror and shrugged. I was no candidate for Team Sparkle, but it would do. Now I just had to get around my father.

I walked downstairs and found my mom sitting in the living room watching TV. She gaped at me and looked me up and down.

"Maddie? Is that you in there?"

I grinned back at her.

"You're wearing heels." She bent down and examined them. "I must have bought you those a year ago." She glanced up at me, worried. "Do you have a fever?"

I rolled my eyes. "Is it all right if I go out with Clare?"

"Who's Clare?" she asked.

"She's just a friend."

My mom raised both eyebrows at this. "You dressed up like this for a girlfriend?"

"We're going to a club." I glanced down the hall. "Where's Dad?"

"He's on a conference call right now." She met my eyes. "You're just going with Clare, right?" she asked. I nodded because it was the truth, but her eyes were skeptical. "Then I guess it's all right, but only for a few hours."

❀

Twenty minutes later our train arrived at the Westside stop. The club was hot and loud and packed with people when we walked in. A band was setting up in the corner and people were already filling up the dance floor in front of the stage. Clare and I slid into an open booth we snagged just as a group got up to leave. She grabbed both my hands in hers and leaned toward me across the table.

"I just want you to know I'm really sorry about what happened at Scott's apartment."

I nodded and squeezed her hands back before she let go. "It's all right. You didn't know I'd be accosted."

She rolled her eyes. "Scott can be such a drama queen. It never crossed his mind that mocking and ridiculing you to your face might not be the wisest strategy to convince you to join our side."

I laughed lightly and shook my head.

"Maybe I should have told you all along," she said.

"Justin should have told me the truth," I reminded her. "But I think I understand why he didn't."

I looked out at the crowd, a mix of mostly young people our age. The band was starting to do sound checks.

"Anyway," she said. "I want you to know that I don't care if you *join our side* or whatever Scott calls it. I still want to be friends, no matter what happens."

I raised my eyebrows. "What makes you think I've said no?"

Clare leaned away from me. "But I thought you made your decision at Scott's?"

I smiled coyly. "I don't like being put on the spot," I said.

Clare's eyes lit up. "You mean, you're still considering helping us out?"

I shrugged. "I honestly don't know anymore. But if Justin could wait three years to ask me, he can wait a little while for me to decide. I just have to figure out a way to be useful to you guys without going behind my father's back."

Clare smiled at me. Suddenly, a young guy slid into the seat next to her. His thick, curly brown hair fell below his cheekbones. Blue eyes, the identical color and shape of Clare's, looked over at me.

"This is my brother," Clare said. "He makes it a point to interrupt all of my conversations."

"Noah," he said, and extended his long, wiry arm over the table.

"Hey," I said, and reached out to shake his hand. "Madeline."

Noah gave my hand a confident squeeze. His fingers were rough and callused as they pressed against mine.

"He's playing in the band tonight," Clare said.

"I don't think I've seen you before," Noah said to me.

"She grew up less than a mile from us," Clare told him. "Isn't that crazy?"

"What? And we've never met?"

I shrugged. "I'm a victim of DS."

"Oh, I get it," Noah said, and gave his sister a mocking stare. "You've only recently been liberated by the freedom fighters?"

I laughed at this and Clare rolled her eyes. Noah looked back at me with a grin. It felt so good to laugh again.

"Somebody's got to fight for a good cause," she reminded him.

"And somebody's got to write music about it," Noah pointed out.

"Noah's not quite as dedicated to changing the world as some of us," Clare said.

He shrugged. "I appreciate the effort though. When my little sister saves the human race from our dark demise, I will definitely buy her a beer and play at the party."

I laughed again and Clare sighed.

"Nice to meet you," he said, and strolled off toward the bar. I watched him go with a smile.

"He's adorable," I said.

"A lot of girls think so," Clare added. We glanced around the room at the growing number of women that were packing the dance floor.

Noah came back to our table with two drinks. "My treat," he said. He winked at his sister. "Clare's favorite," he said with a wide grin before he walked away.

I stared down at the pink fizzling drinks.

"What are these?" I asked.

Clare grimaced. "They're these new energy drinks. I swear, it's legalized crack, but no one has caught on yet."

I took a sip and it was so sweet it gave me a head rush.

"That's disgusting," I said.

"I know," Clare said. "Noah lives off of them. He only ordered it to annoy me. You've got to love brothers."

We looked over at the stage when the band began to play. A young girl sang lead vocals and her voice was low and seductive. It was the kind of voice that made you want to sink inside someone's arms. Clare and I were quiet for a few minutes listening to the band. Noah played the bass and his hair fell over his eyes, which I could see made half the girls in the crowd swoon. Their music had a reggae-rock sound.

"So," I asked Clare, "is Scott the leader of this whole thing?"

She shook her head. "He likes to think he is. He has the most technical experience out of any of us. I guess you could say he's the brains. He's hacked into more security systems than anyone. But I'd say Justin's the leader. He has the most respect. And he avoids computers like a virus. He's more active. He needs to be working directly with people to feel like he's making a difference."

"I don't think Molly likes me very much," I said.

Clare smirked. "Molly doesn't like anybody. She's pretty intense. She's eighteen, she already has a master's in psychology, and right now she's working toward a medical degree."

My mouth fell open with amazement.

"I wouldn't want to be that smart," Clare added. "Sometimes the more you know, the harder it is to enjoy life. It's like you lose curiosity or something." She told me if Molly doesn't talk to me, it's probably because she's psychoanalyzing me. It's her little hobby.

"And she's usually right on," Clare said. "She's like the psychic of the group, which comes in handy when you're always trying to figure out who's on your side."

"Where do you fit in to all this?"

Clare took a sip of her drink and her lips puckered from the sweet flavor. "That's a good question. I grew up with these guys so

I'm lucky enough just to know them. Justin likes having me along to meet new recruits and make people feel comfortable. He thinks communication is my strength. I want to help design face-to-face schools, if we ever get to that."

"What about the rest of the group?"

"Riley's really good with electronics. He can fix anything—cars, computers—I've seen him fix a public ZipShuttle that broke down and left some people stranded. In his spare time he flies planes."

"Oh," I said, like these were common hobbies for a teenager.

"It's crazy, these guys all have some sort of superhuman power. Pat's kind of like Justin. More hands-on. Fearless. Really good at being the gopher. When he was sixteen he set a record for the most interceptions in one year."

"I can't believe I've never found you guys, even before my sites were blocked. Believe me, I've been looking."

Clare smiled. "You can't find us. That's the point. We're impossible to trace."

"What do you mean?"

"Simple. We don't exist."

I stared back at her and waited for her to continue.

"There's no name that defines us. We don't have a fan site, believe me, we'd all get arrested if we drew attention to ourselves. We're connected with people all over the country," she said, "but the best way to keep secret is to stay invisible. It's a lot harder to find something that doesn't exist in the first place."

"Then how do you gain supporters?"

Clare shrugged. "We seek people out that we're confident will join our side. No one seeks us out. It's the safest way to move forward. We don't keep digital records."

Her eyes were serious, which for Clare was a rare sight. It made me tune out all the noise and movement around me. "Most of what we do just depends on trust and faith. I only see Justin once every few months. He fills us in on what's happening. What's to come. And we all support and trust each other. We believe in the process. It hasn't failed us yet."

Clare coughed on another sip of her drink and I offered to get us some water. I wandered over to the bar and noticed, for the first time I could ever recall, men watching me as I crossed the room. I observed, self-consciously, that some of their looks lingered and traced me up and down.

I set my hands on the smooth bar and ordered two waters. While I waited I observed groups of people dancing. I scanned the crowded room and stopped when my eyes met a familiar glance. My stomach twisted into knots.

Justin sat in the back corner of the room, at a booth with Spencer and Ray. He gave me a slow nod but his eyes were cautious. I instantly felt the energy in the room shift as if the lights dimmed or an air current changed direction. He was wearing a short-sleeved shirt that showed off his long, toned arms and his hair was a mess, as usual, tousled and shining and perfect. Of course he had to show up the one night I decided to go out and look effortlessly beautiful, just when I was trying to get over him.

I quickly looked away, grabbed my drinks, and headed back to the booth where I could avoid his eyes.

Clare looked at my frazzled expression.

"What's wrong?"

"Justin's here."

She nodded. "I know." She looked at my wide eyes. "Oh, you didn't know?"

"Of course not," I said, and ducked my head low like I was trying to hide.

"I thought you knew he was in town."

I groaned and ran my fingers through my hair.

"He's been here the whole time. I thought you saw him."

"I didn't."

"Well, it's no big deal. He's not going to come over here. He can sense when people don't want to talk to him."

I chewed my nails anxiously. "I know, it's just that his presence is a little—"

"Noticeable?"

I sighed. "Suffocating."

I took a long drink of water and waited for my heart to settle down. I tried to distract myself by asking Clare about her ideas for face-to-face school, and when Noah's band took a break he came over to sit with us. He was exactly the diversion I needed. Noah kept us entertained with traveling stories from playing gigs on the road. His stare didn't consume me like Justin's did and for the moment, I really needed that. After a twenty-minute break, Noah got up to join the band for its second set. They started off with a fast beat and Clare pulled me to the dance floor. We wove through the crowd until we were in the middle of the pack. A young guy, about my age, danced his way next to us with a friend at his side. He was a little taller than me and wore a blue button-down shirt that matched his eyes.

"Mike," he yelled over the music to introduce himself.

"Madeline," I yelled back.

He had beads of sweat on his forehead from dancing and his hair was dark and wavy. He looked like a business type, with his collared shirt buttoned all the way to the top and tucked into khaki dress pants.

"Is that your boyfriend?" he asked, nodding in Noah's direction. I laughed and shook my head.

"No, I just met him tonight."

"Oh," he said, "good to know." Mike danced closer to me, and his friend, who introduced himself as Chris, inched next to Clare.

After dancing for a few songs and feeling sweat roll down my back, I told Mike I needed something to drink. We picked our way through the crowd and I found a stool at the bar. I gulped down another glass of water while Mike slammed a shot of tequila. He offered me one but the smell coming off his breath alone was enough to make my stomach queasy.

"No thanks," I said. Mike took another shot and his face was flushed pink around his cheeks and his words slurred as he told me about his computer accounting job. When Mike reached his hand out and started playing with the ends of my hair, I stood up.

"I should probably find Clare," I said, and he followed me into the crowd like he was attached by a leash. I sighed, clueless on how to get rid of him. He knew I was single and the bar was one giant room. It's not like I could escape. We dug our way through the packed dance floor. I raised my chin to look over the crowd and frowned to see Clare sitting at a table with Chris, engrossed in conversation. I turned around in the middle of the dance floor to find Mike standing behind me. He extended his hand to me and lifted his eyebrows. I tentatively offered him my arm and he grabbed it and pulled me against him. He wrapped his arms tightly around my waist and I leaned away.

"I need some space," I yelled over the music. I smiled to try and ease the rejection. I didn't mind dancing next to Mike, but in his arms was another story.

He looked at me with a frown.

"It's really hot," I said, and fanned myself with my hand. You're also drunk and you smell like a liquor bottle, I wanted to add.

Mike took a step back but he kept his hands firmly on my waist. "What, I offer to buy you a drink and you won't even dance with me?"

I narrowed my eyes at him. "I didn't take your drink. Besides, it doesn't entitle you to grope me." I pushed his hands off my waist.

"I'm not groping you. It's called dancing. Let me show you."

He grabbed me again, pulling one hand tightly around my waist and bringing his face within inches of mine.

I glared at him and twisted my lips together. I glanced over at the table again but Clare was oblivious. Great, I thought, she'll never stop talking. Mike ran his hand up my waist and I reached down to cut him off while I balled my other hand into a fist. Obviously, this guy wasn't taking the hint.

Suddenly, I felt a tall presence standing next to me. Mike looked up at Justin and froze.

"I don't think you're getting the hint," Justin said, staring Mike down with dark eyes that stated there was no room to argue.

I looked back at Mike and felt his hands loosen around me.

"I'm cutting in," Justin stated.

"Why don't we let her decide that?" he retorted, but his voice sounded unsteady.

It didn't take me a second to make up my mind as I uncoiled myself from Mike's grasp. He snickered and shoved his way through the crowd. I watched him disappear just as the song playing came to an end. The crowd turned to clap and I glanced at Justin. His eyes were on the band but they were angry and his body was tense. The band transitioned into the next song, which had a slow beat.

Couples paired up around us, gathering close in each other's arms. The singer belted out low, sultry lyrics that I recognized from an old classic: *You'd better please hear my cry, and let your arrow fly.* I turned to face Justin and couldn't help but grin. He knew what he got himself into. People around us melted against each other and I waited for him to make a move. He looked over at me. He didn't have to ask what I wanted. I stood my ground stubbornly and he knew.

He let out a deep breath of defeat and took a step closer to me.

He slid one arm slowly around my waist and with his free hand he hesitated. His eyes warned me not to read too much into this. He placed his other hand over mine and interlocked our fingers.

He took another step closer to me. I had to consciously remind myself to move my feet to the music. I stared at his eyes, drinking them in. They were closer to me than ever before and so dark I could see shades of light reflecting off of them.

The music simmered the air around us. *You'd better draw back your bow, and let your arrow flow.* I lightly pressed my fingers against his hand like I was memorizing the feeling of skin, as if this was the first and last time we'd ever touch. It was difficult to move my legs with so many waves of electricity shooting through my body with both of his hands on me. It was my greatest fantasy coming to life, except that my dance partner looked slightly less enthused.

Justin wouldn't meet my gaze. He looked over my shoulder or at the band, but never directly at me. There was a crease between his eyes like he was frustrated. He held his chest straight and his head high while we danced as if to show people we weren't together, just friends, no feelings attached. I, on the other hand, sank closer toward him like my bones were made of wax and they were melting in his presence.

Since he was so determined to avoid me, I took the chance to stare at every feature on his face. The way his deep eyes caught the light. How soft his lips looked. His messy hair that was teasing me to run my hands through it. I could feel my breath start to come out shaky. I wanted Justin more than I had ever wanted *anything*. And if I couldn't tell him, maybe I could show him.

He moved his hand lower on my waist. With any subtle movement he made, my heart responded by drumming in my chest. He kept his face a safe distance from mine, despite the closeness of our bodies.

"You cause trouble wherever you go, don't you?" he asked me.

"Clubs should hand out 'Sorry, Not Interested' cards for those kinds of situations," I said.

His lip twitched slightly. "You could just be honest with people, you know."

He looked down at our hands for a moment, locked together, and finally, his eyes met mine. They were careful, like shields were up behind them.

"I didn't expect you to be here," I said.

"Is it so bad to see me?" he asked. "I thought we were friends."

"You told me you couldn't be my friend," I reminded him.

"Maybe I was wrong," he said, and slid his hand a little lower on my waist. "So, is this a truce?"

I didn't answer. I decided to show him instead. I moved closer until our chests touched. Maybe it was the power of the music that gave me confidence, or maybe I had given up on trying to act like Justin didn't mean anything to me. He reacted exactly as I expected. His back shot straight up and his body went rigid as he tried to keep his distance.

"Thanks for getting rid of that guy," I said, and leaned my head toward his neck while I talked. I was trying to be sexy, which I had never attempted before. I had no idea if it was working.

He tightened his lips. "I was just trying to help you out, Maddie," he said flatly.

"I was about to slap him," I said, and grinned. He wrinkled his eyebrows at this. I couldn't tell if it was from my comment, my closeness, or both.

"I took a self-defense class," I added.

He raised an eyebrow. The gesture only made him sexier.

"Online? What did you learn, push the up and down arrow keys really fast to get away?"

Instead of arguing with him, I dropped my hand out of his. I moved my arms up around his neck until they rested at the base of his hair. I could feel his chest expand against mine.

I cocked my head to the side. "Does this bother you?" I asked innocently. I kept my gaze steady on his. I knew my dad's eyes were capable of getting what they wanted. Maybe I could experiment tonight.

I twirled my fingers through the soft ends of his hair. He narrowed his eyes at me. He knew exactly what I was doing.

"I'm just trying to use all these nerve endings," I said, and let my fingertips play. My skin was burning. "Isn't that what I'm designed to do?"

Our faces were just inches apart. His eyes glared down at me but didn't lean away this time. Then, he surprised me. He looked right at my lips. For a second I thought he was going to kiss me. I could feel his heart beat through his T-shirt and I know he could feel mine. He slowly traced one of his hands up my arm to my shoulder. He hesitantly allowed his fingers to move through my hair, to my chin, and he lightly brushed my cheek. My stomach kicked so hard it made my breath catch in my chest. I could feel my knees starting to shake.

I watched a world of thought being processed behind his eyes. He slowly scanned my face as if he had never allowed himself to fully notice me. As if he was memorizing my features.

Too soon, the song ended and he dropped his hands from my waist. I felt the muscles in his neck tighten and I reluctantly dropped my hands. I slid them down his warm chest and he took a step back. The crowd around us applauded the band but the sound felt worlds away. Justin backed up a full step. Questions multiplied in my head. Do you like me at all? Do you hate me? Why can't you let anyone care about you?

A faster beat filled the room and couples separated on the floor.

He ran a hand through his hair and turned to me. His face was flushed. "I don't really dance," he said.

I stared at him. People moved in circles around us, music blared, and all I could feel was my heart screaming in my chest, all I could see was light reflecting in his eyes.

"I'll see you around," he said quickly. "Try to stay out of trouble."

I watched him go with frustration. I wanted to scream after him as the light and energy that made my world glow evaporated out of the room as the door swung shut behind him.

CHAPTER *fourteen*

I expected the house to be dark when I got home and was surprised to see so many lights on in the downstairs windows. Baley greeted me at the door and I paused when I heard voices in the living room. Deep voices. My intuition kicked in and a cold chill crept over me. My dad called my name as I shut the door behind me.

Goose bumps rose up on my arms as I headed into the living room and I stopped abruptly in the doorway. Paul and Damon Thompson were inside, talking to my mom and dad. They all fell quiet when they saw me. All the wall screens in the house were turned off. There wasn't a single noise, only loud silence. Even my mother's face was sullen.

I was in trouble.

"Where have you been?" Dad asked. He sat next to my mom on the couch.

"I went out with Clare," I said, and managed to keep my voice steady.

"I didn't ask who you were with, I asked where you were," he repeated.

I studied each face and tried to guess what I did wrong tonight. Leaving the house wasn't against my probation terms. I took a deep breath to keep calm.

"Clare's brother Noah is in a band and we went downtown to watch it," I said plainly. "I don't think the club has a name, it's just on the Westside."

Damon crossed his arms. "Noah and Clare Powell? These are your daughter's friends?" he asked in my father's direction with a patronizing tone. I pressed my hands against my hips.

"I think I'm old enough to choose my friends, Damon. I don't need a babysitter."

My dad stood up from the couch. "Watch your mouth," he said. "I demand respect in this house."

"You mean control?" I said.

"When you're on your own, you can choose your friends," he said.

I threw my hands up in the air. "Dad, I'm almost eighteen. What's the difference? Am I going to wake up when I turn eighteen and magically make all the right decisions?"

"Not according to your track record," he retorted.

Paul interjected, "We're just looking out for you, Madeline."

"Well, you don't need to," I snapped back at him. "I'm fine. I'm happier than I've ever been. I'm meeting people that I actually want to spend time with, so don't worry about me."

My dad interrupted us. "Madeline, Damon came over tonight to discuss some options for you."

I creased my eyebrows. "Options?"

My dad nodded. "It seems that having you on probation hasn't been a serious enough consequence." He paused for a moment and met my eyes. "We have no other choice."

I stared between my dad and Damon.

"They're sending you to a detention center, Maddie," my mom said, her voice uneven. "In Iowa."

"Iowa?"

"You'll be disciplined there," Dad added. "Something your mother and I haven't adequately been able to do with you."

I looked from my dad to my mom and saw her lips were pressed together firmly. She looked dazed as she listened to my father.

"Is anybody going to tell me what I did wrong?" I glared at my dad. "This is insane."

His eyes were livid. "What's insane is my daughter has pulled a three-sixty ever since she's been interacting with a certain Justin Solvi."

"Dad—"

"And you broke your parole assisting him in the escape of a young man being held in custody in Toledo. A young man who broke the law and should suffer the consequences. He belonged in a detention center. People have to pay for their mistakes."

I stared at my father in shock. "I didn't do anything wrong, I swear."

He shook his head. "DNA testing is a great way to solve these kinds of mysteries, Maddie, although I am grateful your leg healed up okay," he said and nodded at my scar.

I gulped and my throat felt tight.

"We heard from the police today. When your mom could testify that Justin came over and picked you up that night in the same car the police saw you three drive off in, after you gashed your leg on an exposed drainage pipe, well, they didn't need much proof beyond that."

I looked over at my mom. She refused to meet my eyes, her face unreadable.

My voice trembled when I spoke.

"I'm sorry, Mom, I didn't mean to lie." Tears pooled in my eyes. "I swear I didn't assist in anything."

Damon spoke up. "As far as we're concerned, associating with someone like Justin Solvi and his friends is breaking your probation. You should have known better than to get mixed up with those kinds of people. They're all DS protesters. Do you know who Justin's parents are?"

I looked over and pleaded with my mom to step in. To believe me. My father spoke up.

"There's nothing more to discuss. Damon and Paul will take you to the airport."

I stared between my parents. "Can't I explain my side of this?"

My dad took a step closer to me. "Didn't I tell you not to see that young man?"

I nodded.

"Didn't I warn you he wouldn't be a good influence?" he asked, and I nodded again.

"Were you not the third person in that car in Toledo?"

I looked down at the ground.

My dad shook his head. "I can't get you out of it this time, Maddie. I can't afford to draw any more attention to this family. You knew all along that if there was the slightest evidence showing you were fighting DS, you'd go to a detention center."

I stared back at him.

"You have to learn to deal with the repercussions of your actions. Actions are dangerous."

"If you cooperate, you'll be released in six months," Damon added.

"Six months! Mom?" I cried. She followed behind me.

"There's nothing we can do, Maddie. If the news finds out you were involved in the Toledo case and we didn't give you the fair punishment, your father could lose his job. This time, there's nothing we can do. You brought this one on yourself."

Hot tears flooded my eyes. She bent down and picked up a pair of my tennis shoes and gripped me in a hug. So quietly, with her mouth pressed against my ear, she said, "In case you need to run."

I blinked back at her with confusion and took the shoes out of her hands. I put them on and Damon gripped my arm so tightly I could feel my skin bruising under his fingers.

My mom handed me my purse, after she took out my phone and flipscreen.

I lifted the strap over my head and stared at my dad the way someone might stare at a puzzle they've worked years to put together and can't solve. I didn't even see my father then. I saw a man as distant to me as a stranger. All the light was gone from his dark eyes as he stared back at me.

Damon's phone rang and he answered it and nodded into the receiver. "The driver just pulled up. Let's go."

My dad glanced out the front window and back at Damon. "You didn't bring your squad car?"

Damon and Paul simultaneously shook their heads. "We don't want to be obvious," Damon insisted. My dad's eyes flickered to me with concern.

"What do you mean obvious?" he asked.

Damon hesitated. "We've been having problems with interceptions lately and squad cars are a dead giveaway. We've had better luck using unmarked public service vehicles."

There was a black car in the driveway with the words *Corvallis Airport Transfer* written across the side. My dad still looked skeptical and Damon put his hand on his shoulder.

"Don't worry, Kevin. I'm sure Paul and I can handle escorting your daughter to the airport. Besides, I don't think she's had too much training in car escapes." Paul chuckled at this and I glared at him.

Damon pulled me outside and opened the door to the back seat. I climbed in next to Paul. I looked out the window and saw my mom standing on the front porch. She was trying to keep it together, trying to be strong for me. But I saw the devastation in her eyes and the way her hand clung to my dad's arm. I looked at him and saw a brief expression change on his face. For a moment he looked as pained as my mom. Maybe I pretended to see it because just as quickly as it came it fled and was replaced by a scowl. I preferred the grimace to the look I saw on my dad's face for that fleeting instant. It was as if someone dear to him died and I couldn't help but wonder if that's the way he saw me right now.

The driver, who was young, about my age, started the engine. As we pulled away I fought to keep my mind focused. I thought about what Justin had said. Think on my feet. Know my strengths. I closed my eyes and immersed myself in the situation to try and come up with a plan. There wasn't time to cry.

The car headed down the street and picked up speed. I studied the door. There was no handle that I could see, as if I was already in some sort of a locked cell. I watched the road ahead and estimated I had about twenty minutes before we got to the airport.

Think, Madeline.

I looked at Paul; he was staring straight ahead and his chin was held high. His back was held straight against the seat and he clamped his hands tightly to his sides like he was some kind of soldier. He was acting so tough, but I knew him better than that. I remember when we were little and our families would get together for holidays. Paul was always so whiny. He complained if he got the tiniest scrape, he'd cry if he didn't get his way. That's when an idea came to mind.

The driver took a sharp turn and the tires squealed against the road.

My hands went to my stomach.

"I get carsick really easily," I whispered to Paul. He glared back at me as the car pulled another fast turn. I held one hand against the window and the other one I kept on my stomach. I pretended to concentrate on my breathing. Paul watched me skeptically.

"You'll be fine," he said.

I held my hands against my stomach and grimaced. "Can he slow down a little? I feel like I'm going to throw up," I said. Paul's eyes widened, like he was remembering the same memory I did. He hesitated and looked at the driver and back at me. The car swerved between lanes, passing a ZipShuttle and a light-rail train. I groaned from the movements.

"Can you at least roll the window down?" I pleaded as the driver swerved again. "Maybe some air will help."

"Slow it down a little," Paul said to the driver as he scooted away from me. The driver glanced over his shoulder at Paul for a second and swerved out of the lane. He almost hit a ZipShuttle and quickly jerked the car to avoid it.

"Oh, god," I muttered, and started to cough. I leaned my head between my legs.

"Dad!" Paul yelled.

Damon swore with disgust and rolled down my window halfway.

I slowly lifted my head and took a deep breath of fresh air. I glanced at the window but it wasn't wide enough for me to squeeze through if they ever did happen to slow down. I could try and shatter the glass, but if it was bulletproof it would probably take more than my elbow to break it. I lowered my head between my legs again and stuck my finger down my throat until I could taste acid creep up the back of my mouth. If I did throw up, it might actually get them to pull over.

Paul moved as far away from me as he could. "Hey, pull over. She really is sick."

"We're not pulling over," Damon shot back. "She'll puke in your lap before she escapes."

I whimpered with the realization that I was royally screwed. Just as I accepted my fate, the driver spoke up.

"You might be okay with her puking, but you're not the one that'll have to clean it up," he said, and pulled the car off the highway onto an exit ramp. Damon swore at the driver as he pulled in to a rest stop.

"Dad, she's just using the bathroom," Paul said. I sat up too fast and almost did feel queasy as the car slammed to a stop. Damon looked back at me, his face red with stress.

"You get two minutes," he said. He told the driver to unlock the car and ordered Paul to go with me. I stumbled out of the car and headed for the front door while Paul argued with his dad. When I got inside, I ran toward the bathroom and kept going when I noticed an exit sign at the end of the hall. I heard someone shout behind me as I bolted through a metal doorway. The dark, fresh air greeted me like open arms. All I needed was a head start. I could find somewhere to hide. I could wait until morning and try to find Justin. I could do it.

I mentally thanked my mom for making me put on tennis shoes. There's no way I'd manage a sprint escape in heels.

I heard the metal door swing open and Paul yelled after me. He wasn't far behind. I ran harder down the alley, the breeze scattering my hair and my eyes watering from the wind in my eyes. I pumped my arms from side to side to gain momentum. Paul yelled out for me to stop.

"There's no point, Maddie," he shouted. "You're only making this worse."

My legs sprang harder off the cement and I cut through a yard filled with trees to help shade me from the street. I leaned against the side of a house to catch my breath and try to think of a plan. As soon as I leaned against it, a security siren wailed. I jumped away from the house and outside lights snapped on, flooding the entire yard with bright spotlights.

I sprinted away from the house and saw, in the distance, headlights coming down the street. I ran into another yard and this one also had motion-detecting alarms. Ground lights blinked off and on to warn the family inside and another siren pierced the air. I continued to run, setting off security alarms with each yard I passed. Not quite the inconspicuous plan I had in mind. I saw a park across the street at the end of the block. As I set off another yard security system, Paul grabbed my arms and jerked me roughly against him. I pulled away and fell down onto the turf, taking Paul with me. We struggled on the ground as he tried to hold my wrists down. I kicked out at him.

He finally caught ahold of my flailing wrists and pinned them together against my chest.

"There's no point in fighting me," he said, his face close to mine. He was straddling me and just as I opened my mouth to shout at him, a deep voice boomed over us.

"What the hell is going on here?" a man yelled. The next thing I knew, Paul was yanked off me and dragged to his feet. I sat up and stared at a middle-aged man, tall and stocky, who held Paul's arms behind his back. His son stood next to him in the yard and had a similar build. They both looked down at me and noticed my messy hair and shirt that was balled halfway up my waist. I tugged it down.

"He—he pushed me down," I said, which wasn't a complete lie. The older man held Paul as he squirmed to break free.

"I'm a cop," Paul said as he swung his arms.

The son laughed. "A cop, good one. What are you, sixteen?"

"My dad's Damon Thompson, I work for him," he said.

"I don't care who your dad is, he obviously didn't teach you how to treat women."

Paul broke out of the man's grip, but his son was there to catch him. In a blur, he shoved Paul so hard in the chest he flipped him onto his back. I winced and watched Paul struggle to get up, but the older man was there to catch him.

I heard a car engine in the distance and I turned to run. I crossed the street and headed for the park. There were small trees and benches scattered, but nothing looked big enough to hide behind. I ran to the other side of the park, and just as I passed a row of trees, a dark arm reached out from behind a tree trunk and grabbed me around the waist. I screamed as I felt myself being lifted off the ground, and a strong hand pressed against my mouth. I elbowed the sides of my captor and bit down on the finger that had lodged itself between my teeth.

I heard a low grunt and kicked my legs out. He managed to keep hold of me until we got to a silver sports car.

"Damn it, I'm trying to help you," an unfamiliar voice told me. I squirmed and he finally set me down but kept a strong hand around my bicep.

"I'm not getting in that car." I stood eye level next to him. He was stocky, young, and dressed in a black hooded sweatshirt. His dark, furious eyes stared back at me as he shook out the finger I just clamped down on.

"I work with Justin. Now get in before I throw you in." At this point I didn't trust anyone but myself.

"You'll have to throw me in," I insisted, and before I knew it he picked me up again, opened the car door, and shoved me inside, slamming the door in my face.

He got in the seat beside me and started the engine. "I've got to say, you are the most defiant girl I've ever tried to intercept." He stuck an earpod in his ear and soon he was mumbling so fast I couldn't understand him. He turned the corner and we were met with headlights sailing in our direction. Blue and red flashing lights snapped on as the car pummeled toward us. The driver swore as we narrowly missed hitting the car head-on. We drove onto the sidewalk and over a few turf lawns before we flew back on the road. My head was thrown back against the headrest. I looked over my shoulder and the car peeled in a sharp turn to follow us. The driver took a corner too fast and my head smashed against the glass before I could catch myself.

"Fasten your seat belt!" he yelled. He spoke into his earpod again and took another corner suddenly, as if he was being directed. The cop car was still on our tail. I grabbed the belt, my hand shaking. The speed of the car made me fall deeper into the seat and I tried to slide the belt into the lock but I could barely sit up. I widened my eyes at the speedometer to see the car needle climbing to 100 mph. I could see 25-mph speed limit signs pass by in the residential neighborhood we were careening through.

I touched my forehead, where my head had bashed the window, and warm, sticky blood was seeping out. He found a sign for a freeway entrance and peeled the corner in time to catch it. Even with a seat belt on my body was jerked against the passenger door again and I jammed my wrist against the window. I turned and glared at him.

"Sorry," he mumbled.

I turned to see the flashing blue lights farther back in the distance.

Just as we gained speed he scowled at something and I heard him mumble "Are you serious?" Instead of entering the freeway, we turned and sped down an alleyway that was barely wide enough for the car to fit through. The cement walls nearly grazed the sides of the car. We bumped and skidded over boxes and trash on the ground. We hit a rubber trash can and sent it flying into the air, dumping its contents behind us before it crashed against the building and rolled to a stop.

He stepped on the brakes when the alley abruptly ended and turned toward an industrial park. The tires squealed as we curved along the edge of the park until we were behind a warehouse in a loading dock. He followed the end of the road and it opened up to a railway track and he sped across it, onto a gravel road that kicked up so much dirt we could barely see out of the windows. The car jumped and jostled over the rocks and I squeezed my eyes shut. It felt like my brain was being knocked against the sides of my skull. I could hear trains next to us, but there wasn't enough visibility to see how close we were. We stayed on the rough gravel for miles, sweeping up a tunnel of dirt with us, which I realized was keeping us camouflaged.

When I thought my body couldn't take any more jostling, I felt the car turn. We cut over the tracks again and the car bounced and jerked over brush and turf until we made it back on the smooth pavement.

We drove down a commercial business street for a few miles and passed dark, barren office buildings. He was still talking to somebody into his headset; I could hear him asking for directions.

Streets flew by, traffic signals passed, and it felt like hours before we slowed down again. He braked suddenly and I looked around, weary and my throat parched, at a quiet residential area. We pulled in to the driveway of a dark house and the garage door automatically opened. He pulled the car in and when the door slid safely shut, he opened his door and a dim overhead garage light snapped on.

"Where are we?" I asked.

He grabbed a bag out of the back seat. "We need to keep off the road for a couple hours" was all he said.

When we walked inside the house, I smelled stale, dusty air and from the loud echoes of our footsteps assumed the house was empty. He checked the front door to make sure it was locked and aimed a flashlight down the hallway. I followed behind him and he opened the first door we came to. He motioned for me to follow him downstairs and I grabbed the hand railing to support my shaking legs.

Once downstairs, he manually turned on a naked light bulb dangling from the ceiling. I studied him, finally having a chance to see his face. He had short brown hair and thick eyebrows and looked barely old enough to drive, maybe fifteen.

He sat down at a round table in the center of the large room. The floor was a cold gray cement and the walls, made of cinder blocks, were the same dull color. It smelled musty and a damp chill filled the air. A row of shotguns leaned against the wall and my stomach clenched. I glanced back at him. He could have told me he worked with Justin just so I would cooperate. I took a step back and looked for any kind of an escape but it was a windowless cellar with all the homey charm of a dungeon. There was no way out other than the stairs. The boy continued to talk into his earpod.

"She was with a cop," he said. I watched the hard look on his face as he listened to someone on the other end. "Fine. Okay. If you say so."

He turned off the phone and stood up, rummaging through a cabinet, and seemed satisfied with something he found. He sat back at the table and looked at me for the first time. I held his gaze and waited. He opened his mouth and offered a bored explanation.

"We stay here for the night. They're searching east and west but they'll look north next, up toward the border. That's when we make our move and head south."

I looked up at the dank, water-damaged ceiling. "Where are we?"

He opened his flipscreen and ignored my question.

"In the morning we drive. It's about seven hours." He glanced back at me and I returned his look with a glare for skimming around my question. He jerked his thumb toward a door underneath the stairwell.

"That's the bathroom. There are some bandages in there if you want to clean yourself up."

My fingers went to my forehead and I winced as I felt the swollen skin and dried blood that formed on top of it.

"I'd try to get some rest," he said, and pointed to the cot at the back end of the basement. "There's a change of clothes in here," he added, and kicked the duffel bag in my direction. The bag stopped a few inches from my feet. He looked down at the screen—apparently the hospitality session was over.

"You think I can sleep right now?"

His expression stayed flat. "How would I know?"

"Who are you?"

"The less you know at this point the better. I can't tell you anything so don't bother asking. I'm just the interceptor."

The interceptor with amazing social skills, I wanted to add.

"Let me talk to Justin," I said.

He shook his head. "There are three other interceptions going on tonight. He's a little busy right now."

I watched him spread a map over the table. "Can you just answer one question?"

He raised his head.

"I don't know if I should be scared or relieved right now."

"Maybe a little of both. But I'd lean on the relieved side." I nodded and a heavy sigh escaped my chest. With nothing better to do, I walked across the room to the cot and sat down. The mattress squeaked and I could feel springs poking through but it felt good to be sitting on something stable that wasn't traveling at a hundred miles an hour. I stretched my legs out and leaned my back against the cool surface of the wall.

The next few hours were the longest I'd ever experienced. The basement was cold and dreary. My mysterious captor, who refused to tell me his name, made at least a dozen phone calls. The only time he acknowledged me was to tell me there was food in the fridge. My mouth was dry and my throat was still parched but my appetite was gone. I missed Baley. I missed my mom. It made my heart ache to think I let her down.

Time crept by and I counted the cinder blocks and ceiling tiles. The walls of gray concrete enclosed me like cold arms. I stood up for a moment to stretch and forgot I still had my purse strapped over my chest. I opened it up and felt something inside I didn't expect. Something thick and leathery. I pulled out the journal my mom had given me. I didn't remember ever putting it in my bag. I felt around in the bottom of my purse and pulled out two pens. I sat back against the wall and tucked my knees up close to my chest to use as a desk. I rested an open page against my lap and contemplated what to write.

My mom used to tell me that whenever she felt scared or lonely or upset, instead of trying to ignore her feelings, she allowed herself to dwell in them. She told me if she acknowledged her problems, instead of avoiding them, they seemed more manageable and more in her control. She told me problems don't go away by slamming a door in their face. It's better to invite them in, have a long talk, and try to reach an understanding.

I looked down at the blank canvas of paper. There was only one memory on my mind tonight and even though I wanted to ignore it, I decided to face it, to write about it for the first time. The worst memory of all.

July 8, 2060

Digital schools haven't always been around. My mom went to public school, and I started off attending a public elementary school. Until March 28th. Nearly eleven years ago today. It's a day of silence now, a day of reflecting, referred to in history books as M28.

My memory of it is slight. I was in kindergarten and all I remember is we were suddenly dismissed from school early, which is thrilling when you're six years old. I remember seeing the expression on my mom's face when she came to pick me up. She wrapped her arms around me so possessively, so desperately, I thought my ribs were going to crack. Her tears scared me and I cried too at seeing my mom so upset, her face white, her eyes red and swollen. I could only guess the worst: my dog died. I knew friends whose dogs died; we talked about it one day in class when the school rabbit died. It's a part of life, I was told.

Mom took me home that day and my world changed forever. A world that was bustling with activity fell silent. A world I felt safe in transformed into one I should fear. I once was taught the world was my playground. Then I learned that playground was only safe behind a screen.

My parents sat me down in front of what would become my future world, a giant wall screen. I was introduced to Millie, my new kindergarten teacher. She smiled and introduced me to all my new friends who were all digital images, smiling and waving back at me. I thought it was so entertaining. School became one long television show. We sang and danced. We played virtual kickball and read stories in a circle and whenever I had a question, Millie's automated assistant, Pebbles, would pop up on my screen and help me. He was a blue puppet with bright green eyes and had a pink Afro that danced on his head. He made me laugh and promised me we were best friends.

I'll never forget a story Millie read to the class one day. It was about a monster with sharp teeth and pointy fangs that could lash out at me. She said it lived outside. It lurked around the city. In the park. Even inside stores and buildings. It was dangerous, she said, because it was invisible. It could jump out without any notice. But she promised me the monster couldn't come into my house. It couldn't find me in my bedroom. It couldn't crawl through a computer screen. And I believed her because I was six years old and that's when your teachers are your protectors and your imagination is ripe and developing and it's easy to shape and bend. So, I stopped going outside. My home became my world. My computer became my life.

Before M28, schools were becoming more and more violent. More shootings, stabbings, rapes, drugs, deaths. My mom remembers seeing so many posters for student funerals in the hallways of her high school that she stopped noticing them after a while. Posters for memorial services were hung next to posters for club meetings and fundraisers. Shootings began in smaller numbers, usually in a classroom or outside of school. But killers became hungry for attention. Shootings broke out in auditoriums, cafeterias, sporting events, pep rallies, where one hundred lives could be taken effortlessly. Most of the shootings happened in high schools and colleges. Apparently these kids could obtain the weapons easier. These kids knew how to use them. These kids mentally cracked.

More and more students opted for taking digital classes, even when my mom was young. Parents started pulling their kids from schools. They turned to computers more than ever, as a way to fix the problem. The news only sensationalized the violence. Pretty soon, people cut themselves off from each other. Parents canceled play dates. People were encouraged to work from home. Socialize at home. Date online instead of meeting in person.

About thirty years ago security fences became mandatory around all schools, policemen were stationed at every entrance, and metal detectors made going to class like passing through airport security. Students were stripped of all metal devices and had to check their coats and bags to be searched. They were only allowed to carry their books to and from class until the end of the day, when they were permitted to pick up their bags again. Ironically, this tightened security only made kids more creative. It became a challenge to smuggle guns into the schools. Shootings escalated.

School bombings also became more frequent in the news. One hundred and eighty students were killed when the south side of a high school was leveled in Tulsa, Oklahoma. I wasn't born yet, but my mom remembered. More and more kids were pulled out of public schools and placed in private ones by their parents. Private schools couldn't be built fast enough. Until those schools became the targets. In Milwaukee, Wisconsin, three private schools were bombed simultaneously. An instant attack, on March 3. People call this day in history 3-Day for the date—3/03. Three quickly became an unlucky number.

After 3-Day, my father began designing and implementing year-round digital school programs for all ages. He was a high school principal and also the best prosecuting lawyer in the state of Oregon (all principals needed a law degree at this point, since most of the disputes they resolved were of a criminal nature). My dad was head adminis-

trator at a high school where seven students were shot in the hallway outside of his office. He was the one who shot the student on a killing rampage. All principals carried guns at this point and were trained how to use them.

My dad couldn't keep up with the number of parents enrolling their students in digital school. He resigned as principal to set up online curriculums for kindergarten through twelfth grade, as if he knew what was ahead. His program swept through the country like wildfire.

On March 28, eleven years ago, the largest attack to ever hit America actually hit the most vulnerable. The children. Seventeen elementary schools were bombed on that single day, all within the same hour, on all sides of the country. Ten thousand children died. In one single hour. Three thousand more were injured. Five hundred of those died in hospitals that didn't have enough workers to aid all the victims. The attack was led by a radical group in America who called themselves the Spades. The Spades were famous for the violent riots they led against reproduction. They fought for sterilization to reduce the overpopulation of the planet. They rose to tenacious measures to get it.

❀

When I left school on that day, March 28th, a piece of my life was stripped away. A part of my growth was stunted. A life ended forever, for everyone in my shoes. Some people say that until bomber babies have passed on and a new generation takes over that wasn't a witness to those catastrophic events, everyone will suffer. The sun will refuse to shine its brightest and laughter will forever be muffled, as if the smoke from those bombs left a perpetual layer of soot over our souls for the lives robbed that day. A joy was stolen from every heart in the world.

The repercussion led to digital schools 1–4. Now there is no choice. Even going to a public tutoring session is new; this has only been approved in the last few years. It's still banned in many states. A digital screen is like a bulletproof jacket. It isn't porous like our skin. Nothing can leak through. So why meet face to face anymore? People are far too untrusting of one another. Far too unwilling to let go. Far too secure in the virtual worlds they've created in order to feel safe and hide from the pain.

CHAPTER fifteen

Just as I was beginning to nod off on the cot, the driver pushed his chair back and stood up.

"It's time to go," he said. I nodded without a word and went into the bathroom to change. I wiped the dried blood off my forehead and a purple bruise stained my temple and the skin was swollen, but so was my heart and my mind and I didn't have the energy to care. We walked upstairs as quietly as we came down. I followed him outside and waited while he pulled the car out of the garage and turned on the alarm system on the panel next to the door. I looked up at the pink sleepy sky beginning to wake up over the rooftops. The neighborhood was silent. Even the trees were still. I breathed in deeply. It smelled like my neighborhood. The turf and trees expelled a subtle plastic odor.

I slid inside the car and as we pulled away the driver spoke into his earpod, leaving me alone with my thoughts. My eyes ached for sleep but my mind was too overwhelmed. I looked out the window at the sky and watched it shift from pink to gray as we drove down an unending gated highway. The ten-foot concrete wall seldom offered relief or open space. Most highways had tall barriers run-

179

ning along either side so neighborhoods could be built right up against them. Land had become so valuable that some of the highways were constructed to rise above the city buildings. For all I knew we were driving over businesses right now. I watched signs of city names pass us by, all strange names I didn't recognize.

My mind felt tinted like the car windows, dulling all my thoughts into a bleak gray. I had too much time to think the last few hours. Too much time to reflect, to doubt, to overanalyze. The journal in my purse felt as heavy as a brick resting on my lap. I looked down at it with frustration. What was the point of wasting my time remembering the past? I couldn't change it, I couldn't help it. *I couldn't help it.* My heart thudded hard in my chest and I blinked heavily out the window. I hated the world that passed by me and the people in it I couldn't trust. I hated the unknown future in store.

Hours crawled by filled with empty thoughts. My eyes were open but I didn't see. My body was intact but I didn't feel whole. I was breathing, my heart was beating, but I didn't feel alive.

Suddenly the driver interrupted my trance.

"We should be there in an hour," he said. I didn't bother asking where because I didn't want to know what basement I'd be holed up in like a prisoner. I blinked out the front window. I didn't feel like talking. I had become accustomed to the silence. My mouth felt sewn shut.

I pulled the hood of my sweatshirt over my head and continued to stare blankly ahead. I fell into a daydreaming haze again and didn't come out of it until I felt the car slow down. I straightened up in my seat and watched as we pulled off the main road on to a residential street that dipped down a steep hill. I hardly noticed the sun had come out now that the thick marina fog had lifted. The sky was a crystal clear blue. When we came over the crest of the hill, in the distance below us was a blue, rippling horizon sparkling under the sunshine.

I stared at the expanse of ocean in front of us. The water stretched out into the distance until it held hands with the sky. As soon as I saw the curling ocean waves, glittering like thousands of diamonds in the sun's rays, my spirits started to lift. The sight of the water has a strange way of cleansing your mind and making you feel new again, like it exfoliates the rough edges of your thoughts.

Before we reached the beach, we turned a corner and slowed down in front of a small, one-story brick house. When the car stopped, a tall presence suddenly appeared next to my door and I could feel my heart beating again when I realized who it was.

Justin opened my door as soon as we pulled to a stop. He grabbed my wrist to help me out and before I could stop myself I dropped into his arms, hugging him like I was embracing sunshine and love and happiness and all these things I was craving. I buried my head into his white cotton shirt, warm against his chest. I didn't realize how much I needed to touch somebody. I took a deep breath and felt the hollowness inside of my chest slowly curl in on itself. It's strange that a single person can be as nourishing, as necessary as food to make you feel alive.

He was tense, surprised by my forwardness. He didn't wrap his arms around me, but he slowly rubbed his hands up and down my back to calm me down. I could feel tears of relief pool in the corners of my eyes. I took a long, shaky breath and he continued to rub my back and his voice was close and soothing.

"You're safe, Maddie," he said. "I won't let anything happen to you."

He didn't need to say it; I couldn't feel safer anywhere else.

I pulled away and started to stumble backwards until he

reached out to steady me. I pushed back my sweatshirt hood and felt dizzy, like the ground beneath me was moving. I pressed my fingers against my throbbing temple and winced from pushing too hard against the bruise.

He studied me and reached his hand out as if he was going to touch the tender spot on my forehead but then he dropped his hand.

"Are you all right?" he asked me. I nodded and told him I was fine. He continued to examine my face with a frown. I was too exhausted to care how disheveled I looked. "Didn't you sleep?" he asked.

The sound of his voice and the attention of his eyes lifted me up and carried me back to my old self. To the best version of myself. The hole inside of me not only closed but changed into something altogether.

"Sleep?" I said. I put a finger up to my mouth to contemplate this bizarre idea. "Well, let's think about that. In the past sixteen hours I've broken probation, been disowned by my family—and my dog," I added to emphasize the drama. "I was kidnapped twice and held hostage in a place comparable to hell. That doesn't really create a sleep-friendly environment."

Justin watched me while the driver lifted a few bags out of the trunk.

"Leave it to you to be sarcastic right now," he said.

I shrugged. "I think I'm just overtired."

"You've got to be hungry," he said, and grabbed one of the bags from the driver. He slung it over his shoulder and turned to grin at me. "How do you feel about pancakes?"

I followed him inside and prepared myself for more cots and windowless basements. When I walked in, real hardwood floors welcomed my feet. I stared down at the ground with fascination. I'd never seen hardwood floors before, since these days floors are made out of fireproof plastic. I bent down and rubbed my fingers against the scratches and dents and wondered where all the wear came from. The flaws gave the wood character, history of all the people that had been there. I took a step and the beams creaked under my feet. I walked back and forth along the creaky spots with amazement until I looked over and discovered Justin and the driver were studying me like I had gone temporarily insane.

The driver shook his head and walked down the hallway.

"You are overtired," Justin pointed out, and followed behind him.

My eyes scanned the rest of the living room, full of hanging plants that were real and filled with air with an earthy scent. Two red armchairs sat on either side of an antique fireplace. The house had to be at least one hundred years old. They didn't make fireplaces anymore; like our house they were all converted to digital images of a fire.

I followed the sound of voices and headed down the hallway into the kitchen. I heard Justin ask, "So, Eric, were there any problems with the interception?"

"Nah," he said when I walked in, "other than her running for god-knows-where and biting me and kicking me in the goods." He held up his index finger to show off the red teeth marks where I'd broken skin.

Justin laughed and I crossed my arms in front of my chest.

"I'm sorry about that," I said. "I'm just not accustomed to being grabbed and thrown into a car against my will."

"Maddie, I expected nothing less from you," Justin said, and took some plates out of the cabinet. "What I want to know is how did you convince a cop to pull over? And don't tell me you used the bathroom line."

I gave him a hurt expression. "I can do better than that."

"Exactly."

I scooted a chair back from the kitchen table and sat down. "I pretended to be carsick."

Justin and Eric both looked skeptically at me.

"I know Paul's weakness—our families have always been friends. We used to get together for Easter every year when Paul and I were kids. One Easter, I think I was five, I inhaled a basket of Easter candy and then Paul and I went outside and jumped on the trampoline in his backyard."

Eric winced at this.

"Yeah, trampolines and overeating don't really go together. I threw up Easter candy all over him. It got in his hair, down his shirt."

They both grimaced.

"He's been pretty squeamish after that."

Eric rolled his eyes. "Understandably."

"Impressive," Justin said.

"It got me out of the car, didn't it?"

"No, I appreciate it," Justin said. "We would have had to pull an airport escape and those can get tricky."

Justin and Eric started talking details of the night while Justin pulled a bowl out of the fridge and heated a skillet on the oven. I watched him with amazement since I could count on one hand how many times I'd seen my mom cook in my life.

Eric broke down the interception chase by mile marker while I gazed around the kitchen. The primitive atmosphere still surprised me. Silver metal bowls and pots were piled on a wood shelf along one wall. A set of cups hung from small hooks under a row of cabinets above the countertop. I opened a small tin on the table and found sugar cubes inside. I popped one in my mouth and let it dissolve on my tongue. I couldn't help but feel at home in such a rustic place.

Justin set a plate with two pancakes in front of me. I looked down at the round cakes with curiosity. I'd seen them in photographs before, but I'd never tried one. Justin and Eric sat down and I could feel them watching me. I looked at my silverware but shrugged, and tried rolling my pancake tightly into the shape of a fat cigar. I picked up the roll, starving, and took a huge bite. They both watched me, comically.

"What?" I asked with my mouth full. Suddenly my mouth went dry, drowning in a mouthful of dough. I grabbed a glass of orange juice on the table and tried to wash the soggy wad down. For how many times I've heard pancakes were a slice of heaven, I was disappointed to discover they had absolutely no flavor at all. What a letdown.

Eric laughed and Justin poured me another glass of juice. I drank it and felt the dough slide down my throat.

"What do you think?" Justin asked.

"It's pretty bland," I admitted. "It's a little disappointing. I heard pancakes were these amazing, phenomenal—"

As I went to stick another bite in my mouth, Justin caught my hand in his.

"Oh," I said, and set the pancake down. "Should I be using silverware?" He wrinkled his eyebrows and grinned at me while Eric laughed. I felt my face turn red from the attention.

"Would you just slow down? Here." He handed me a bowl of strawberries, a bottle of something I didn't recognize, and a stick of butter. I watched him scrap the butter onto his own plate, spoon strawberries on top, and finally drizzle gooey brown liquid from the bottle.

"What's that?" I asked, and pointed at the liquid.

"Syrup—liquid sugar. You can't beat it." Justin licked some off his finger and then licked his lips with a smile. I mentally scolded myself for staring too long at his lips.

I followed Justin and Eric's lead and decorated my pancakes with fruit and syrup. I used my fork this time to pick up a piece, melted with butter, dripping in syrup, and heaped with berries. The juicy, sweet dough floated in my mouth.

"Wow," I swooned. "Now I can see why they're famous."

I was suddenly famished and devoured the rest of my breakfast. I noticed Justin had dark circles underneath his eyes and realized he must have been up all night directing interceptions. He and Eric continued to talk logistics and I found myself zoning out after my stomach was full. When they finally paused in conversation, I seized the opportunity. I set down my fork and crossed my arms.

"I think it's my turn for questions."

They both stared at me again, Justin with a hint of amusement.

"Not that I don't appreciate all of this rescuing and cooking for me business, but you guys have yet to tell me exactly what's going on."

Justin looked at me and waited. "There's a lot going on," he finally said.

I sighed. "For starters, where am I?"

Justin chewed on another bite of his breakfast. "Bayside."

"Am I still in Oregon?"

"No," he said. "You're in California. Oregon's not a good place for you right now. It won't be for a while."

I frowned. "Where's Bayside?"

"A little north of San Francisco."

I gasped. "Are we in Eden?" I whispered.

Justin shook his head and wiped his mouth with a napkin. "No."

I glanced around the room again, disappointed. "Does anyone else live here?"

"We have a volunteer that stops by. She keeps food stocked and cleans up, but otherwise it's just a safe house."

"What do you do with people after you intercept them? Other than make them pancakes?"

"Every situation's different," he said. "But there are usually three scenarios. One, people can decide they don't want to be rescued and turn themselves back in, although that's never actually happened. Two, people agree to join our side, which happens most of the time. The cops have recruited most of our members for us. We just have Scott hack into their pickup list. It saves us a lot of work."

"You should really send them a thank-you note," I pointed out.

"I'll get right on that," he said.

"What do you do with people who don't want to join your side *or* turn themselves back in?" I asked. I raised my eyebrows since I was especially interested in this scenario. Justin's eyes met mine.

"We kill them," he said.

I set my fork down and waited for him to smile or chuckle or at least say he was kidding but he stared back at me like he was serious.

"You kill them?" I repeated.

"Metaphorically speaking," he said. "We kill their digital lives and help them start real ones. Help them relocate and get back on their feet. Think of it as being a born-again human."

"How do you kill someone digitally?"

"It's not that hard. You just delete the files. That's all people are anymore. A bunch of hardware. We help them set up a new name, new information, new contacts. Start over." He grinned. "Technology does have its perks."

I drummed my fingers on the table and asked him what happens in the meantime.

"The most important thing right now is for you to stay away from computers. That's the only way they track people anymore. As long as you're outside of that world, you don't really exist. It's pretty backward if you think about it."

"So I need to hide out?"

He nodded. "You're a unique case, considering who your father is. So, if it's all right, give me some time to work out a plan."

"Who's your father?" Eric asked.

I shrugged like it was no big deal.

"She's Madeline Freeman," Justin said, pointing at me with his fork. Eric's jaw dropped open.

"You're Kevin Freeman's daughter?" He looked at me with disgust.

I glared back at him. "I take it you don't want my autograph?"

Eric looked between me and Justin. "You're trying to convince the heiress of digital school to join our side?"

Justin grinned at me.

"Would people please stop calling me that?" I said.

Eric shook his head with disbelief. He stood up and stretched and said he wanted to get some sleep before he headed back. Justin got up as well and grabbed our plates. He said we should all sleep for a few hours.

"Come on, I'll show you your room," he said. I followed him down the hallway and he opened a door into a simply furnished guest room. A queen-size bed sat in one corner, windows with the shades half closed lined the farthest wall, and double closet doors lined another. A tall dresser stood near the door and there was a rocking chair next to the bed.

"They keep some clothes in here," he said, and opened the closet. Inside was a dozen pair of shoes on the floor, all tennis shoes or sandals, nothing fancy. There was also a heap of jeans, sweaters, and T-shirts, enough options for any kind of weather.

"Just wash your underwear in the sink. They don't stock extras of those but we can pick some up."

I felt my face redden at discussing my underwear situation, but he spoke plainly as if this was all routine. "Okay," I said.

I opened one of the dresser drawers and found some books, notebooks, a blanket, and a few more sweaters.

"There's a bathroom down the hall with stuff to use, extra toothbrushes, soap, whatever you should want. If you need anything else, just let me know."

"Thanks," I mumbled. I wasn't used to being treated as a guest. As I stood there, I realized this was my first time sleeping away from my family.

"I'll be downstairs," he said, and headed for the door.

I sucked in a deep breath and turned toward him, panic flaring up in my chest like steam. I didn't want to be alone. He understood my expression, like he'd seen it hundreds of times before. He took a step closer to me and kept his eyes steady on mine.

"Look, Maddie, I know you've been through a lot, but I can guarantee you're safe. I'm not going to let anything happen to you. All right?"

I nodded and looked down at my feet.

"Try and rest for a while and then we'll talk. I'll be right downstairs if you need anything."

He shut the door behind him. I walked over to the other side of the room and pulled the window curtains closed. I stretched out on a soft quilt and suddenly it was impossible to keep my eyes open. My mind and body crashed with exhaustion and before I had another thought, I drifted to sleep.

CHAPTER sixteen

I woke up and opened my eyes to a room that was dim with fading sunlight streaming through the curtains. I blinked up at the ceiling above me and frowned. Where was I? Where was my ceiling canvas? I reached over to my nightstand, but it was gone, replaced by a rocking chair. I stared at it, surprised. Did my mom redecorate my room? Why would I want a rocking chair? I rubbed my eyes with confusion. My toes felt constricted and I glanced down to see my tennis shoes sticking out from underneath a throw blanket. I sat up in bed and looked around the room with blue walls and a single painting of a boat harbor hanging in front of an old dresser.

I shook my head and slowly the pieces fell together. It wasn't a dream. I had actually managed to escape and was hiding away in, what town? Bayview? I looked down at the blue blanket and didn't remember having it on me before I fell asleep. I also noticed a folded white towel and washcloth were set out for me on the dresser.

I opened the closet and scanned my choices. I grabbed a dark red T-shirt that looked worn and soft. I held a pair of blue jeans up to my waist and they looked about the right size.

After a long, hot shower, I scampered toward the kitchen, ringing my hair out with a towel. When I walked in, Justin was sitting at the table and his presence caused a flurry of movement in my stomach. He looked up from his flipscreen and asked me if I was hungry. I felt my stomach rumble staring at him, but I couldn't describe what my body was craving. I set my towel down on the chair and frowned at being so needy.

"You're not going to cook all my meals. And you don't have to set out towels on my dresser and tuck me in," I said.

He grinned. "Actually, that was Stacey, the woman who volunteers for us."

"Oh," I said, and blushed.

"She brought groceries over. But I asked her to check on you, if that counts for something. And," he said as he stood up, "I'm not going to cook for you. I'm going to teach you."

"Teach me?"

He turned to face me. "How to fend for yourself."

I glanced around the kitchen. "Where's Eric?"

"He left a little while ago."

I had to fight a smile and I could feel my heart applauding in my chest. I was alone with Justin. All alone in a house on the ocean. Secluded. Quiet. My life instantly turned from a tragedy into paradise. Crazy how a guy can have that kind of psychological power. *And pathetic.*

He leaned against the kitchen counter and I watched his dimples form half-moon indentations around his mouth. "So, how much cooking have you done?"

I thought hard, which was difficult with him staring at me.

"My grandma used to bake around the holidays, but she passed away when I was ten," I said. "So, I'm a little rusty."

He motioned for me to go on. I stared at him, confused with what he was waiting for. "What did you make?" he asked.

I shrugged. "I remember melting butter over the stove once."

He nodded and stood to his full height. "Okay. I have one basic rule, Maddie. When you're with me you eat real food, not preprocessed, scientifically engineered, supplement-enriched, genetically altered, chemically fortified crap that you've been tricked into believing is food." He took a deep breath.

"Wow. I guess you hate all modern conveniences."

He shook his head. "It's not convenience that bothers me, it's people's obsession with saving time. Everything's a race. I just don't get who or what we're constantly racing against." He waved his hand in the air. "You know what, don't even get me started. Like I said, when you're around me you're not going to eat a piece of cardboard that some fancy food scientist claims is full of vitamins."

I raised an eyebrow. "Are you putting down my mom's cooking?"

"Yes."

I watched with interest while he emptied the grocery bags and set the food on the table. He pointed out sandwich options to me: deli meat, cheese, mustard, mayo, peanut butter, lettuce, cucumbers, and tomatoes. He set two slices of bread on a plate and told me to choose whatever fixings I wanted. It was my first cooking lesson. I examined the choices and grabbed the peanut butter first. I swiped it over the bread and threw a few sliced tomatoes on top.

"There," I said. "My first homemade sandwich." I looked at Justin. "Did I pass?"

He chuckled. "Um, *I* wouldn't eat that."

"Why not?"

I studied my open-faced sandwich with indifference. It seemed appetizing enough.

"You just don't want to mix certain flavors. There's an art to it."

"There's an art to eating?"

He pulled the tomatoes off my sandwich. He popped them into his mouth and chewed them. I could hear the juicy texture squishing between his teeth.

"Go for it," he said, and nodded to the table. I reached for the lettuce this time and set a few leaves over the peanut butter. I scanned the rest of the condiments. I opened up a container of mustard and squirted a design of stars and swirls on the bread like it was paint. I smiled at my picture and held it up for Justin to admire, but he just creased his eyebrows.

"You said eating was art," I pointed out.

I pressed the slices of bread together and he watched me take an enormous bite of my peanut butter, mustard, and lettuce sandwich. I swallowed and tried to ignore my gag reflex kicking in.

Justin gauged my reaction and fought to control his features.

"Well?" he asked.

I licked my lips and forced a smile. "It's so good. You have no idea what you're missing," I taunted him.

"Right," he said with a grin.

"Try a bite." I waved the sandwich in front of his face. I knew I was flirting, but I couldn't help myself. It was too much fun to make him smile. He pushed my arm back and grabbed the sandwich out of my hand. He threw it in the garbage and got out two new slices of bread.

"You know, Maddie, for how book-smart you are, your lack of common sense is a little scary."

I frowned at him. "Why didn't you warn me? You're the teacher." He lathered up another slice of bread with peanut butter. He looked at me over his shoulder.

"I can't watch your every move. You've got to make mistakes once in a while. It's the only way you learn."

He opened the refrigerator and leaned down to grab something from the back shelf. He stood up with a jar full of thick red sauce.

"It's jelly," he said. "Usually goes better with this."

I stared at the jelly with suspicion. He smeared some on the other slice of bread, stuck the two together, and handed it to me on a plate. He grabbed a banana off the table and set it on my plate as well.

"Thanks." I sat down at the kitchen table just as Justin's phone rang.

He checked the caller ID. "I gotta take this," he said. I nodded and he walked out of the room. I looked out the window at a sky that was creeping toward sunset.

After I finished dinner, I rinsed off my plate and headed into the living room. I bounced up and down on the balls of my feet. It just occurred to me how much time I'd been cooped up.

Justin walked into the room and noticed my restlessness. "What's up?" he asked.

I didn't want him to feel like he had to entertain me. I knew he needed to work.

"I'm just antsy," I said. I looked around the living room. "Is there a running machine here?"

He shook his head and glanced out the window. "Are you into sunsets?" he asked.

"I've seen them online," I said.

Justin rolled his eyes and stuck his phone in his pocket. He grabbed his sweatshirt off the couch. "Come on," he said.

❂

I found an old pair of red Converse tennis shoes in the closet, a little big, but they would work. I tied up the laces, pulled on a sweatshirt, and fastened my hair into a ponytail.

Justin was waiting in the front yard and I followed him down the street. I took a deep breath of the thick, salty air. The cool breeze gave me the second wind I needed and I easily kept up with his long strides. We turned the street corner and headed west, toward the beach.

The blacktop street gave way to gravel, which gave way to soft sand. The coastline, I noticed, was nothing close to the thrashing, powerful waves of Oregon I remember seeing when I was little. These waves were timid and passive as if the water was on vacation and life was too calm and easy to bother getting worked up about. Or maybe I had grown up and the things that used to scare me didn't seem as threatening anymore. I took off my shoes and rolled up the bottom of my jeans. I left my shoes on the sand and Justin kicked off his sandals next to them.

I asked him what Eric's job was exactly. He explained Eric was a gopher, somebody that intercepted people, like me, that were being detained or sent to a detention center for trying to rebel against DS.

"Do you know what goes on in detention centers?" I asked.

He shook his head and told me all they know is that they're rehabilitation clinics for rebellious teenagers. They hold people until they're deemed safe to go back into society, meaning they won't stir up any more trouble.

"But you can't cure people from having an opinion about their lives," he said. "That's just human nature."

I looked over at Justin. "Were you ever a gopher?"

"I did it for a while," he said. "It's good training, good discipline, but it's too predictable. Now I direct more of them like I did with you and Eric."

Predictable, I thought. That would hardly be the word I'd use to describe the two interceptions I experienced. I'd hate to know what his idea of surprising was.

"Once you intercept, all you do is drive for eight hours or hide out in someone's basement. Not much to it," he said.

"Justin, we were shot at," I pointed out.

He laughed. "Bullets can't kill you. Remember the law they passed? All firearms can do now is stun people for a few minutes. The most dangerous bullets out there are about as lethal as a dose of sleeping pills. It's the whole movement toward more peace, less violence. It's one of the few laws I agree with."

I stopped and gazed out at the sky and Justin stood next to me. We were both quiet. A string of clouds floated over the horizon and the sun was setting behind them, splashing icy metallic blue and silvery pink light across the water. A cold wind blew off the ocean and Justin pulled his hood up over his head. He shoved his hands in the pockets of his sweatshirt and turned to look at me.

"It's been an intense twenty-four hours," he said.

"It's been intense since the day we met," I corrected him.

"How are you feeling about all this?" he asked. His eyes were sincere like they always were when he was listening.

I smirked and kicked at the sand. "You've probably seen this case hundreds of times. How am I handling it compared to other girls?"

"What's that supposed to mean? You know, most people in your shoes are a little more freaked out right now. They're scared or angry or relieved or bawling their eyes out. But they're showing some sort of emotion. You don't have to be so guarded all the time, you know."

I stared back at him. "Maybe I'm still in shock."

"Maybe you're not used to being honest. Maybe you're so used to telling people exactly what they want to hear you forget how to think for yourself. Or maybe you only know how to express your-self behind a screen because that's easier than looking people in the eye."

"Why are you attacking me?"

His face softened. "I'm sorry," he said. "I just get the feeling you're afraid to open up because you were always reprimanded for it. I don't want you to feel that way around me. You have a mind and a voice and thoughts for a reason. So use them."

I turned away and crossed my arms over my chest. I couldn't argue with this because it was true and for the first time in years, someone actually cared what I thought and I didn't have to tiptoe around my dad and whisper my feelings to my mom like they were secrets I should be ashamed of.

I started to walk down the beach as I considered this.

"You might as well tell me what's on your mind," he said after me. "I'm not your dad. I'm not going to ground you if you have an opinion." I turned and glared at him.

"I'm fine," I said, and he returned the stare.

"If you need to get something off your chest, I'm here to listen. Believe me, trying to hold everything in doesn't work. Eventually it makes you crack."

I took a long breath. What he didn't realize was that at this moment, standing here alone with him in the open air, all my thoughts and questions and concerns weren't about myself, or my parents or even my situation. My thoughts circled and spiraled and all came crashing down like the waves and they all revolved around him, as if getting through to him would be solving the greatest mystery in my life.

"Okay," I said. "You want to know what's annoying me more than anything? You are."

"Me? What did I do?"

"You help people every day, people trust you and worship you and adore you. But you never let anybody get too close. I watch you. You set up a wall against everyone, even your friends. It's like you draw some invisible line no one can penetrate."

He looked at me for too long and his eyes turned golden brown in the reflection of the sunset. He nodded slowly.

"You're right."

I blinked back at him. "I am?" I asked, confused he gave in so easily without a fight.

"I don't let myself get attached to people," he said simply, as if this would answer all my questions.

"Why not?"

He narrowed his eyes with frustration. He turned and started walking down the beach and I caught up to him.

"Hey," I said, "you're the one that wanted to open up about feelings. It's interesting," I added. "You can talk about anything, but when it comes back to you, you get—"

"Annoyed?" he finished for me. "I told you before, people can't depend on me. I need to be in too many places at once."

I shook my head. "I don't think that's true. I depend on you more than anyone."

Justin stopped and fixed his eyes on me. They hardened now. "You shouldn't do that."

"Why?" I asked.

"My life"—he paused for a moment to find the right words— "is not normal."

"So what? Everybody's battling something. But do you really want to let your problems dictate your life? Because you don't strike me as that kind of a person."

His face lightened with surprise. "See, doesn't it feel good to speak your mind?"

I couldn't help but smile. It did feel good, like something toxic and heavy was leaving my body, like your mind can get clogged with the soot and grit of too many thoughts if you don't sweep it out once in a while.

"I live in about forty different cities," he said. "I drive sixty-five different cars. I sleep when I can fit it in. You can only have so many commitments in life, and I've chosen mine. Friends are a commitment and I don't have time for that."

"Maybe it's all you've known up until this point, but it doesn't mean it has to be that way forever."

Justin took a long, deep breath before he answered. "I love what I do. Do you know how many people I've helped in your shoes? Hundreds. Maybe a thousand. We're intercepting half the people that are sent to detention centers. This is what I want to commit my life to. We're losing our freedom more and more every day, Maddie. Fighting digital school is more important to me than anything. And with every choice you make you have to compromise other things."

"What are you giving up?"

He threw his hands in the air like it was obvious. "Relationships. I can't live like this and ask someone to be okay with seeing me once a month, if that. I'd never want to bring anyone into this kind of lifestyle. That's way too selfish, because my job will *always* come first."

I felt desperate to convince him. "You mean just because your mission is to make other people's lives better, you can't enjoy your own?"

He tightened his lips. "I do enjoy it," he stated.

"Not if you're cutting yourself off from the very reason why you're human."

"That's my choice and I promised myself I'd never bring another person into this. I work better alone."

There was a finality in his voice to show me this conversation was over. I turned out and looked at the water and tried to make sense of his words. Justin woke me up to experience a world that

I was missing out on. But maybe he needed someone to wake him up to the things he couldn't see.

He understood me better than anybody and for the first time, it occurred to me I might be the only one stubborn enough to try and understand him.

I watched the sun dip below the horizon and it lit up the clouds like an orange flame.

"This is the best part," he said.

He sat down on the sand and I sat next to him. I pulled my knees up and hugged them against my chest. The wind picked up and I pulled a stocking cap out of my jacket pocket and tugged it on. We sat in silence and watched the water and the sky and the clouds perform magic for us. I pretended my problems could be whisked up and churned under the waves, one at a time, and disappear forever. It relaxed me to watch a rhythm that was so constant it could hypnotize you. I shifted in the sand, overly aware that I was only inches from Justin. I looked over at him and he was sitting exactly as I was, with his arms wrapped around his legs, his eyes fixed on the light show in the distance.

"This is what I'm fighting for. This moment, right now." He stared intently around him. "Look down the beach, it's deserted." I gazed down the north and south stretch of beach and he was right. There wasn't another soul there to appreciate the sunset.

"This is the real world, right now happening in front of us, and everybody's missing it. It's like hearing you have a cousin or a relative but only knowing them through pictures and stories. You never actually meet. You never really get to know each other. We don't know the world anymore. Everybody's moved inside. People learn about the ocean, but they've never seen one. They know about the sun but they never feel it. The reason to be alive is to appreciate moments like this," he said, and opened his hands to the sunset as if he could hold on to it.

We watched the light slowly stretch and fade below the Pacific. I didn't want to admit this was the first sunset I'd ever seen, or that this moment in my life was possibly the most intimate I'd ever known. I also realized this was my answer. Justin was offering me the entire world at my fingertips. But denying me the one thing I wanted.

CHAPTER seventeen

The next morning I woke up with a start to a banging noise, like a hammer hitting metal. I pulled a pillow over my head and yelled, "Off," which always silenced my computer alarm. The hammering continued. I flipped onto my back and groaned. What kind of a rock song was this? I sat up and blinked and forgot, yet again, that I was a long way from home. The sound was coming from outside.

I walked into the kitchen, my brain still drowsy with sleep. I grabbed a mug off its hook and poured a cup of coffee. Just the smell made my sleepy eyes open wider. I heard more commotion outside and followed the sound out the front door. The sun was shining and it beat down on the driveway. I looked over and saw Justin leaning over the open hood of a car. He had a dark baseball cap on, turned backwards. He wore a white tank top smeared with dirt and oil, and his blue jeans were equally as filthy. The jeans were baggy and slid low on his waist, revealing some of his green boxers.

I cleared my throat and he turned around and grinned at me, a friendly grin but with an edge to it that I picked up on now. It was an edge that was polite, but never crossed the line.

"So," I said. "You cook and you fix cars? Isn't that an oxymoron?"

He sat down in front of the car, on the warm cement, and I walked over and sat next to him. He leaned his back against the car and took a drink from a water bottle next to him.

"Is it that strange?" he asked. I took a sip of my coffee and studied him. The sun poured rays of light that glowed off of his skin and heated the pavement around us. His face was flushed from working and his hands and nails were dirty with car grease. And he made car grease look really good.

He looked over at me and caught me gaping and I quickly looked away.

"It's just weird to imagine you dodging the police one second and baking an apple pie the next."

He stared at me like I was crazy. "I don't bake pies," he argued, like I insulted his masculinity. "I only make flourless chocolate cake," he stated, and I laughed.

He took a long gulp of water. I watched the muscles in his neck move when he swallowed. I could hear the water slide down his throat. I looked at the light stubble of hair on his chin, around his lips, and below his cheekbones. My eyes were drawn to his shoulders and the muscles in his arms where veins popped out and glistened with sweat. He was oblivious to my staring.

I looked out at the front of the house.

"When do we have to leave?" I asked.

"Not for a few more days."

"You mean we have to stay here?"

He looked worried at this. "Is that all right?"

I shrugged and tried not to stare too long at his eyes, light with the sunshine hitting them.

"It beats a detention center."

He smirked and picked up a screwdriver.

It was then I noticed a pink smooth scar on his shoulder. It began just outside the strap of his tank top but I could see it ran down farther, hidden underneath his shirt. He caught me staring.

"Job injury?" I asked.

He shook his head. "It happened when I was little," he said.

"What happened?" I asked.

He surprised me by reaching behind his back and pulling the tank top over his head. My mouth dropped open at the sight of long, thin scars that stretched across his chest. From his waist up, there were several streaks of pink skin. I also couldn't help but notice his toned stomach and how his chest shined with sweat. The scars made Justin even sexier to me, like he was some kind of a gladiator with battle wounds to prove it.

I leaned in close to study the marks. I could tell the accident happened when he was young from how faded they were. As he grew, the scars had stretched and lengthened out so the skin wasn't puckered, just smooth and light compared to the golden tone of the rest of his skin.

"They look like burns," I said.

He nodded and took another drink of water. He didn't look embarrassed at all by his flawed skin. He seemed proud.

"What happened?"

"I've always had a thing for fire," he said. "I've just been drawn to it, ever since I was little. When I was three years old, my parents took me camping."

Justin squinted into the sun as he told me this and I watched his eyes turn amber in the rays of light.

"They built a campfire one night and turned their backs for a second and I walked right into it. I fell across some of the burning branches and it scorched my skin up pretty good."

I looked down at his chest and winced.

"The weird thing is, when it happened I didn't even scream, even when the pain of the burn really set in. After you break contact from the heat, it still keeps charring your skin, that's one of the reasons burns scar so bad. We were in the middle of nowhere when it happened. My parents backpacked in with me so all they could do was put cold rags on my skin. But they said I was completely calm." He glanced over at me and grinned. "Ever since then, my parents joke I'm fireproof."

I looked at one of the lighter scars across his chest, below his collarbone. I hesitated and reached my hand out toward it, slowly skimming my finger along its smooth surface. I saw Justin's chest quickly respond to my touch with a sharp intake of breath. I thought maybe I scared him, or my finger was cold. I rubbed the scar and it felt delicate, like tissue paper. He watched me and something in his eyes was cautious but he didn't stop me.

I dropped my hand and looked away. "I've never seen a fire," I said.

Justin leaned his head back against the car. "It's incredible."

I stared at his scars skeptically. "Why?" I asked.

"Everything. The crackling sound it makes, the smoky smell— the color of the flames. They turn blue, green, orange, yellow, purple. The way fire moves, it consumes you. It's so beautiful you want to touch it but you know you can't. I think that's part of its draw."

He looked over at me.

"And the heat," he continued. "That's the best part." His eyes were on mine but they were distracted. I could see him picturing it. Feeling it again. "It's the most powerful force that exists. But people hate fire because they can't contain it."

I looked at his chest again. In digital school I learned fire was a threat, something uncontrollable that devoured everything in its path. I grew up watching news coverage of forest fires, building fires, wars, bombs, heat—fire stole more life than any other element. Fireplaces and wood-burning stoves were all illegal now.

"It sounds scary to me," I said.

He shook his head. "It isn't. You've just been taught to believe that. The trick is to respect it. People don't understand nature is stronger than we are. It always will be. People hate to be the underdogs."

I smiled at this. "Not everyone is fireproof."

He rubbed his chest with one hand. "I could easily fix this," he said about his scars. I looked down and couldn't imagine it. They were magnificent. "But I don't want to," he said. "I like defects. It's what sets us apart."

I followed his gaze and noticed he was looking at my calf.

"That's my only scar," I said. Justin reached his hand out and ran his fingers delicately along the tender spot on my leg where the skin was swollen and puckering under the wound. Healing. His fingers sent waves of electricity up my leg, through my knee, all the way to my thigh. He met my eyes again, his fingers still on my leg.

He smiled. "It's a good one," he said.

I couldn't look away from him. My eyes were locked and my head was dazed. Justin slowly moved his fingers to my wrist and flipped my hand over so my palm was facing him. My heart pounded at the touch of his skin. He studied my wrist and lightly rubbed his fingers along the outline of my tattoo. I felt my breath stick in my chest.

"I like this," he said. The wind picked up and sent a breeze toward us, ruffling my hair around my shoulders. The sunshine was so warm I felt a bead of sweat trickle down my neck. I was acutely aware of my senses again. That always happened when I was with Justin. The heat of the sun intensified, the trees rustled like music, the smell of engine oil was thick in the air, and the touch of his skin heated my entire arm up to my chest and down to my stomach. He looked away and I felt my breath begin to come back.

I hesitated and found the courage to pull my arm down until the palm of my hand rested against his. I brushed my fingers against his warm, rough ones. This moment, this tiny gesture, was one of my bravest acts. One of my greatest risks. After a long moment he pulled his hand away. He sat up straighter and his jaw tightened and the liquid in his eyes hardened, even against the sun.

He took a deep breath. "You're driving me insane, you know that?"

I couldn't help but smile since that's what he did to me on a daily basis.

"You're the one stripping," I informed him, and waved my hand over his bare chest. He stared at me, completely baffled like it never occurred to him what kind of effect he had on women. For the first time, I realized he probably didn't know. Justin didn't think about himself.

"Maddie, this can't happen," he told me. "And torturing me isn't fair."

I lifted one shoulder. "I'm not trying to torture you," I said. "I'm just dropping subtle hints."

He raised his eyebrows at me. "Subtle?" he said. "Is that what you call your little dance of seduction at the club the other night?" He looked at me square in the eye and I felt my face heat up.

I tried to play innocent. "I just got lost in the music."

"Oh, is that what that was?"

I looked out at the yard and laughed with embarrassment. "Maybe you're making a bigger deal out of this than it needs to be," I said.

"*I'm* making a big deal out of it?"

"It's not like I'm asking you to marry me."

He blinked back at me and creased his forehead.

"I'd be happy just to make out. If you want to, I'm cool with it, that's all I'm saying." I stared down at my feet and wondered where I was getting the nerve to speak my mind.

"You are the strangest girl I've ever met," he said, like he thought I was joking. He picked up his water bottle and gave me a sideways glance. "Have you ever kissed anybody?" he asked, and took a sip.

I smirked. "There aren't a whole lot of opportunities in the digital world. I did practice on my hand once. It didn't do anything for me."

Justin coughed on the water he was swallowing and I slapped my hand over my mouth.

"Did I just say that out loud?" I mumbled.

He was half coughing, half laughing. "Yes, you did," he managed to say.

"Delete, delete, delete," I said, and pushed an imaginary button in the air. "I really miss that feature."

"No, that's the good stuff. People always want to delete the good stuff." His eyes lit up. "That's a cool idea, though. What would you say, right now, if you could immediately delete it, so no one read it?"

I stared at him and blurted out the first words that came to my head. "I love your lips," I said.

Justin pulled his head back with surprise and stared at me.

"Are you serious?" he asked.

"I'm just being honest," I said, and threw my hands up in the air. I stared at his puzzled face and leaned closer. "Do you ever stare at your lips in the mirror and get hypnotized by the sight of them?"

He blinked at me a few times like I was nuts. I watched a red hue stain his cheeks. "Maybe we shouldn't play this game," he said.

"No, no, this was your idea. It's your turn."

He turned and faced me. With his entire body. Then he turned my shoulders so I was facing him as well. His long legs straddled mine. I tried to swallow but my throat was too tight. He held me with his eyes.

"I care about you," he said, and his voice turned low and serious. "More than I feel safe caring. You make my heart do some really weird things."

I stared back at him with shock.

"I'm just being honest," he said with a small grin.

"You want to delete that?" I asked. It was the greatest thing I'd ever heard in my life.

"Yes."

"Why?"

"I don't want to get you mixed up in my life. You don't know what you're getting yourself into. But I do."

"I thought you were attracted to me."

He fixed his eyes on me. "Of course I am. Who wouldn't be? Look at you—you're stunning."

I blushed and looked away. Stunning? Me?

"And you don't even know it, which might be one of the coolest things about you," he added.

"Okay, feelings are mutual," I managed to say. "So then why can't you let it happen?"

Justin shook his head. "Didn't you hear anything I said yesterday?"

"Didn't you hear anything I said?"

"God, you're stubborn."

"You're stubborn and stupid," I said.

He grinned at me, a wide grin that made his dimples stand out. "You're so charming when you're honest."

"Why are you so determined to fight this?" I asked. He scooped up my hands in his. He stared at me, through me.

"I need you to listen to me. Okay?" I nodded and felt my hands burn. "I'm not stupid. I see what's sitting in front of me. But—" He looked away for a moment as if his thoughts were also blurred when our eyes met. "Here's the reality. I'll be gone in a couple days and who knows when I'll see you next. In a month or two? And after that a couple times a year, for a few days here and there? You have too much to give to settle for that. I won't let you settle for that. *You can do better.*"

"Don't worry about hurting me, if that's what you're afraid of. I want to get hurt. At least I'll feel something for a change." I stared him straight in the eyes. It was a relief to finally say these things out loud.

He let go of my hands. He didn't say anything, he just watched me. I stood up and walked toward the house. I knew Justin wouldn't come after me. And he didn't. But maybe I was getting through to him. He forced me to open up all my senses, to imagine a lifestyle different from the one I settled for. Maybe I was having the same effect on him.

CHAPTER *eighteen*

Justin spent the rest of the day working. He went down to the basement and only came upstairs to grab water or something to eat but his earpod was always in and he was always mumbling into it. I didn't want to bother him so I kept to myself. Without my phone, computer, or flipscreen I didn't know what to do. No music, no chatting, no television. I didn't want to complain but a simple TV would have been appreciated.

I wandered into the guest bedroom and rearranged the clothes. I neatly stacked all the sweatshirts and sweaters on shelves in the closet, organized according to size. I coordinated the shirts and blouses in matching color combinations like they do in online stores. I grouped the shoes together neatly on the closet floor from smallest to largest.

I went into the kitchen and made a sandwich. I ate dinner alone. After I was done, I sulked back to my room and sat on the floor with my back against the bed. I picked up my purse and dumped its contents on the carpet, searching through it for anything to entertain me. I found some ChapStick and put that on for nothing better to do. I looked around the room and wanted to scream. The house was too quiet and I ached for my wall stereo or my ceiling canvas.

As if sensing my impatience, someone knocked at the door. I said to come in and Justin slowly tapped the door open. He had showered and changed into sweatpants and a white T-shirt and I could smell soap drifting into the room. His hair was still damp and it looked shiny in the light. He hesitated in the doorway as if there were an invisible barrier blocking him. I sat up straighter against the bed frame.

"Can't you see I'm busy?" I said.

He asked me if I needed anything and my right foot shook back and forth. I reminded him I wasn't used to being so unplugged.

"Unplugged?"

"I've never gone a day without my computer. And I don't have my phone or my music or my ceiling canvas or a TV." I stared up at the ceiling. "This is sort of like an alcoholic going through withdrawal." My foot shook again and I wondered if there wasn't some truth to that. Maybe I had been addicted to technology. Maybe my brain physically was having withdrawal from so much constant stimulation.

He leaned against the door frame and stared down at me.

"If I knew you'd get arrested so fast, we would have tried weaning you off of technology earlier."

I smiled and chewed on one of my nails. "Thanks a lot."

"You just can't be communicating with anyone right now. First we need to figure out what to do with you."

He said this lightly, as if the fact that he assisted in the escape and was housing a girl running from the law was like hosting an out-of-town guest.

"I know. I'm just trying not to go crazy." My foot shook again. I told him I was thinking too much. I was so used to being distracted.

Justin stepped inside the room and pressed his back against the wall. He crossed his arms over his chest and looked thoughtful.

"There are some books in the living room. Did you see those?"

I nodded but I couldn't concentrate on reading. He studied the mess on the carpeting next to me and something caught his attention. I followed his gaze and noticed he was staring at my journal.

"That's yours?" he asked. I nodded and looked away.

"My mom gave it to me. It's authentic—made of real paper."

He raised his eyebrows. "Do you use it?"

I nodded, annoyed even looking at it. "I have."

He watched me carefully. "You write longhand? That's so old school," he teased. He slid down the wall and sat on the floor across from me. Our knees were almost touching. He asked if he could see it and I nodded. He picked it up and examined the cover and flipped through the pages. I stared at his bare feet and baggy sweatpants and the way he propped his elbow on top of his knee.

"Messy," he noted of my penmanship. I shrugged and let out a long sigh. Justin looked at me curiously.

"Do you want me to leave?" he asked. His dark eyes were level with mine. My mouth dropped open with surprise.

"No, why would I want you to leave?"

He tilted his head to the side. "Something's bugging you and it's in this room."

He looked around at the walls and the bed as he tried to locate it. I sighed. He *could* read my eyes.

He glanced down at what he was holding. "Huh," he said. He flipped the pages between his long fingers. "It's this."

I nodded and glared briefly at the journal. He watched me and waited for an explanation. "My mom gave it to me for my last birthday. She collects old books and she's always handing them down to me. She gave me that one when I turned seventeen."

His eyes were absorbed on mine but this time his gaze didn't make me lose track of my thoughts.

"She told me it's therapeutic to write my thoughts down, so that's what I started to do. And I can see what she means, it forces me to slow down and reflect, but . . ."

I picked up a piece of my hair and rubbed it between my fingers. "Nothing really happens to me. Until recently." I paused and Justin nodded for me to go on. I wasn't used to people giving me their undivided attention and his steady gaze pulled the words out of me.

"My first entry was about trees, I guess since that's where paper books come from." I paused and smiled to myself. "It's just funny, I never once thought about trees until I sat down and wrote that entry. Then it all sank in how I lived in a city where none of them grew. It made me wonder what everything looked like fifty years ago, before people started moving their lives inside and before all of those huge fires. It made me so upset to think about," I admitted.

Justin looked down and flipped the book over in his hands.

"So, I stopped writing that entry because it was making me depressed. For days all I could think about were those trees that I've never even seen. And then it made me angry, the idea that I never had a chance to see that world. And the fact that people could give up so easily. Some inventor came out with plastic trees and it was a quick fix and everyone jumped on it. Everyone just wanted instant gratification. Even with nature."

I looked at the journal Justin still held in his hands. "Every time I pick it up, I surprise myself with what I write. Almost every entry is depressing. It's making me doubt whether I've ever had a true friend, if I've been living inside one huge lie. It's making me doubt who my parents are, who I am, what love is." I shook my head and grinned sadly. "Maybe my life is depressing."

I pulled at the small threads on the carpeting.

"The worst was the other night," I said. I felt a cold chill run up my arms all the way to the top of my head. "When I was staying wherever I was staying. Something about that basement—it was like a morgue. All I could think about was M28 and all of those kids." I could hear my voice getting shaky so I took a deep breath.

"I just kept writing, all about DS and how it started. I never let myself think about it, you know? No one ever talks about it, you just don't go there. My dad was a high school principal at one of the schools that had a shooting. Seven students died." I stared at Justin. His eyes were intense on mine. "My dad killed the student who had the gun."

"I heard about that," he said quietly. "I'm sorry, Maddie."

"It hurt to write all that. It physically hurt. I felt so sick after I thought so much about it."

He nodded. "Maybe it woke you up to what's happening around you though."

I took another long breath.

"Knowledge can hurt because you can't turn away from things anymore. You can't pretend you're blind to what's happening," he said. "It's a lot easier to ignore something you don't want to accept than to face it."

"You don't ignore anything," I said.

He shook his head. "My mom made me keep a journal, ever since I can remember," he said. "Sometimes I feel like you do right now. But I think your mom's right. It is good for you. And you never know, you might have some good news to write in it someday."

Justin stood up. I looked down at the journal on the floor next to me. I didn't loathe it as much anymore.

"You should get some sleep," he said. "Tomorrow's a big day."
I raised my eyebrows.
"Why?"
He smiled, a huge smile that made my heart beat irregularly.
"It's a surprise."

CHAPTER *nineteen*

I heard an engine roaring in the driveway and I turned over and moaned into my pillow. The clock on the wall said it was 9:30 but I was still exhausted. Sleep came in sporadic waves throughout the night, only to snap me awake with images of my parents or the police standing outside the door. I rolled out of bed and dragged my feet toward the kitchen.

I looked down at the stove and saw a skillet covered up. I opened the lid and scrambled eggs were inside mixed with what looked like tomatoes and something green and leafy. As I dished it up, I shook my head and wondered if Justin ever tired of having to introduce me to everything. I wished there was something I could teach him, some way to make myself useful other than being the needy, scared, hungry teen delinquent in the house.

Just as I picked up my fork to try the first bite, I heard the garage door open. I grabbed my plate and walked out the front door to find Justin standing next to a box lying on the driveway. I took a bite of the scrambled eggs and Justin looked over at me.

"Hey," he said. It looked like he just worked out, his hair was windblown and strokes of red stained his cheeks.

"Morning," I answered back. I held my plate high in the air. "Sorry you have to feed me all the time," I said.

He rolled his eyes. "Maddie, stop apologizing every time I cook something."

I nodded and took another bite. "Deal." I sat down on the ground and crossed my legs and focused on my breakfast. I glanced at the box next to him.

"You could do me a favor if you want," he said.

I perked up at this.

"Make me a list of all your dad's passwords, a burned copy of his files, step-by-step instructions on how to access his profiles . . ."

I frowned. "I thought we were talking about food." I looked down at my plate, annoyed that he still saw me as a connection. Like I was some sort of business opportunity to pursue. It was irritating, since I saw him as possibly the love of my life.

"Clare told me you were reconsidering, that's all," he said. I dropped my fork.

"You talked to Clare?" I asked. Justin stared at me.

"Sure."

"How is she?" I asked. "Whatever happened with that Chris guy at the club? Did her brother lose that groupie? What happened to that nasty Mike guy?"

Justin stared at me. "Okay, whatever that just was, I don't do that."

"Do what?" I asked.

"Gossip, girl talk, whatever."

I set my plate down on the ground. "Justin, I can't talk to anyone. You need to be my go-between."

"I don't talk to Clare about boys. My reputation's on the line."

I picked at my food. "Sorry, I'm just feeling a little isolated right now."

"It's temporary," he reminded me.

"What's this surprise you had in store?" I asked. Justin's eyes lit up and I watched him suspiciously. "What is that?" I asked, and pointed at the box.

"It just came in the mail." He had a mischievous grin on his face.

"How do you get a delivery when no one's supposed to know we're here?"

"Well," he said, and hesitated for a moment. "It's my birthday today."

My mouth flew open. "Justin—"

He held his hand up in the air. "No, it's not a big deal. I don't really celebrate it. At least, not like most people."

I stared back at him and wrinkled my eyebrows. "What do you mean 'not like most people'?"

"I'm usually working on my birthday so I don't make a big deal about it. But my dad always sends me something." His eyebrows rose. "You want to see?"

I nodded and he opened the box and pulled out something covered in bubble wrap. He set it on the ground and ripped the plastic away to reveal a metal shell about the size of a football with wires sticking out of one end. He picked it up and rolled it around in his hands like he was holding a precious stone. I stood up and walked over to get a closer look.

"Your dad sent you junk metal for a birthday present?" I asked with confusion.

Justin smiled. "He likes to tinker," he said, and his eyes caught mine. They had a daring edge, which made me a little anxious. "Usually with aerodynamic . . . things."

I took a step back. "Aerodynamic things?" I asked.

He nodded. "He's a retired inventor. But he still dabbles. I usually get the most random ones to test out. His latest . . .

apparatus . . . had a few problems with the engine so he built a new one for me to try."

"Good for you," I said, still confused what this tiny mound of scrap metal was supposed to accomplish.

He pointed over his shoulder toward the garage and I turned to look. Inside was a small vehicle, about the size of a go-cart. I walked inside the garage to examine it. The black frame of the car was small, just large enough to fit two people. The side doors didn't open, you had to climb over them to get in. The front of the car narrowed into a cone-shaped tip, giving it a sleek, bullet shape.

Justin grabbed a tool off the workbench. I noticed the words *Sand Rocket* spelled out in red letters on one side.

"What is this thing?" I asked. I bent down and examined the wheels. They were too small and delicate to be meant for driving any long distance.

"I'm not exactly sure," he said. "We'll have to wait and see."

"We?"

I watched Justin attach the small engine to the back of the car. I ran my hand along the side and noticed the body of the car was soft, like it was made out of rubber.

"Are your dad's inventions safe?" I asked.

"Define 'safe,'" he said.

"Predictable."

He smiled. "What's the fun in that?"

I backed up and studied the car again. "Have you ever tried driving it?" I asked.

He shook his head. He tightened a few more screws and walked over to the driver's seat. He turned on the power switch and the car coughed to life. The engine sounded strange, not like a car engine. More of a hissing sound, like a snake. Justin's eyes met mine. They were wild, which I found both sexy and terrifying.

"You want to try it out?"

I gulped. "Where?"

He looked at me like it was obvious. "On the beach."

I attempted a weak smile.

"Maybe I could just watch you, safely, from the side?" I offered. I saw the excitement in his eyes flicker with a hint of disappointment. I nodded in defeat and agreed I'd go with him after I changed.

I ran inside and threw on a pair of shorts and a tank top. The sky was a clear blue and the sun was making the humid air hot and muggy. I came back to the garage, fastening my hair in a ponytail, and Justin was still fiddling with the motor. It was attached somehow, but I was still skeptical it would do anything.

"Ready?" he asked.

I nodded and hopped inside the car.

Justin jumped in next to me. "You sure?"

"Let's just go before I change my mind," I answered. I fastened the seat belt as tight around my chest as it would fit without suffocating me and said a silent prayer this wouldn't be the final hour of my life. I wondered if we crashed, maybe Justin would hold me in his arms and kiss me on my last breath of life. This idea made death seem a little less tragic.

We were so low to the ground I could reach my hand out and touch the garage floor. Justin fastened his seat belt and grabbed a hold of the steering wheel. He eased the car out of the garage and when we reached the driveway he tapped his foot lightly on the gas pedal.

The engine hissed and I felt my hair blow back as the car flew ahead. My eyes squeezed shut and I felt my body jerk forward and then snap back against the seat with a sudden stop. I slowly opened my eyes and we were across the street, on the neighbor's front lawn, only a few feet away from crashing into the front door. We both blinked at the door and back at each other. I tried my best to laugh but it came out more like a long whine.

"Are you okay?" he asked.

I rubbed the back of my neck. "Yeah, just a little whiplash. It's fine," I assured him. "Neck muscles are overrated."

Once Justin was convinced I was fine he looked back at the steering wheel and beamed. "That's great pickup." He laughed. "This baby's going to work just fine."

I tried to share his enthusiasm as he pulled out on to the street again and we drove the few short blocks to the beach. The little car moved as smoothly on the street as a skate gliding over ice. I couldn't even feel the bumps in the road.

We pulled on to the sandy beach and turned to face the south shoreline. We looked both ways and couldn't see anybody walking in the distance. Justin drove the car closer to the water where the sand was smooth and firm from being packed down by the tide.

"You ready?" he asked.

I looked back at him. My mouth dropped open as he revved the hissing engine.

"I think so?" I said.

"You think so?" he yelled over the wild roar of the engine.

"Yeah, but . . ." My eyes pleaded with him. "You said you thought I would like this!" I reminded him.

He motioned to my arm with his eyes.

"What's on your wrist?"

I looked down. "A bird," I said, stating the obvious.

"That's why I think you'll like it, if it works. Hold on." Before I could argue, Justin slammed his foot on the accelerator and we flew forward down the beach. I could barely inhale as my breath was ripped away by the speed of the car. I opened my mouth to shout but my voice was covered by the sound of the engine.

In the next second, there was a loud crack, like a piece of the car broke off. I screamed and realized there was something flapping in the air. A plastic sheet unfolded like an accordion on each side of the car. The fabric pulled smooth and snapped tightly in place to form wide wings. I held on to my seat belt and felt the car slowly angle upward and lift off the ground. I squeezed my eyes closed. It couldn't actually fly, I told myself. Maybe we'll just hover off the ground a little bit. Justin's laugh made me open my eyes in time to watch the ground beneath us pull away. The hissing engine quieted down as we rose over the ocean. My mouth fell open in amazement. There were the calm waves, a hundred feet below us. I looked around and took in the bird's-eye view of the coastline, the cliffs along the shore, and the brown and red mountains in the distance. We could see a giant white-peaked mountain, at least a hundred miles away, that I never would have seen from the ground.

"It isn't made to fly very long," he shouted over the wind tossing our hair. "It can lift us up, but then we coast the rest of the way down."

I barely noticed what he said, too mesmerized by the view. We glided with the wind and Justin told me the white-peaked mountain in the distance was Mount Shasta and he pointed out the skyline of San Francisco, faintly noticeable on the horizon. The ocean below us looked as smooth as blue stained glass. I could see ships out in the distance and sea caves and sand dunes along the shore. The coastline curled and twisted with the water's edge, like a seductive dance.

We were both so distracted with the scenery, we forgot to notice we were cruising closer and closer to the ground.

I stared down at the water and started to panic. The ocean was coming faster and we were nearly a mile from the shore.

"Don't worry, we won't crash and burn," he said.

"Yeah," I said and swallowed. "More like crash and sink?"

I glanced at Justin but he looked more thoughtful than worried. We were coasting low now, the dark water creeping close.

"Let's see what this does," he said, and pressed a lever below his seat. We both leaned forward when another hissing sound erupted underneath us.

"What's happening?" I asked. Suddenly, the two wings of the car unclipped from the sides. I met Justin's eyes for a terrifying second.

"Maybe I shouldn't have done that," he mumbled quickly. I moved to try to catch the wing, as if I could physically hold it to the car. The wings slipped off of both sides and we plunged ten feet into the ocean, sending up a wave that drenched us.

"We're dying, we're dying," I yelled into my hands. I waited to sink inside the freezing water, but nothing happened. Justin nudged my arm and pointed to the sides of the car. The rubber lining had filled up with air and expanded like a raft. We were floating in a giant inner tube.

We looked at each other, stunned, soaking wet, while the water rocked us slowly back and forth.

"That was awesome," Justin said. He pulled his fingers through his hair to ring the water out. "Want to try it again?"

I shook my head and pressed my hand against my chest to try to lower my heart rate. He smiled and we both turned to see the shoreline, a long ways away from us.

"Here's the ultimate test," he said. "Either we paddle with our hands to get back, or this engine will still work."

He turned the car on and the engine revved into life.

"My old man still has it," he said. The car gained speed as we accelerated toward the shore.

"Wait," I said, and grabbed Justin's arm. He took his foot off the pedal and turned to look at me, his eyes alarmed.

"What's wrong?"

"Can we just sit here for a while? I mean, it's not every day you get to float out on the ocean like this."

He nodded in agreement. He turned off the engine and the world became quiet. We each sat back in our seats and let the craft float with the motion of the tide. I laid my head back and opened my eyes to drink in the blue cloudless sky. Justin leaned his head back as well and stretched his arms out, crossing them behind his head. I glanced over to see his eyes were closed. He took a deep breath and slowly let it out.

Neither of us spoke the distance it took to get back to the beach. I wanted to listen. I wanted to concentrate on the sound of the water bubbling around me. I pressed my hand against the ocean's cold surface until my fingers broke through and splashed cold water on my face and arms. I licked my lips to taste its salty, bitter flavor. I wanted to savor the image of the smooth sandy beach that waited patiently for us, and the wispy clouds on the edge of the sky that looked like a ribbon floating over the horizon.

I stared up at the blue canvas above me and wanted to freeze this moment to make it last forever. But sometimes it's dangerous to stare too long at the sky. It makes you a dreamer. It makes you believe anything is attainable. And anyone.

We floated back to the beach and when the bottom of the car scratched against sandy ocean floor, Justin unclipped his seat belt. He pulled his body easily out of the seat and landed down next to the car with a splash. I unclipped my belt and he came around to help pull me out. He dragged the car onto the shore and we waited for the wings to wash up. We rolled them up and he threw them on top of the car. The car was light, so Justin grabbed a handle on the back and dragged it behind us.

We walked back to the house and Justin pushed the car into the garage. I looked down at my arms, pink from the sunshine.

He closed the garage door and looked over at me. I watched him and felt that energy again, the electricity that coursed through me when he was too close. His face was lightly sunburned, and it made his dark eyes stand out.

"Thanks for the ride," I said. "And flight. And float."

"Sorry you thought you were going to die."

"Oh, that was just for effect. I wasn't scared."

"Right," he said, and grinned. I smiled back at him and the wind picked up my hair and tossed wisps of it across my face. He surprised me and reached out his hand and tucked a piece of my hair behind my ear. He let his fingers linger there, longer than necessary.

I stared back at him and waited. I couldn't breathe. I couldn't move.

But, just as easily as he let himself go, he tensed up and dropped his hand.

"We need to leave in the morning," he said suddenly, like he was trying to shift the moment with words.

"Tomorrow?" I asked. I only had one more night with him?

"I can't," he said. "We can't . . ." He trailed off. "I need to get back to work," he reminded me.

"Where are we going?"

"I'm taking you to stay with my parents."

"Eden?" I said with surprise. It was like telling me I was traveling to another planet, the idea was so foreign. "Will you be there?" I asked.

"I'm going to be pretty busy for a while," he said. "I have a lot to catch up on. But I'll check in with you." His tone turned businesslike. Unemotional.

"Oh" is all I could say.

"I'll make sure you get settled there before I take off."

I nodded at this but my mind felt numb. I heard Justin's words but they sounded far away, like he was talking through walls.

"Why don't you pack a few changes of clothes tonight? We'll leave early," he said, and without another word, he breezed past me through the door.

CHAPTER *twenty*

I sat in the living room that night and tried to concentrate on a book but my mind wandered away from the words and followed my thoughts toward one person. I knew he was downstairs but I didn't want to bother him. He spent all afternoon with me, which I understood was a privilege considering how valuable his time was. But now I was so used to his presence I had grown to need it. He had become like a second layer of skin.

I could hear faint sounds coming from the basement and curiosity pulled me out of my seat. I walked down the hallway and listened through the open doorway. I didn't want to interrupt a phone call, but it wasn't Justin talking. It sounded like a television was turned on. The door creaked open and I walked down the stairs slowly. When I got to the bottom, Justin looked up at me. He was sitting on the couch, a soda in his hand, looking content. I walked all the way down and turned to gape at the television.

"We've had this the whole time?" I asked.

I looked around the basement. There was a desk in one corner with a computer sitting on it and monitors and flipscreens were sprawled out on a long table in the wide-open space. The couch and television were sectioned off in the corner of the room. A rug was spread out over the floor in front of the couch. I looked at the basketball game on the screen and back at Justin.

"It's my thing," he said. "It's how I relax." He took a sip of his soda and grinned. His cheeks were rosy from the sun.

"Well," I said. "Since it's your birthday I'll let it go. I guess there has to be some perk to baby-sitting me," I added.

Justin watched me. Something in his eyes looked carefully before he spoke.

"Do you want to join me?"

Part of me wanted to turn away, to pretend like I didn't crave his constant presence.

"I don't want to bother you. You probably like your alone time."

"You don't," he said bluntly, and he was right. I didn't know how to be alone with just my thoughts and no distractions.

"I'm working on it."

"Yeah," he said, and sat up straighter. "It takes practice."

He stood up from the couch and walked toward me. My heart raced as I had the ridiculous idea he was going to reach out for me. He passed me without even a glance and walked to the refrigerator. He came back behind me and sat down with a chocolate bar in his hand.

He opened it up and offered me some but I shook my head.

"These are your vices?" I asked. "Chocolate and basketball?"

The light from the television reflected in his eyes when he looked at me.

"Uh-huh," he said, and popped a piece in his mouth. He grinned at me, a lazy grin that made his dimples stand out.

I walked over to the couch and sat down. Sitting so close, my arm only inches from his, made breathing more of an effort. I could feel heat coming off of his skin. I forced my eyes on the basketball game but every movement he made was a distraction.

Every time I saw his chest move, his arm lift the soda to his mouth, or his throat muscles flex when he swallowed, my eyes were drawn to him out of the corner of my eye. I kept my arms crossed tightly over my chest. I looked over at him when the game went to a commercial break and he was watching me. His lips looked soft and red in the light.

"You okay?" he asked.

And suddenly I wasn't. All my nerves were unraveled. I had no idea what to expect in Eden, who would be there, how long I'd stay in hiding. I wondered if I'd ever be welcome in my home again. I felt in the pit of my stomach that anything I had ever imagined as normal was gone forever. Things were changing too fast, like a tornado spinning my life into a wreck.

Justin set down his soda and turned to give me his full attention.

"Talk," he said.

"I don't know what to say." He was right. I was closed off. And I didn't want to be. Not with him. I met his eyes and they were so intense, so aware, they made my thoughts spin. Why couldn't I just have a normal conversation with him? Why did my stomach and chest and heart have to do cartwheels every time he looked at me?

"Is it your parents?" he asked.

"It's everything. I went from a life that was so regimented to this blank slate. And now you won't even be there."

"I'll be there a day or two," he offered.

I tried not to wince at this. I knew he'd already given me more time than he gives anyone. I was spoiled.

"Maddie?"

Panic gripped my chest and held tight. It felt like the oxygen was trapped in the base of my throat and I had to make an effort to pull it through.

I met his eyes again.

"I know it's easy to say this and difficult to comprehend it right now, but you will be fine." He said the words slowly to emphasize them. "You'll be more than fine. Where I'm taking you is so great."

"Yeah," I said. If only it was easy to imagine that, being more than fine. If only he understood I couldn't be more than fine without him.

"I know it isn't home," he said as he watched me. "But it's your life now. You're going to have choices."

Tears rolled down my face and I quickly wiped them away.

"I'm not brave," I said. "I don't know what you thought, but I'm not."

His voice was sincere. "Yes you are."

I shook my head again. "No I'm not. I'm afraid of spiders. And attics. I won't even go in my basement alone at night."

I could hear him smile next to me.

"Now I'm having a panic attack," I said.

"You have a soft heart," he said. "That's a good thing. You know, there are so many things you can't control in life, like what happens to you or how people are going to react to what you do. It's wasted energy to worry about it. But you can control how *you* react. That's the trick."

We both fell silent and I tried to steady my breathing, but it still caught in my throat like someone was trying to strangle me. Justin turned so his whole body was facing me. He set one arm up on top of the couch and leaned against the back cushions.

"Can I teach you something that might help you relax?" he asked.

I shrugged, convinced I was incapable of relaxing at this point.

"You need to learn to escape. It's hard for you to handle silence because you've always been bombarded with noise and distractions. You barely ever have to think because a machine is always doing it for you." I wiped my eyes and nodded.

"So, with that and with everything else that has happened, you probably feel—"

"Terrified?"

He smiled. "You need to find peace in quiet, not panic attacks."

"I'll try."

"Okay," he said. He turned off the television and the room turned darker, lit only by a light in the opposite corner of the basement. He focused on me. "Lay your head back and close your eyes."

I glanced at him with disbelief but did as he said. I leaned my head against the couch and closed my eyes. In the silent room I was only aware of my heart beating and the sound of my breath.

"I want you to picture a place where you feel like nothing could ever hurt you. Your utopia."

I pressed my lips together with concentration and hoped an image would pop into my head. "Okay."

"What do you see?"

I stared as hard as I could. "The back of my eyelids."

Justin waited patiently while I thought about it. I couldn't *see* anything.

"Maybe I don't have a perfect place."

"Picture a place that's calming. Where you feel safe."

I squinted harder. I only saw darkness.

"I don't see anything," I said.

His voice was steady. "It's because you're looking with your eyes, Maddie. Look with your mind. Imagine a place you love."

I exhaled deeply and thought about how wonderful the day had been with him.

"The beach," I said finally.

"Good. Now describe what it looks like."

I creased my forehead. "What do you mean?" I asked, and opened my eyes to stare at him. "It's a beach."

His eyes were patient and his mouth curled up at one side. "You need to concentrate on this. Really imagine it."

I took a deep breath and looked away. I squeezed my eyes tight and still envisioned a postcard picture of a beach.

"Try and describe it," he said again in a soothing voice.

The details were obvious. "There's an ocean and there's brown sand and blue sky."

I felt Justin move next to me. Suddenly annoyed, I opened my eyes and got up to my feet, pressing my hands against my hips.

"I'm sorry, but making me feel like an idiot isn't helping me unwind."

He sat calmly on the couch and studied me. "I'm making you use your mind. A part of your mind you don't use often enough in DS."

"Well, what's the point of closing my eyes and pretending?"

He leaned forward. "The point is *imagining*. Letting your mind go."

I gestured at the back wall of the basement. "The beach is right down the street, you know what it looks like. There's over a million pictures online if you want to look at them. I'm sorry, but this isn't the relaxing escape I was planning on."

He watched me with a hint of amusement on his face. "Are you finished?"

"I'm finished playing the 'describe my happy place' game. Because I can't."

He cocked his head to the side. "I don't take you for a quitter."

I frowned and played with the zipper on my sweatshirt.

He kept his eyes steady on mine and I noticed a cautious edge inside of them slip away, like the shields were finally coming down. Their dark brown pool of color, in the dimness across from me, moved like liquid.

"I'll help you if you're willing to try," he said. "And don't say 'I can't.' Those words really irritate me." Justin leaned forward and patted the rug in front of the couch, right in front of his legs. I sighed and took a seat, my back inches from his knees.

"Okay," I said as I hugged my knees to my chest. "Let the learning begin."

"Lean back," he said.

This I didn't expect. Justin gently guided my shoulders back between his legs until my neck was resting against the cushioned seat of the couch. I could feel his legs lightly resting against my shoulders. My chest inhaled rapidly as he lifted my arms up and rested them on top of his knees like armrests. I instinctively closed my eyes.

"Remember when you asked me what makes us human?" he asked.

I nodded and tried not to gasp as he carefully, hesitantly, ran his fingers through my hair.

"It's our senses. That's another thing that sets us apart from computers. Smelling, seeing, hearing, touching, tasting. I don't care what virtual world those computer programs can create. Are you telling me a computer can do this?" he asked, as he slipped his fingers softly through my hair. I gulped.

"No," I managed to whisper.

"Okay," Justin said, his voice smooth and velvety. "Don't just look at the ocean, Maddie. Be there, walk along it, breathe it in, hear it. Use your senses."

With his fingers slowly sifting through my hair, I went back to the ocean. I remember once when I was little, when my grandma was still alive, she took me to Newport and we stayed overnight at a hotel on the beach. I remember an early morning walk we took together on a cloudy, windy day and how happy and invigorated I felt being outside and holding her hand.

"I see it," I said finally. Justin wove his fingers through my hair and lightly rubbed my scalp and the feeling made me want to moan.

"What time of day is it?"

"It's morning," I said. "The sun is still low in the sky. It's just starting to rise over the cliffs and there's a heavy marina fog."

"Describe the fog."

I grinned and my face relaxed as he traced his hands lightly across my cheekbones.

"So foggy you can feel the air, like you're walking in a layer of clouds."

I was quiet as I felt the ocean air resting heavy around me.

"Look out at the water," he said.

"It's wild. The waves are somersaulting over each other. They're breaking eight waves back. Some are crashing down so hard they kick up spiraling funnels in the sky."

I was there. I saw it all. I felt it all. Justin's fingers flooded into my dream as if his hands were the wind tossing my hair.

"It's humid but the wind's cool. I have a jacket on and a stocking cap. My shoes are off and the wet, hard sand's freezing cold on my feet. I can feel it squeeze between my toes with each step. Rock stacks are scattered down the beach. People are out walking but I can't make them out in the fog. They look like floating shadows."

My arms were so light they could have floated off of Justin's legs. "I can feel the sun rays filtering through the fog. The air smells damp and salty."

I breathed a full, deep breath that filled my body until every crevice of my lungs expanded. And then I let go. With a long exhale, my worries were pushed away. I was utterly calm.

I was so content sitting there, I hardly noticed Justin lift my arms off of his legs. He slid down on the floor next to me and I could smell salt in his hair and sun on his skin. I turned and his face was only inches from mine. The next thing I felt were both of his hands on my face, lightly drawing me closer, and then his eyes closed and his lips softly touched mine. I closed my eyes and my lips caught on fire the moment he kissed me. The skin on my face was burning from all the trails he left with his fingers. He opened his mouth and I opened mine and he tasted so sweet.

It was weird because it wasn't weird. At all. It's like we were designed to do this. Like we should have been doing this all along.

The kiss deepened and he pressed his lips harder against mine. I reached up and pulled my hands through his hair and his tongue was in my mouth and I could feel a moan come out of his throat.

I balled his T-shirt in my fist to pull him closer just as he did the same thing to me and I felt his mouth smile against mine.

All my doubts melted away. My head was spinning and my heart and my stomach and my soul. I knew he wasn't doing this because I asked him to. I could finally feel how bad he wanted it. His hands weren't just on me, they were exploring me, like he'd been waiting all his life to touch me. He kept kissing me and I sank against him and melted into his arms and he just held my face in his hands, lightly tracing my jaw and my cheeks and my neck. He touched me like he could break me. I wanted him to touch me forever. His hands took his time but his mouth was hard against mine. I couldn't breathe.

He leaned his head back for a second and our mouths separated, but his hands still cradled my face like he couldn't let go. His breaths came out short and uneven like mine. His eyes were wild and confused and overwhelmed. We both tried to catch our breath as we stared at each other.

I couldn't help but smile.

"I like this part of the exercise," I said. He slowly dropped his hands and ran his fingers through his hair, which I had messed with my knotting and pulling. He rubbed his hand against his flushed face. His lips were stained dark red and I stared, wanting to taste them again.

"That's not normally how it works," he insisted. I didn't want him to think. I wouldn't give him the time to second-guess what was happening.

Still high off of his kiss I leaned into him, craving more. "It should be," I said, and pressed my lips to his again as if this was common behavior for us. He kissed me back and his long arms wove their way around me.

"You taste like chocolate," I mumbled into his mouth.

"You taste amazing," he said, and I caught his words on my tongue and grinned because it was one of the coolest things I had ever felt.

I knotted my hand in his thick hair and pulled his face so close against mine I practically suffocated us.

We lost track of time.

We moved from the floor back to the couch, only to end up back on the floor again. My face felt perpetually flushed from my heart racing the entire night.

We only stopped to catch our breath.

Justin's mood changed that night. He was warmer to me than I ever knew he was capable of. He had always been so careful with me, so hesitant. Now his hands were constantly busy, either touching my hair, my face, my arms, my waist. It seemed so natural for him to be this intimate, I was amazed he had the discipline to fight it off. He was too good at being sensual to imagine him being unemotional with people.

"Feel that," Justin said at one point, and pressed my hand over his heart. Through his warm shirt, it felt like a tiny drummer was hammering away inside his chest. At least I wasn't the only one who had a minor heart attack every time we touched.

I grinned back at him. I had everything I wanted in my hand. If I had to choose my eternity, I'd choose this moment, right now, with him. Because there's no place else I'd rather be.

CHAPTER twenty-one

Hope and courage and risk dwell inside of us on an uncharted island and if we learn to look for it and tap into it, our possibilities are endless. That's what I focused on during the drive to Eden. Hope that my future wouldn't always be about running from my past. And most of all, hope that what happened between Justin and me was more than just giving in to the moment. More than a fleeting night. He didn't bring it up during the drive and neither did I because sometimes you ruin the moment with words.

I was starting to think, maybe you need to feel your way more through life—just turn off the lights and follow your senses, even if you stumble once in a while. Maybe that's what falling in love is like. Just feeling your way through the darkness until you find something solid to hold on to.

We exited the highway and turned onto a main street of town, with a bright yellow sign greeting us in blue letters: WELCOME TO EDGEWATER. It was an old-fashioned wood sign, not a digital screen like advertisements in the city. I waited to see gates and security guards standing ready to check us in but as we drove into downtown we didn't hit the security booths I imagined.

"Where are we?"

Justin looked over at me with surprise. "This is it. Eden, as you like to call it." I stared out the window at the main street, packed with shops and people sitting outside and families strolling down the sidewalks.

The city didn't look anything like I imagined. We drove down a cobblestone road and passed a grocery store, restaurants, and coffee shops. We passed a city park with a gazebo in the center and people picnicking on the grass. There was even an Edgewater Hotel. I blinked up at the painted sign suspended over a green awning. Who would come here to visit? Train tracks curved along the side of the street parallel to the road and a light rail buzzed by.

My eyes searched for the fences. "How do they keep track of who comes and goes?"

He wrinkled his eyebrows. "What?"

"They allow random visitors here?" I asked with astonishment. "Shouldn't we have to register somewhere?"

"Good god, Maddie, what were you expecting? A mental institution?"

I stared, dumbly. "I don't know. Something barricaded at least."

"Your idea of Eden is something barricaded?" He gave me a quizzical stare and I shrugged my shoulders.

"I thought it was a place people were exiled to."

He shook his head. "No, that's what the government wants people to think. The rest of us are the ones who are barricaded." Justin looked out the window at the street. "Everyone that's here chooses to be here. As long as they keep quiet and don't cause trouble the government ignores them. There are a lot of cities like this, all over the country, but you'd never know because they're not on maps. Cities where trees grow. Where people walk outside, where fear doesn't rule people's lives. My parents don't even have locks on their doors."

I stared down at the shaggy grass that lined the sidewalk and asked Justin to pull over. He parked along the curb and before the car fully stopped I opened the door and jumped out. I had felt real grass once before, at a zoo in Portland. It was soft and mushy and terribly fragile. If you pushed into it too hard, it gave way to thick, chalky dirt. If you dug your fingernails into it, you could easily rip it out of the ground. It amazed me how people lived with such a delicate plant. The turf ground I grew up with could hold up under anything. It didn't get trampled with use or dried out in the sun. It persevered under the human lifestyle, which so much of nature didn't.

I kneeled down on the ground and ran my fingers through it, taking in its unusual shape. Some spots of the grass were fuller, some blades shorter, some greener. It had its own personality. It was softer than the turf grass and more giving under my fingers. Justin leaned against a tree and watched me and that's when I looked up to study it. First, the smell of the tree was so much more intense. This one carried a musty, earthy smell. The branches and leaves swayed and sounded more like soft rain when they moved, more like a whisper than the clatter plastic leaves made. The plastic leaves cackled and chattered but these hushed and sighed. I stood up and rubbed a leaf between my fingers, feeling its smooth, velvety surface. Tiny veins ran through the leaves that looked as real and alive as the veins under my skin.

"Pretty amazing, isn't it?"

I nodded, overwhelmed. I pressed my palm on the trunk as if I'd be able to feel a pulse underneath it.

"It puts things in perspective," he said.

I looked over at Justin. "What do you mean?"

He studied the tree trunk. "This planet will outlive us all. People are just lucky enough to pass through. But we're so self-absorbed— we don't get it. People are deluded enough to think we can con-

quer the planet. Or that we're powerful enough to destroy it."
Justin shook his head and stepped back. "But we'll never have that
kind of power. Humans are like every other species. We'll come
and go. We're just passing through."

I rubbed my fingers along the jagged bark.

"It's hard to believe your parents can live here so freely. It's like
they break the law and their punishment is to go on vacation the
rest of their lives."

"Maddie, there's something you need to know," he said, his
face serious. "Your dad thinks my parents are dead."

My eyes narrowed skeptically. "What? Why would he think
that?"

"Because he was part of the team that prosecuted their case
four years ago. When my parents broke parole and were convicted,
your dad requested the death sentence. His word carries a lot of
weight."

I stared at him. My own father would order for someone to be
killed? I backed away and shook my head.

"I wasn't going to tell you, but there's no point in keeping anything from you. My parents have such a long criminal record
fighting digital school they qualified as terrorists," he said, laughing to himself. "And these days most terrorists are executed."

"I can't believe my dad would do that."

"I don't think you understand how powerful he is," Justin said.
"He designed the most influential program in our country. I
mean, the president calls your dad to ask him for advice."

"How did your parents escape?" I asked.

"They never told me the whole story. But they obviously knew
someone inside that helped them break out. They were released
the night before their execution but their deaths were recorded.
Someone signed off as witnessing it. For all your dad knows, they
were killed."

I lowered my head. "And you can allow yourself to care about me? The daughter of the man who tried to kill your parents?"

His eyes were sincere. "I've never thought of you that way. And my parents worship you for what you did."

"Because they didn't know who I was," I pointed out. "When they found out it was Kevin Freeman's daughter, what did they think then?"

"You can use power for good or bad, for control or freedom. You grew up watching your dad abuse it one way and it made you take the opposite direction. That's what we all think. Everything's about balance. That's what sustains life. Maybe your role is to keep your dad in check?"

I grinned at him. "You're still just using me for my connections, aren't you?" I joked. Justin frowned.

"Do you honestly think that?" he asked. I looked down at the ground and shook my head. I finally was allowing that doubt to shake off.

"Are you ready to keep going?" he asked. I nodded and followed him back to the car.

Justin described his parents' beach house while we drove down the end of the main street of town and headed up a gradually ascending hill to a cluster of homes. He explained it's more like a hotel, always open to people. It's a block from the ocean, built up on a sandy ridge overlooking the sea. It's in walking distance to downtown. His parents get everywhere on bikes and shoes. He told me Edgewater was picking up on tourism. A few DS colleges even offer field trips to the town to study ecology.

The wheels of the car came to a stop in front of a spacious two-story Victorian home. The house looked ancient, even though the yellow paint gave it a fresh, restored glow. A white porch wrapped around the first level of the house and hanging baskets overflowing with pink and orange flowers and ivy lined the rafters. I took a deep breath of relief. I could definitely handle this. Bikes cluttered the front lawn and a narrow trail of flat rocks carved a path to the house.

Justin grabbed my duffel bag out of the trunk just as the front door swung open, and a woman nearly sprinted down the porch steps.

"Justin!" she yelled. I could instantly tell it was his mom; she had the same smile and dimples. Her long dark hair had some streaks of gray in it. She wore red-rimmed glasses and she was small, a few inches shorter than me. She grabbed Justin around the chest and he had to duck down to hug her back. He towered over her.

She leaned away and stared up at her son. "Did you get your father's birthday present?" she asked.

Justin nodded. "It was uplifting."

She waved her hand in the air. "I don't even want to hear about it," she told him. "It would be nice if he'd give you a present on your birthday that didn't endanger your life."

She turned to greet me.

"You must be Madeline," she said. I nodded and she wrapped her arms around my shoulders and pulled me in for a tight hug. She let me go and studied my face. Her eyes widened with surprise.

"Well, aren't you beautiful!" she said.

I felt my face flush with embarrassment. I looked down at my shoes and shook my head.

"Justin, you didn't tell me what a doll she is."

"Probably because I don't use the word *doll* very often," he said.

"Well," she continued, and her bright eyes fell on mine. "You never know these days, with all the crap people eat and nobody gets enough sun or exercise anymore. People are getting uglier by the second. And not just physically, emotionally, mentally. People are turning into pasty computer zombies."

I tried not to laugh. I could see where Justin got his cynicism from. I had a feeling my mom would love Elaine. Too bad that was a family gathering that would never happen.

"What did you imagine?" Justin asked her.

Elaine glanced back at me. "Oh, I don't know. It's just so good to finally meet you, Madeline. We've been looking for you for a long time."

I nodded. "About three years," I said.

She wrapped her fingers around my arm like we were old friends and guided me to the porch. Justin followed behind us. "You're welcome to anything here, so please don't ever feel like you need to ask."

"Thanks," I said sincerely. I glanced around at the porch, full of benches and blooming with flowers. "It's gorgeous here."

She inhaled deeply and nodded. "We love it."

"Where's Thomas?" I was surprised how casually Justin said his father's name. I'd never used my dad's first name. It sounded too impersonal.

"Who knows. He's hiking somewhere on the coast. Rough life."

He looked down at his mom. "You guys earned it, Mom. Stop being so hard on him."

"He'll be back tomorrow. We weren't sure when you'd be getting here." She paused and looked between the two of us as we stood next to each other on the porch. Justin held my duffel bag, swung over his shoulder.

Her face fell with concern. "You both look awfully tired. Did you two sleep at all these past few days?"

Justin turned his mom's shoulders and steered her through the front door before she caught my blush. His eyes found mine for a split second and he grinned. It was a little awkward walking behind his mom when, about eight hours ago, I had been rolling around on the floor with her son with my shirt pulled halfway up my back.

We entered a small foyer and I wiped my shoes off on a sandy rug. A small table against the wall was piled with books and boxes. A row of hooks along the wall was heaped with jackets and hats, and random pairs of shoes were piled by the door. I already loved the cluttered look of the place. Her house, unlike mine, looked lived in.

"I apologize for the mess," she said, and giggled to herself. "But who has time to clean these days? There are far better things to be doing with your life."

"My mom has a saying," Justin began, and waited for her to finish.

She blinked back at him. "I do?" Justin rolled his eyes. "Oh," she said. "Justin, I don't want Madeline to think I'm too critical."

"But you are," he said. I watched her with my eyebrows raised and waited. She glanced over at me and threw her hands up.

"Oh, I just think a neat house is the sign of an extremely boring person, that's all. And I don't really like to associate with boring people if I can help it."

"I can live with that," I said.

She looked over at me. "People come and go so often here, Madeline, it's hard to keep anything neat. It's one big free-for-all. But," she added, "I have rooms upstairs ready for you both." She slapped a hand over her mouth suddenly. "Oh, you two must be starving. It's a good thing Erica brought over some leftovers."

Justin leaned in to whisper to me. "She doesn't really cook either. That's my dad's job," he told me.

"I heard that!" she yelled over her shoulder.

We walked through the foyer and down the hall. The house smelled like wood and coffee. Our house didn't have any smells. I also wasn't used to this much color in a house. The foyer walls were a bright citrus yellow and the walls in the hallway were a bright ocean blue, almost turquoise, but weathered looking and cracked in places. I studied the color as I passed. In our house, fireproof beige carpeting or laminate floors covered every square inch of it, and most of the walls were stark white.

I wasn't very hungry, more tired than anything, but Elaine poured me a bowl of soup and set a plate in front of me stacked with biscuits. The warm chicken broth was salty and thick and I sat at the table and drank it down. It started to fill me up, which just made me more tired.

"Justin, this poor girl's exhausted. What have you done to her?"

I tried not to blush again and Justin looked indifferent as he rummaged through the pantry shelves.

"Haven't you been feeding her? She's so thin," she scolded him.

"I haven't been able to sleep much," I said, which was partly true. I just didn't go into why, exactly, I hadn't slept last night.

"Well, you can relax here. Maybe you should turn in early tonight, both of you, and get a good night's sleep." After another helping of soup, Justin walked me back toward the foyer. I said good night to Elaine and thanked her for dinner. She gave me another tight hug before I followed Justin up the stairs and down the hallway. He led me to a room in the corner of the house. I walked inside and it was small, with a slanting ceiling and a large window that looked out at the ocean. He threw my bag down on the bed.

"If you need anything, let me know," he said. I nodded and walked over to the window and peered out. The night was calm and clear and a cool breeze swept in that smelled like the ocean. I stared at him and he stared back at me and it felt like we were both fighting something. He hesitated, like he was going to take a step forward but he backed up instead. He took a deep breath and ran his fingers through his hair, making it wild.

"Good night, Maddie," he said, and turned away without another word. I stared at the empty space across my room. He hardly touched me today. He kept a polite, friendly distance. And I was worried. I wanted to crawl inside his mind and open up all the doors and windows that I was afraid he was trying to close again.

❀

I rolled over in bed and gazed out at the moon, visible through the thin white curtains that were stirring from the breeze. My mind was exhausted, but my body wasn't and there was one person to blame. Just as I was about to throw my sheets off and find him, I heard my door tap open. I could feel his energy pass through the room before I could make out his tall presence in the darkness and I propped my head up on my elbow, glaring at him. He leaned against the door until it clicked closed. He moved closer and I could smell his soapy skin and hair. I pulled the sheets back.

"Is this all right?" he asked as he crawled into bed with me. Our eyes met in the shadowy darkness and his hand found my face and his lips found my mouth.

"What took you so long?" I whined when he started to kiss me.

"I had to wait for my mom to fall asleep," he complained, sounding as annoyed as I had felt.

"You didn't even kiss me good night," I mumbled, our lips still attached. He lifted his head back and stared into my eyes.

"You think I could have stopped with one kiss?" he asked like I was insane. He touched my lips with one finger and shook his head. He leaned back into me.

I didn't want to think. I could barely breathe. All I could do was feel. I traced my hand over his arm and up to his face because I couldn't get enough of that feeling, of the warmth that came off of his skin, and we just hid inside the darkness. The more I kissed him the more I needed to kiss him, like his lips were a drug. I tasted his mouth with my tongue. He grabbed one of my legs and pulled me on top of him.

It was safe, with all the lights off and no one around to point and stare. In the night it's easy to indulge. It was just the two of us—we didn't have to think about who we were or what this meant or where it was going. It was like an escape. It's easy to forget at this moment billions of people exist and far-off galaxies are being born and stars collide. Kissing is its own kind of collision, it produces its own planetarium of lights inside your head. For me, it was like seeing colors for the first time after living in a black-and-white world. A single person can be just as wide and vast and spellbinding as any sky full of stars. They can make you think the world stops and night can last forever. I laced my fingers around his and squeezed his hand and he squeezed mine back and it made something ache in my chest.

CHAPTER twenty-two

I walked downstairs the next morning to find a party in the living room. I stared with shock at about twenty people, milling around, drinking coffee, the front screen door slamming open and closed. There were kids running around and dogs loose and I almost tripped over a soccer ball that suddenly rolled past my feet. A young boy ran up to me, grinned shyly, and kicked it away, disappearing down the hall, and another boy sprinted around the corner and yelled after him. I walked into the kitchen and Elaine was in there with about six other women and there were heaps of food spread out on the kitchen table. I felt a pang of guilt seeing this, because it reminded me of my mom and how much she would love all this noise and commotion. Elaine was talking and gesturing wildly and the other women were talking and I just watched with fascination. When Elaine saw me, she smiled and quickly came over to plant a huge, motherly kiss on my forehead. I blushed in return.

"This gorgeous young woman is our guest of honor," she announced to her friends and quickly introduced me, rattling off so many names I couldn't keep up, so I just smiled and nodded at all the friendly faces. Someone handed me a cup of coffee and before I could respond Elaine handed me a plate piled with muffins.

"Madeline, can you take these out back? Thomas is on the deck with Justin. You need to go introduce yourself, he can't wait to meet you," she encouraged me. The next thing I knew I was being ushered toward the back door.

I walked outside to find Justin sitting on a wide deck that overlooked the ocean. The waves crashed in the distance, just past a sandy hill scattered with some brush and stalks of weeds. Justin turned to me and so did the man sitting next to him, a man who had Justin's build. He smiled and stood up. He had the same intense eyes as Justin, the same confident stance. I squinted up at him in the bright daylight.

"I see Elaine's already put you to work," he said, and grabbed the plate from me just as I was starting to tip it over. He shook my hand and studied me. He smiled broadly, like I was a close family friend, which made me uncomfortable since I was more like a family enemy.

"Madeline," he said. "It's been a long time."

I stared back at him and creased my eyebrows. He was talking like he'd already met me.

"We've been looking for you a long time, is what I mean," he told me, and I nodded. "Have you been given the full tour?" he asked. Justin and I both shook our heads and I watched the two of them, equal build, equal height, walk in front of me toward the house. Thomas gave his son a surprised glance. "You haven't shown her the computer room?"

"I wanted to give you the honor," Justin said. He looked at me over his shoulder. "It's one of his toy rooms," he said.

I looked back and forth between them and waited for the punch line. "You have computers here?" I asked with surprise.

"Madeline," Thomas told me, "we may be backward in our ways but we like to know what we're up against."

I followed them down the hallway and he opened a door that led into a giant storage closet and food pantry. When I assumed the back wall was a dead end, Thomas pressed a code into a panel on the wall. One of the shelved walls swung open and a metal door appeared behind it, like the opening to a bomb shelter.

I stared at Thomas. Something told me this old Victorian house didn't come built with a disguised, security-encoded entryway. He scanned his fingerprint and the door buzzed open. A narrow stairway illuminated as soon as Thomas walked through. I followed behind him and when we met the foot of the stairs I looked around at a room the size of a conference center. Screens filled every inch of wall space. Dozens of computers sat on white tabletops sprawled throughout the room. I walked past the screens and marveled at them, as if being reintroduced to a drug addiction. In the center of the room was a large circular table with four monitors spread out.

I ran my fingers along one of the keyboards and smiled to myself. It was like greeting an old friend that you've grown apart from. I wasn't sure if our relationship could ever be the same again. My fingers and eyes had seen and touched so much in the past few weeks; it was strange to think this keypad and all these buttons had been my world practically my entire life.

I walked past the monitors and did a double take when I noticed a Cerberix on the table, plugged into one of the computer outlets. I studied it closer with disbelief. A Cerberix is decoding software, designed to infiltrate any website. It can tap into anything from someone's personal bank account to a corporation's most secured data files. The software could override any password or security code and find information whether it was in use, saved, or being transferred. I knew there were only a handful of people in the country that had access to one. I knew that because my father was one of them and a few years ago, I taught myself how to use it. When kids my age were chatting and flirting and going to digital concerts I was hacking into confidential government sites and downloading information.

"Where did you get this?" I asked, pointing at the *c*-shaped computer drive.

Thomas looked back at me. "I have ways of acquiring things."

I was shocked at his easygoing reaction, as if we were talking about a new television model, not a stolen piece of highly specialized government equipment. I put my hands on my hips.

"Do you know what would happen if you were caught with this?" I asked.

"Certain and immediate execution, I suppose," he said lightly, and I cringed since he was already "executed" once before. I stared skeptically between him and Justin. Did this whole family think they were immortal?

"I'm not too worried, Madeline," he said. "I designed them, you see, so no one's going to find out that I have a few extras lying around."

"You designed Cerberix software?" I asked with shock.

"He invented it," Justin said.

Thomas nodded. "Biggest mistake of my life," he said with a sigh. He pulled a chair back and we all sat around the computer table. I stared at Thomas like he was part hero, part villain to invent something so controversial, something that allowed the government to spy on anyone they wanted.

"I was working at a computer engineering firm in Phoenix when I was Justin's age. It was a company specializing in warfare communication. When I designed the software, I was told the program would be used by the military as a means of protection. We'd use it to hack into enemy sites and freeze their communication or try to intercept attack plans. This is when the U.S. was being threatened with nuclear attacks from China, before the Big Freeze in 2040."

I knew about the treaty signed in 2040. Every country in the world with nuclear warheads came together and agreed to dispose of their weapons. It was the most peaceful day recorded in history. The treaty, still called the Big Freeze, has been signed every subsequent ten years and is in effect today.

"I was willing to do anything to stop the threat of a nuclear world war," he continued. "That's why I agreed to design it. But it turned out the software had nothing to do with safety. The government turned my invention into a giant spy system. They used it to monitor everything we're doing. They know what we watch, what we eat, who we talk to. They can read every single chat message we write. There's no privacy left. That's the kind of power I gave the government."

"But if you invented it, can't you figure out a way to shut it down?" I asked.

He shook his head.

"By the time I realized what they were planning to use it for, it was too late. They owned every file I ever created. And I was so young back then, so trusting, I didn't think of creating a loophole. It's easy to put too much faith in technology and think discovery and innovation are always going to be a step forward. When you get too excited about the possibilities, you don't stop to consider the consequences. Just when you get too cocky, life has a way of putting you in your place."

"So, now you're trying to make up for what you did?" I asked.

"Well," he said, "I've found a way to use it for a better cause. A peaceful cause, as it was intended."

"You're using it to fight digital school," I said, amazed to meet the man whose invention had such an impact on my own life. "But if you've had a Cerberix this whole time, why couldn't you steal my dad's files five years ago like you tried to?" I asked.

Thomas grinned. "That's a good question. There are a few limitations to a Cerberix. They act as protection against other hackers. It's like a permanent security guard. Since your father has one, there are only about a dozen people in the U.S. who do, and we hit a dead end. Two Cerberixes cancel each other out.

"When Justin and I realized your father's files were accessed from his own computer, it made perfect sense. That's the only way it would have been possible. No one could have broken in unless they got to his computer and dismantled the security themselves, which I assume is what you did."

I shook my head because I didn't dismantle anything. He raised his eyebrows with surprise.

"How did you do it?" he asked me with a grin. It was so strange to see someone proud of what I did. I'd only explained it once, to my father and Damon, and they weren't quite as encouraging.

"When I was little, I always played in my dad's office when he was working, because he was always working. When I got older, I'd read in his office and watch the news with him; it was the only way I could spend time with him. I watched him work on the computer, but he didn't know I was paying such close attention. My dad sometimes used a dozen passwords to get on a single site. So I started memorizing what he did because I was impressed and I wanted to see if I could do it, like it was a game."

Justin and Thomas both watched me with the same intense expressions.

"Kids always mimic what their parents do," I pointed out. "It just so happens my dad is the CEO of digital school, so that's what I tried to be."

"But isn't his computer sensitive to his fingerprints?" Thomas asked me, and it was true. The keyboard in his office only responded to his touch, which was another security measure.

"I used a MindReader to do it," I said. "My dad bought one, when they first came out. Since I knew all of his passwords and where the files were, I just used the MindReader to access them."

"Very clever," Thomas said with a grin.

"It was easy," I said. I stared back at him and wished this was the way my own father would look at me, with admiration in his eyes, not constant disappointment.

"Let me show you what kind of a difference you made," he said. I hardly noticed Justin stand up and walk upstairs, I was too mesmerized by the charts and graphs and statistics Thomas was showing me on the monitors, the lists and profiles of thousands of supporters they gained after my Rebellion. I never knew the inspiration it motivated. My dad made it his mission to make sure I never knew. No wonder Justin committed nearly three years to track me down. He was right. I was the key they needed.

For the rest of the afternoon, Thomas showed me some of the research they collected on me over the past few years, where I was going online, who they thought I was. It was like watching a documentary of myself. For the first time in my life, I was proud of what I did. Maybe it wasn't a mistake. It was just my way in the door, into a world in which I'd always belonged.

I glanced around at the sheer size of the basement. "What do you do with all this room?" I asked.

"Training, mostly. We bring in people older than me and younger than you who want to bring down digital school and start over again. Get this world back on a wellness plan," he said. "We wait until we have about forty people to train and bring them all in at once."

Thomas looked up when Justin came back downstairs.

"Maddie," he said, "there's somebody here to see you." Before I could ask what he meant, a voice interrupted us from upstairs.

"Madeline, you're here!" Clare yelled. I jumped out of my chair, almost knocking it over, and raced up the stairs to meet her. Clare stood in the kitchen next to Pat and Noah and I practically fell into her arms.

"What are you doing here?" I asked as we separated. I stared at the three of them with surprise.

"Justin told me you'd be here. I couldn't believe it when I heard what happened," Clare began rambling. Pat and Noah were already helping themselves to food, and people were still coming and going like this was a community kitchen.

"So much has happened," Clare said. "First the whole power outage in Toledo—I could have guessed that was Justin's doing." She raised her eyebrows at him as he walked into the kitchen. My stomach did flips at the sight of him and I wondered if that sensation would ever stop happening every time he walked in the room.

"Then, we heard about the interception and how you got away from the cops yourself. How did you manage that one?" Clare went on before I could answer. "Anyway, we knew you escaped, but we didn't hear anything from Justin for two days. What was *that* about?" Clare stopped to glare at him and he just wrinkled his eyebrows back at her.

"I didn't know I had to check in with you for daily Madeline updates," he said.

I looked over at Pat and Noah and asked them how long they'd be staying. Clare's face fell when the question left my lips. Noah rolled his eyes.

"Kid, I can't live at home forever," he said. Clare shook her head.

"It's stupid, Noah. You haven't even finished DS four," she said. I looked between her and Noah for an explanation.

"Noah desperately wants more band groupies," Pat offered.

"No, well, yeah," Noah said and he looked back at me with a grin. "My band and I are moving to L.A. Pat's coming with me."

"Los Angeles?" I said with surprise.

Clare pouted. "Not only is my brother leaving, but he's taking his band and stealing one of my best friends," she whined. "And now you won't be in Corvallis, which means Justin won't. This year is going to suck." Clare slouched down on a chair next to the table.

I set my hand on her shoulder. "You'll have Molly and Scott."

"Great," she said. "They really know how to let loose."

"At least you're not in hiding because you broke your probation and were disowned by your family," I pointed out.

Pat and Noah both nodded in agreement.

"See, Clare," Pat said. "Whenever you catch yourself feeling bad, just remember poor Maddie here. Your life isn't close to as depressing as hers." I rolled my eyes at him.

"Thanks for being sensitive in my time of grief," I said.

"I do what I can," he said, and smiled at me. I glanced over at Justin and his eyes were studying Pat's thoughtfully. I saw something flicker, like an idea flashing through his head. Then, just as quickly, it was gone. He was as good as my father at keeping his emotions camouflaged.

Justin excused himself and walked down the hallway toward the basement.

Noah and Pat stood up and announced they needed to bring their stuff in. Clare grabbed my hand and stood up from the chair. "I need to talk to you," she said, and pulled me toward the back door. A cool breeze whipped past us when we got outside, and Clare locked her arm around mine. We jumped down the porch steps and headed for the beach.

Clare glanced over her shoulder to make sure no one was around.

"Okay," she said, and her eyes focused on mine. "What's really been going on the past few days?"

All she needed to see was the grin on my face and the glow in my eyes to know the answer to her question. Her mouth dropped open.

"I can't believe it. Somebody brought down the walls of the impenetrable Justin Solvi."

I creased my eyebrows. "What do you mean?" We stepped around scrawny bushes lining the path to the beach.

"I mean, Justin Solvi is unattainable," she said. She said his name like he was some kind of celebrity and I guessed, in her circle, he was. "I've never seen him so much as second-glance at a girl." She stared at me and her blue eyes widened with shock. "Wow. He must be in love with you."

My stomach flipped at the words but I quickly argued them away.

"Clare," I said, and shook my head. "Be serious."

"I am," she insisted. "Justin is about work. When he comes here, he works. When he's hanging out with his friends, it's *all about work*. That's all he knows."

I frowned. "That's not right."

"Do you know he's never taken a day off? Ever! In the ten years I've known him, he's never just taken a day to himself. Thought about himself."

"He doesn't think about himself," I said. "I don't even think he sees a *self*, he sees us all as interconnected or something."

"I know, it's so saintlike it's annoying." I laughed, but Clare's eyes were serious. "I'm not kidding. Justin makes me feel so selfish sometimes because he never, ever thinks about himself. It's crazy."

We were both quiet for a few seconds.

"So, are you guys dating?" she asked. I laughed because the idea still sounded so bizarre to me.

I shrugged. "I don't know what's going on. All I know is Justin's leaving soon and who knows when we'll see each other again."

She nodded. "You've definitely picked a challenging guy to like," she said.

"Or love unconditionally," I said.

Clare stopped and looked at me. "You really love him?" she asked. I nodded without hesitating.

"I just want to warn you, Maddie, he closes himself off to people, sometimes in the snap of a finger. It's weird, I love Justin like a brother, but I'd never want one of my good friends to date him. I think he's going to follow in a path similar to his parents."

I could feel my heart sink. I looked out at the ocean waves curling in the distance.

"Justin won't admit it," Clare said, "but I think growing up without his parents around really affected him. All he knows is how to distance himself from people. And I don't think he would ever want to drag another person into that kind of lifestyle. He was always left behind and even though there's no bitterness or resentment, it's not ideal to be tossed around, never knowing where you're wanted, like you're a piece of luggage someone needs to store. I think the way he sees it is he needs to choose one life or the other."

I nodded because I was afraid of the same thing. I was scared that once we were separated, once his routine was back in place, he'd let the distance naturally grow. Clare squeezed my hand.

"But," she said, "that was before he met you. And no matter how headstrong someone is, you meet one person and your world can change forever."

The sun was starting to set by the time Clare and I made it back to the house. The sky faded into a dark purple canvas and the air turned chilly so I ran upstairs to grab a fleece. When I came back down, I was met by Justin and his mom, who both looked up at me with a dare in their eyes.

"What?" I asked.

"We like to welcome our guests with a little display," Elaine said. "Something to get you fired up, if you know what I mean?"

I looked between her and Justin.

"Come on, let's go outside," he said. I followed him and Elaine out the front door and down the steps to the side of the house. People were gathered in a tight circle and I joined them to see what they were staring at. I looked down at a shallow hole carved in the ground with stones tracing a circular border around it. A pile of sticks and leaves and branches were piled inside.

People were pulling up chairs and blankets and somebody started strumming a guitar. Justin held something out to me.

"Do you want to do the honors?" he asked.

I took the matchbox out of his hand and nodded. I'd never lit a real match before, but I'd had seen people do it in movies. I took a match out and swiped it across the side of the box. The flame caught with a whisper and I stared at the tiny glow I was holding like it was magic. I could smell sulfur and smoke from the flame. I realized what Justin meant. It was tempting to want to touch the precarious orange light.

Justin nodded to the fire pit and I flung the match on top. Before it even hit the ground, flames shot up with a roaring gust. I jumped back as the fire reached into the air like slithering arms grabbing for something to devour. Clare, Pat, and Noah leaned toward the growing flames, stretching their hands and fingers out to the heat. I backed up until I reached the safety of the porch. The fire danced imperiously in front of me. I could hear the flames eating away at the wood inside of it. Branches snapped and crackled and I felt waves of heat and smoke drift over to me.

"Oh my god," I whispered to Justin when he approached. The flames were hissing and it reminded me of all the times I'd seen fires on the news, scorching and killing and burning. All I knew fire was capable of was death and destruction. How could you appreciate something you could never trust?

"This couldn't be safe," I said.

"It's safe," he assured me. "Just don't walk right into it and you'll be fine."

I shook my head.

"It can be used for good, Maddie," he said, as if he could read my mind. He tried to pull me forward but I stayed in place.

"It's too close to the house," I said, remembering all the stories and footage I'd seen of forest fires demolishing homes and neighborhoods. I glared at Justin.

"Your house isn't even fireproof. Are you insane?" I asked. A few people standing around the flames turned to watch me. Elaine's eyes flickered to mine.

His voice stayed calm and even. "We have fires almost every night here. It's not the enemy the news makes it out to be. Experience it for yourself before you judge it."

I didn't answer him, I only stared ahead. I watched Elaine pull up a seat at the edge of the roaring flames and relax next to it. Others sat down on blankets and lawn chairs. I kept my distance and shivered in the chilly darkness.

"Look at me," Justin said.

He cupped my chin in his fingers and pulled my gaze away from the fire, but I could still see it reflected in his eyes.

"Your whole life you've been shown and told what to believe. But I don't think you know anything until you experience it firsthand. So, form your own opinions."

I looked back at the fire while I listened to him.

"Right now," he said, "your mind is like a rope that's been twisted so much in one direction it's coiled up. I need you to unwind. Do you know what I mean?"

I stared back at him.

"Unwind? You mean let go of everything I've ever known? What I was taught to fear, I now need to accept and I probably need to fear what I've always been taught to trust?"

Justin's eyes were patient. "Hopefully you won't fear anything. You'll just see the truth."

"You make it sound so easy."

He took a step closer to me. "Listen to me. You need to trust everything I tell you. You can question it and make me explain it a hundred times, but you need to open yourself up to try things. I'll never try to conform you to believe something false. And neither will anyone here. Can you understand that?"

I nodded slowly. I took a deep breath and edged my way toward the fire pit and sat next to Clare on a blanket. Pat sat down close to my other side and Justin took a seat on the opposite side of the fire, next to Thomas.

I stared at the flames and listened—they had a voice of their own, a sound and a rhythm that whispered around us. For the next few hours, I watched how the fire brought people close together. Clare and Pat and I spread out on the blanket, like our own private island. Pat told stories about traveling with the band. He didn't play, but he worked as the band's manager and promoter. Anytime he brought up the move to California, Clare argued about it.

"You were getting plenty of work in Oregon," Clare reminded Noah. "And your fans actually care about you there."

"Yeah, well Oregon has about twenty venues. And California has over two hundred," Noah reminded her.

I watched the fire flicker off of everyone's faces while they talked and paint dancing shadows along the ground.

"I'll have to tell my brother to see your show, he lives in L.A.," I told Noah. I sensed Justin watching me and looked over in time to catch a flicker in his eyes. My intuition made me want to pull him aside and ask him what he was thinking but his father whispered something to him and the two of them were lost in conversation.

When the fire was starting to die down, people slowly dispersed. I went inside to get a glass of water from the kitchen but I stopped in the hallway when I heard Clare's voice.

"What's your problem?" she asked. "Pat's your cousin."

"I think he likes her," I heard Justin say, trying to keep his voice low. I stood frozen against the wall, too surprised to move.

"You care about her, Justin, why can't you admit it?" Clare was struggling to keep her voice to a whisper.

"Of course I can admit it," he argued. "It doesn't mean I have a right."

"You're ridiculous. Do you honestly think she's going to fall for Pat because *you* think it's a good idea?"

"I can't be there for her if she needs me. Pat can. It makes sense."

I rested my head against the wall and stared up at the ceiling. So, I realized, that's why he was giving me space tonight.

"There's a slight problem with your plan. She's in love with you, you stupid idiot."

My stomach flipped at how easily Clare could speak those words.

"Don't call me a stupid idiot," I heard him say.

"Sorry, stupid jackass?"

"That's a lot better." I heard Justin let out a deep sigh. "The best thing I can do is leave her alone," I heard him say. "I don't want her to get hurt."

"Why don't you take your own advice?" she said. "Your mind's all coiled up in one direction. Why don't you let it unwind and see where it goes?"

I was standing next to the bathroom door and I made a show to shut it loudly. I heard their talking stop. I walked into the kitchen and pretended to be oblivious.

"Hey," I said.

"Hey," Clare said, and turned to me and smiled, but the smile didn't reach her eyes. I poured a cup of water from a blue pitcher on the table and Justin walked out of the room. I watched him go and looked back at Clare. She sighed and walked out as well to join the rest of the group outside. I set my glass down on the table and realized my hands were shaking.

CHAPTER twenty-three

I wanted to pretend like everything was fine, that I didn't know Justin was trying to break things off with me. I trudged upstairs to my bedroom, curled up in a chair next to the window, and pushed the drapes back until the ocean was in view. The silvery moon cast a trail of light along the surface of the water and I had the urge to follow its path like it was reaching out for me, teasing me to dream. I don't know how long I sat there, lost in my thoughts, hypnotized by the distant, shimmering waves.

I heard my door creak open and I turned, snapped out of my daydreaming. Justin walked in. His skin looked dark against his T-shirt and I could smell the smoky scent of his clothes. He sat down on the edge of the bed.

I loved having him there. I hated how much I loved it.

"Everyone's going to bed," he told me. His voice was low and raspy in the darkness.

I nodded but focused my gaze out the window. Justin studied me quietly and I slipped out of the chair and climbed onto his lap. He was surprised at first by my forwardness, but then his shoulders relaxed and he wrapped his arms around me. I rested my head under the crook of his neck and concentrated on the rhythm of his heart.

He whispered in my ear, "I'm leaving for Portland tomorrow."

I nodded because I knew what was coming next.

"I'll be gone for a while." He leaned away so he could read my eyes. "Do you think you'll be all right here?"

I nodded again because I didn't want to make him worry. I didn't want to be needy and clingy and all these things that would hold Justin back. I knew how important his mission was.

"I know what you were doing tonight," I said.

His eyes narrowed for an instant but he slowly nodded.

I stared back at him. "Do you want me?" I asked him.

I felt his chest rise in a deep intake of breath. He reached his hand out and lightly traced the skin under my collarbone, above my chest, where my heart was pounding. He let his hand rest there for a few seconds to feel the pulse. His eyes met mine and they were torn.

"Don't waste this on me," he said, and added pressure to his fingertips. I knew he could feel how fast my heart was beating.

"Why not?" I heard myself whisper, and he pressed his palm flat against my heart.

"It's too amazing," he said. "And I can't give you mine." His eyes looked pained and guilty and it made my heart wince. "You deserve someone that can," he said, and dropped his hand.

"Stop trying to turn your feelings off," I said. "I'll just seduce you again."

He grabbed me in his arms and lifted me onto the bed next to him like I was as light as a pillow. He held my head between both of his hands and studied me. I stared back into his dark eyes. He was too perfect.

"I'm not trying to turn my feelings off," he said. "I tried that already and it was a waste of energy. Remember when you told me you needed some time to adjust to being unplugged? Well, you need to give me some time, too. Up until a few days ago, I never thought I'd let this happen. You're the first person that's ever called me out on it. And you're right. I've committed my life to helping people be more human and I'm denying myself one of the core reasons that make me human. Sometimes you don't see those things until someone wakes you up to it. But give me some time to figure this out. That's all I ask."

"Do your parents know anything?" I asked.

He nodded and it made me blush with embarrassment.

"Am I that obvious?"

He leaned away and looked at me. "No, it was me. My mom called me out on it the minute I told her I met you. She knows me way too well."

"What did you tell them? That we're dating?"

He laid his head back on the pillow. "We never really labeled this," he said.

I nodded and tapped my fingers against his chest. "How would you label it?"

He shrugged and studied me. "I've never thought about defining you."

I nodded and laid my head next to his until our foreheads touched. I stared at his long eyelashes. "I wouldn't call you my friend," I said.

He thought about this. "I hate the word *girlfriend*. It's too generic." He traced his fingers up the side of my waist and lightly touched his lips to mine. "Nothing really explains this scenario," he said.

I ran my fingers through his hair and sighed. "So what are we, superfriends?"

"I like that." He rolled to his side and propped his head up on his elbow. With his other hand he pulled me tight against him.

His mouth turned up into a grin. "I hate to sound incredibly un-romantic, but I'm starting to think of you as my best friend."

I grimaced at this. "As long as you want to kiss your best friend."

Instead of answering me he leaned in and slowly brushed his lips against mine, barely kissing me. With his lips touching mine, he muttered, "That's why this drives me crazy," he said, and pulled back to look at me. "I love how your mind works, and sometimes how it doesn't work." I rolled my eyes and he continued. "But most of all," he said, "I love watching you wake up. It's like you see the world with new eyes every day. I never know how you're going to react."

I nodded at this. *He and I both.* He grabbed my face in his hand and pulled me close and this time he kissed me, really kissed me, and I opened up my mouth and my heart and my soul and he flooded in.

❁

The next morning I woke up alone and I could sense an emptiness in the house, through the walls. Something was missing. I knew he was gone. I could feel him when he was in the house. Even if he wasn't in the same room as me. The air was charged with his prox-imity, as if he carried an electric current only I could feel. I stared at the ceiling and knew I should get up. I heard a faint knock at my door and Clare's face peered in. I could see her out of the corner of my eye but I didn't move my gaze from the ceiling.

"Maddie, you okay?" she asked. I was still in bed with my arms crossed behind my head, motionless, my drapes closed, and a dim yellow light filtering through the room. She came all the way in and stared at me, her hands crossed over her chest. "It's almost noon."

I blinked at the ceiling.

"Am I supposed to be somewhere?" I asked with a stale tone, as if my voice was tired from overuse.

"Maddie, get up." She threw the covers off me but I was too dazed to move. She sat down on the edge of the bed and studied me.

"It's not like you're never going to see him again," she said.

"It's not just that," I said. I sat up and Clare watched me with concern. "I don't know what I'm doing here. I'm endangering his family being here. I haven't committed to helping anyone, so it's not like I'm even a part of this group. Meanwhile, I'm supposed to just hang out and sit by the fire every night like I'm on vacation?"

Clare smiled apologetically. "Listen, I know this is hard. Sometimes there are phases in your life that feel like a waiting room. And there's nothing you can do about it. You're transitioning. But you're not endangering anyone by being here, so get that thought out of your head right now. And it's still too soon for you to be out in public, so swiping your fingerprint and catching a train is pointless. You're stuck here until we figure out a plan. So make the most of it."

I sighed and felt selfish. I should be grateful for everything. Why is it easier to sit around feeling sorry for yourself than it is to drag yourself out of bed and appreciate what you have? Why is it so much easier to dwell on what you lack?

"Pat and I will stay for a few weeks and keep you company."

I nodded. "What about Noah?"

Clare's face fell. "He's leaving for L.A. tomorrow. He's recording an album and after that Pat's going to meet him to look for apartments."

I rubbed Clare's back and nodded. At least I wasn't the only person feeling sorry for myself.

❀

The next few weeks crawled by. I tried to make myself useful to Elaine and Thomas but everything I tried to do required teaching. Pat taught me how to mow the lawn, the strangest job I've ever experienced since I grew up my whole life on plastic grass.

Pat explained how to push the mower back and forth in even sections, and I loved everything about it, the smell of cut grass and the even paths the mower made, like I was making my mark on the earth. It was also a great way to get a suntan.

Elaine taught me how to write a grocery list as well as navigate myself through the market aisles to find foreign products like pimentos and leeks. Thomas trusted me enough to encode my fingerprint on the basement door so I could use the computers whenever I wanted. He and I spent hours going over sites and groups that had been blocked from my computer for years. He showed me how they hacked into police reports to trace for people to intercept.

Clare distracted me with long walks on the beach and Pat entertained us at night by teaching me card games, and we watched movies and sometimes we walked into town and listened to live music and got coffee. But my life lacked an energy that only one person could fill.

Three weeks after Justin left, I sat with Elaine next to the fire. Clare and Pat were inside watching one of Noah's concerts on the wall screen with Thomas. For some reason being in the basement made me feel queasy. All of the sterile wall screens and digital images depressed me. I found myself constantly craving the outdoors, where I felt less isolated by the living, growing life that surrounded me. Or maybe it just reminded me of someone. The fresh air became my sanctuary and I slept with my window open every night, even if I woke up freezing from the cold ocean breeze.

I stared into the fire, thinking about Justin, and I frowned at the flickers of blue, gold, and orange flames. He hadn't tried to contact me once since he left. Even to check in. Three weeks feels like three years when you spend all your time missing someone.

"What's on your mind, Maddie?"

I looked over at Elaine. Even when I studied her, I mostly saw Justin, in her eyes and skin and thoughtful expressions. I stared back at the flames.

"I just feel useless here. Justin's out there, risking his life every day. Saving hundreds of people. And I'm learning how to mow the lawn. Water plants. Boil pasta noodles."

Elaine nodded slowly. Her voice was light. "Change happens slowly. And it only happens one person at a time, one day at a time. Everyone who accepts this way of life has to start over, just like you are. You're learning a brand-new culture."

I nodded and tried to believe that in a small way I was moving forward.

"You need to be content with small steps. That's all life is. Small steps that you take every day so when you look back down the road it all adds up and you know you covered some distance. It took me a long time to accept that, but it's true. You need to have patience."

I stared at the flames. "I just miss him."

"Of course you do," Elaine said. "So do I. You can feel distance. It carries a weight that's heavier than anything."

I rubbed the space over my heart like it was a sore muscle. "It hurts," I admitted. "It feels like something's cracked."

"But you need to be able to fill that space on your own, Maddie," she warned me. "You should never have to rely on another person to make you feel whole. That life is dangerous."

I frowned at Elaine. "You mean I'm not supposed to care about your son?" I asked.

She shook her head and her eyes were kind. "Of course you should care. But you shouldn't *need* him. You need to feel complete first, with living in your own skin. Maybe take some time to get to know who you are and what you want to do before you worry too much about Justin."

I stared into the fire. "He's determined to be alone and that's what bothers me. It isn't healthy to be such a loner. Shouldn't there be a balance?"

Elaine watched me curiously. Then, something lightened in her eyes and the youthful grin I'd grown to love about her grew on her face.

"That's interesting. I wonder if you would have felt that way a year ago?" She looked back at the fire. "You're a confident woman. I think that's what Justin loves most about you."

I blinked at the fire and shook my head. "My dad always says I'm naive."

She smiled. "That's just what grownups like to call young confidence. Sometimes adults want you to see it as a weakness, when really, it's a gift. Justin sees it in you." Her eyes focused on mine. "It's a very attractive trait, Maddie, don't lose it. If you have confidence, if you believe in yourself, you can go anywhere. And you'll be fine."

She stood up and rubbed a hand on my shoulder before she left me alone next to the fire. I stared into the orange blaze and felt a smile creep on my face. She was testing me tonight. And I passed.

CHAPTER *twenty-four*

I was in the kitchen trying to make a grilled cheese sandwich without much luck. I charcoaled one side black and the cheese inside hadn't even melted. I turned down the heat on the stove and suddenly Clare flew through the kitchen door, scaring me. I screamed and dropped the spatula out of my hand.

"Madeline, quick, come downstairs." Her face was white and her eyes were tense with panic. I turned the burner off and followed Clare down the steps. Elaine and Thomas were already there, sitting in front of a wall screen, their faces tight with concern.

I turned the corner and saw Scott and Molly looking back at me from the screen. There was a silence hovering through the room and I knew it was something serious.

"What is it?" I asked.

"Your father's in Portland holding a press conference," Elaine said to me. "And thousands of people are there *supporting* DS." She flipped on another wall screen to show news coverage of the outdoor event. A camera panned a crowd of wild DS supporters standing in front of the stage where my father was scheduled to speak. They waved signs and cheered at the cameras.

I stared at the scene with confusion. Supporters never attended press conferences. People who supported DS stayed quiet and safe and invisible behind their computers at home. They didn't leave their homes. As if Molly read my mind, she spoke up.

"We've never seen anything like this before," she said. "The only people that show up to these kinds of events are protesters."

The crowd covered the pavilion square, and the grounds were packed with people young and old chanting in support of DS. It made a chill run up my back.

"Where are all the protesters?" I asked.

"We don't know," Scott said flatly. "That's the problem. There should be hundreds of them there."

"Last we heard from Justin things were getting out of hand, but that was hours ago."

"Justin's there?" I asked, and felt goose bumps rise up on my arms.

"We can't reach him," Thomas said. "Pat's with him and we can't get a hold of Pat. Everyone we're trying to contact is cut off. Something isn't right."

"We're assuming it was a mass arrest," Scott said. "It's the only thing that would explain how we're suddenly cut off from everyone."

"We need to get him out of there," Elaine whispered.

"How much time do we have before the speech starts?" Thomas asked Scott.

"An hour, tops," Scott said, and looked straight at me. "Maybe you can convince your dad to let him go. Hand yourself over and take his place."

Thomas shook his head. "No. Justin would want himself arrested before we lose Maddie. She can do more for us."

I stared back at his father. But he's your *son*.

Molly rolled her eyes. "She can, hypothetically. She's done nothing at this point except be a risk to all of us." Her icy brown eyes flickered over to me. "And we're not going to waste time while she writes a pro and con list about whether or not to join our side while people that are actually fighting to make a difference are going to jail."

I narrowed my eyes at her and stood up.

"Then let's stop wasting time," I said. "I've been to some of these conferences. I might be able to help."

We quickly arranged for Clare and me to catch a plane to Portland. Minutes later we were in the car speeding to a private airport outside of town where Scott chartered a jet. During the drive we watched the press coverage of the event but it still seemed unbelievable.

Thomas scanned an ID card to open the airport entrance gates and we pulled up to the Jetway. He handed me a backpack with a flipscreen and phone inside. His eyes held mine for a moment before I got out of the car. A world of thought traveled in his expression and I nodded as I grabbed the backpack and sprinted after Clare.

When we sat down in the plane, Clare took something out of her pocket and handed it to me. It looked like a tube of lipstick.

I frowned at her. "Is this really the time to swap makeup?" I asked.

She grinned. "It's a hand taser. My parents make me carry one." She took the cap off and pointed to the metal edge. "If someone attacks you, you press the tip against their skin and it shoots out a charge."

I looked down at it. "Does it last long?"

She shook her head. "It's pretty harmless. Noah and Pat used to play taser tag around the house when I was growing up. It freezes people for about a minute, long enough to run away."

She told me it might come in handy. I thanked her and stuffed the tube in my jeans pocket.

We landed in Portland at another private airport and a black van was waiting for us, parked at the edge of the runway.

"Why don't we take a ZipShuttle?" I asked as we ran toward the car. "Wouldn't it be faster?"

Clare pulled me along. "Yes, but you can't use your fingerprint right now. The police are still looking for you. The second your fingerprint is scanned anywhere, you'll hear sirens."

I groaned as we got in the car. "Maybe I should have stayed behind," I said. "I'm more of a risk than anything right now."

Clare shook her head. "No, you're helping to bring back Justin. We all would risk anything for him."

Riley was in the driver's seat and told us my dad had just started his speech. The digital screen inside the car was on so we could watch the press conference.

"Has anyone heard from Justin yet?" I asked. Riley shook his head and said there wasn't a single protester there.

We crossed over Freemont Bridge toward the sky-rises of downtown Portland. I stared out the window, looking for a mob of supporters, but the city looked placid and still. The van twisted and turned, speeding past trains and ZipShuttles. We approached the historic downtown and sped down a street bordering the Willamette River. We slowed when we approached Waterfront Park, a wide green expanse along the river's edge and encircled by a border of synthetic shrubs and trees. In the distance I could see a stage and the unmistakable cluster of reporters and photographers that followed my dad around like a shadow.

Onstage, surrounded by the event security, my father made his presence. He stood behind a podium stacked high with microphones. About a hundred yards behind the stage was a cluster of people crammed together like cattle in a confined, rectangular space.

"So that's what happened to the protesters," Clare said. She flipped the channel on the screen in the car until Scott and Molly appeared, sitting in Scott's living room.

"It looks like an electric fence is holding them in," she said. "Have you ever seen anything like that?" She pointed the camera lens of her phone out the window so Scott could see it.

I stared out at the park but I didn't see the crowd of supporters.

"This couldn't be the right conference," I said to Riley. "Where are all the people?" I looked back at the screen. "Scott, what are you seeing?" He turned and looked at a screen behind him. From his viewpoint, there were thousands of people screaming and holding signs, cheering on my father's speech. I stared back at the stage. The park, except for the media and the contained protesters, was completely empty.

Riley pulled off to a side street and we all jumped out of the car. Clare still had Scott's image on her phone.

"There's no one here, Scott. What's going on?"

"That's impossible," he said. We headed down the street while we watched the news coverage on Riley's phone screen, still showing hordes of people. Clare scanned the area of the conference in front of us so Scott could see the reality. Not one single supporter.

Scott swore into the phone.

"I can't believe it," he said. "They're projecting an image of fans using a hologram. It's all a media hoax."

"They would never do that," I said, but after we cleared a row of trees, we noticed the wide blue screen stretching along the opposite side of the stage. When the cameras panned the empty screen, the rest of the country saw a crowd.

"They're containing all the protesters so they don't get in the way of the cameras," Scott pointed out.

"Very clever," Molly said.

"Why would they go to all the trouble to stage this?" I asked.

"To make society think everyone loves DS. You're a lot less likely to rebel against something when you think you're all alone," Scott pointed out.

As we got closer, we could hear my father's voice carried through the speakers mounted around the stage. I stared at him, humiliated that he could go along with such a blatant lie. It was all an act. And he *knew* it. He knew, yet he was still going through with it. He was a liar and a coward.

I looked over at the protesters. "How many people do you think are in there?" I asked.

Scott looked down on his monitor for a second. "About four hundred," he said.

I started to cross the street toward the park and headed straight for the security guard standing at the entrance of the gate. Clare grabbed my arm.

"Wait? What if your dad sees you?"

My eyes were wild as I scanned the crowd of protesters.

"I don't care. We need to get them out of there." I turned back and looked at Clare and Riley. "Listen, I need to do this by myself. There's no point in sticking together in case I get caught. I can't handle being responsible for all of you getting arrested in one day." I looked at Riley. "Why don't you figure out a way to get us out of here if this does work by some miracle?"

Riley nodded and said he'd hang back by the car. He put a cell phone in my hand.

"Justin will know what to do if you get him out," he told me.

I nodded and put the phone in my pocket. I looked at Clare but she shook her head and met my eyes stubbornly.

"I'm coming with you," she said. "You can't do this all by yourself." I knew she wouldn't back down so instead of wasting time arguing, I started to cross the street.

"Good luck," Riley called after us.

Clare and I crouched low behind a row of thick bushes to hide the best we could. My dad's back was to us as he talked out to the imaginary crowd. There were two security guards standing in front of the electric fence, one on either side. I squatted down and shrugged off the backpack.

"What are you going to do?" she asked.

"I don't know. I haven't stormed a lot of press conferences and tried to break through electric security gates."

"Maybe you could hack into the conference security and see if you can shut off the electric fence?" Clare offered.

I shook my head. "We don't have time for that," I said. "Besides, I'm sure Scott's tried already." I thought back to what Justin had said. How to take people by surprise by *not* depending on technology.

My father's voice boomed out around us as he began his closing statements. His voice always grew louder when he was drawing to a close. His exit to all of his speeches was to startle. To shock. To keep people faithful to his institution.

I peered around the edge of the shrub at one of the security guards. He was kicking the ground under his feet and looked more bored than intimidating. I scanned the people locked inside the fence, but I couldn't make out Justin or Pat. There had to be a way to shut off the gates. I glanced back at the security guard. He looked about my age, tall and lean. I smiled when an idea took shape.

"Let's do this the old-fashioned way," I said. I peeled off my jacket and stuffed it inside the backpack. I pulled my hair out of its ponytail and raked my fingers through, to make it fall long around me.

"What are you doing?" Clare asked. I looked back at Clare's large, quizzical eyes and hoped this would work.

"You take the security guard closer to the stage," I told her.

"Take him?" she asked.

"Distract him," I said. "Just give me thirty seconds, that's all I need. Keep his eyes off of that fence for thirty seconds."

"That's your plan?" she asked, and I nodded. She looked over at the guard and back at me. "How do I distract him?" she said.

"Flirt with him," I said. "Flash him. I don't care. Use your female powers of persuasion." Clare grinned, catching on to my idea.

"Maddie," she said before she turned away. Her face was serious. "Be careful. If anything happened to you, Justin would . . ." Her voice trailed off. "Just don't let anything happen to you. Promise?"

I nodded and promised her I'd be fine. I ushered her forward and pulled the backpack over my shoulders. We inched our way closer to the open turf grass, toward the barricade.

My heart was pounding in my chest. I could just make out the back of my father's head over the bodyguards that lined up behind him. Cameras were flashing. Standing there, I finally realized what effect my father had over me. It wasn't control. It wasn't intimidation. It was fear. Fear because my father, the one person who should love me no matter what, chose to confine me, to limit me. He created a world full of lies yet he asked me to trust him. And now, standing so close to him, I realized what I feared the most. If my father had to choose who he was loyal to, digital school or his own family, what would his choice be? The fact that I couldn't answer this question made me want to crumble right there, in the middle of the scene.

Instead, I tried to shift my anger into inspiration. Justin was right. Maybe I was here to be a balance. To keep my father in check. Maybe I was the only person brave enough to stand up to him. After all, fear is what fuels you to survive.

"Remember," my dad shouted. "Digital school is the cure to this country's issues of instability, insecurity, and inequality."

Clare and I ducked low behind a tall marble fountain, just on the other side of the fence.

"Under the digital school system," he shouted, "we are all equal. There are no more social distinctions. We are all the same. And that's the way life is intended."

I took a deep breath and prayed this would work.

"We all have the same rights," he shouted. "We all have the same chances. We all can succeed." He took long pauses between each sentence to leave time for his fictional fans to cheer.

I nodded for Clare to go and watched her from behind the fountain. She approached the security guard, who turned his back to the fence in order to talk to her. Once she had his full attention, I sauntered up to the other guard standing by the front gate. He raised his eyebrows when he noticed me and I offered him a wide smile.

"In a world where the future is unknown, let this be known— DS IS FREEDOM," my dad's voice rang out.

I could hear the buzzing from the electronic fence. The security guard cleared his throat.

"Can I help you?" he asked, his voice coarse. I smiled again.

"I have a huge favor," I said, and tossed my hair over one shoulder. His mouth relaxed a little. He pushed his sunglasses up on his forehead and his brown eyes looked me up and down. I took a step closer.

"What's that?" he asked with interest.

I twirled a piece of hair around my finger and smiled.

"DS IS EDUCATION AT ITS BEST," my dad's voice circled around me, like he was yelling right at me.

"I need you to do something for me," I teased. He grinned and his rigid shoulders settled and I knew I had him.

"Well, that depends what it is," he said.

I reached my fingers out and he lifted his hand high enough for me to grab it. His body jumped from the shock of the hand taser. He stumbled over to the ground, his eyes wide with surprise. I bent down and unclipped the holster around his waist, grabbing his gun.

"Sorry," I said. "I just can't have you messing this up right now." I aimed and fired a shot into his shoulder. The gun released a tiny syringe that pierced his skin and knocked him out. His body went limp on the grass.

I turned to the gates, my heart racing.

"DS IS PEACE," my dad shouted to the crowd. I stared up at my father and narrowed my eyes. I grabbed the guard's arm and pressed his fingers against an emergency release switch. The sensor registered his prints and opened the gates.

The electric fence snapped off with a loud crackle and instantly a moving wave of people flooded out. An alarm wailed through the air. I covered my hands over my years to muffle the piercing noise and tried to back away as people sprinted around me. My dad's head snapped around at the sea of people moving through the gate like water breaking through a dam. I saw a guard grab my father and drag him off of the stage, toward a security Zip-Shuttle. The photographers snapped pictures as rioters picked up the signs and banners lying in a heap next to the gates and stormed the steps. I was knocked over in the stampede. Shots rang out and people screamed, pushing and shoving each other. More shots. More screams. Legs and feet pummeled over and around me, stomping me to get to the stage. As I fought with all my strength to stand up, a hand grabbed me and yanked me off the ground.

I looked up at Justin and held on to his hand as we were pushed along with the moving crowd.

"What are you doing here?" he yelled over the noise. He looked furious. "Who sent you here?"

"*I* sent me," I yelled, and I tried to keep hold of his hand as we were pushed and pulled in separate directions.

"You shouldn't have risked it," he yelled back. I tightened my lips together. Leave it to Justin to be protective right now.

"I couldn't let you get arrested."

He looked down at me and his eyes were raging. "Don't worry about me. You're too important."

"No, you're too important."

"I can handle myself."

I gasped when a photographer elbowed me in the stomach. Justin shoved the photographer out of the way and pulled me tight to his side.

"Is this really the time to argue?" I asked when I got my voice back.

We continued to yell as we were pushed and shoved along. I tripped and Justin had to pull me up again before the stampede pummeled me. We reached the edge of the park and both turned back for a second to take in the scene. His angry features finally softened. He pointed to the mob of people in front of us.

"See what I mean about an avalanche?" he said. "This is what you can do."

I looked out at the sea of protesters yelling and using their voices. People stood with signs screaming for a change. A rioter climbed up onstage and she yelled into the microphones.

"Since digital school was established, people spend ninety-five percent less time communicating face to face," she yelled. "American parents spend eighty-five percent less time with their children.

DS ISN'T FIXING OUR PROBLEMS. IT'S JUST CREATING BIGGER ONES."

A roar of people cheered in agreement. Her voice echoed through the speakers before the audio was disconnected with a loud pop. I smiled to see with my own eyes the difference I could make. I wished I could see the look on my father's face right now. Justin grabbed my arm and started pulling me along behind him.

"You're welcome," I yelled at his back. He ignored me and focused on picking our way through people. I looked back at the gates and the security fence was turned on again. Police were trying to contain the rioters that were still screaming.

"Come on," Justin said. We cut through an open area of grass and sprinted toward the river. I ran after him, still dodging people, but it was open enough now to run. We sprinted over a grid of train tracks that curved along the harbor. I handed Justin the phone and he managed to dial a number while he was in full sprint. I pumped my legs and tailed along behind him.

"You've got Clare and Pat?" I heard him say. "Head for northeast. I don't want you guys ten miles from here. Meet me at Sandy Cove. You know where that is?"

We ran down to the harbor, where rows of commercial boats and private sailboats were docked, their sails pulled down, leaving only the skeleton outline of their casts pointing up to the sky.

Justin scanned the series of docks and something caught his eye. He ran down to the end of a pier and grabbed a surfscooter out of the back of a boat.

"It's not my first choice, but it will have to work." I blinked down at the scooter. I had seen them before. People ride them like a surfboard, but these have a motor attached to the back of the board and handlebars to guide the direction. I had seen people do flips and stunts with surfscooters on TV.

"What is it with you and water escapes?" I asked him.

He threw the board on the water. "I'll try and plan ahead better next time. Hop on." He extended his hand to me and I awkwardly climbed on the board, trying to find balance.

"Stop!" I heard a man's voice shout behind us. I turned around to see two security guards running down the dock.

"Hold on," Justin said. He pulled away from the pier just as we heard a gunshot. I squeezed my head against Justin's back as he turned the board around so we were facing the dock.

"That was a warning," one of the guards shouted. "Get back here or we'll make sure not to miss this time."

Both of their guns were aimed directly at me.

"It's not a crime to have an opinion," Justin yelled.

"We want the girl," the guard said. We idled there, in a small wake, the engine purring softly. The water sloshed us lightly back and forth but Justin kept his distance.

"Bring her back or we'll shoot."

I tightened my grip around Justin.

"I wouldn't recommend that," he said, calmly. I studied his profile and saw amusement in his eyes. He stared back at the security guards like he was daring them.

I could feel adrenaline rushing through my body and my hands were starting to sweat. I let my grip ease up around Justin's waist. It was quiet for a few seconds. All I could hear was water slapping the sides of boats docked along the pier.

"Use your head for just a second," Justin yelled. "If you shoot me, we'll tip over. And she can't swim." He nodded at me. "If you shoot her, she's got enough equipment in her bag to pull her straight to the bottom. And you know the penalty for killing an unarmed civilian."

The guards looked at each other and for a fraction of a second and in a brief moment, when their eyes were turned away, I pulled the gun out of my pocket. Two shots rang out. The guards fell over, stunned and limp on the grass.

I stared at the gun in my hand with shock and let it slip out of my shaking fingers and splash into the water.

CHAPTER twenty-five

"I'm really in trouble," I said.

Justin's wide eyes watched the gun sink below a ripple of small waves.

"I wasn't unarmed," I pointed out, as if that detail was still in question.

He stared at me over his shoulder. "Where did you learn how to shoot?"

"I told you, I took a self-defense class," I said.

He looked back over at the men lying asleep on the dock. "You shot two security guards."

He blinked a few times with bewilderment.

I glared at him. "Do you want to sit here and talk about it for a while, or do you want to get out of here?" Justin told me to hold on and he pointed the board out for open water. I fastened my arms tightly around his waist and we wove around the piers until we met the river and headed upstream with the current. The board rolled over waves and kicked up sprays of water around us.

We stayed close to the shore, but far off enough away to avoid piers and pools of harbors. I stared up at the iron bridges that passed us overhead and I looked out at the quiet labyrinth of sky-scrapers built up along the water's edge. If I wasn't running from the law, as usual, I might actually enjoy the view.

We continued north and buildings gave way to apartments and neighborhoods. Justin slowed down and I noticed a soft curve of beach cut out along the river, at the base of a sloping hill. When we hit the breaking waves, Justin took one head-on and we caught a jump. We landed with a splashing thud and I dug my fingers into his waist.

"Sorry," he said over his shoulder. "I couldn't help myself." He drove until we could see the sandy bottom and we both jumped off, our feet splashing into the cold water. He tossed the scooter on the beach and together we ran up a gravel path. The van was parked, waiting for us at the edge of the lookout. We hopped into the back seat and Riley skidded the car away. Pat sat in the front seat next to him.

Clare grabbed my hand as soon as I sat down. "Madeline, you are a genius!" she exclaimed.

"What is Madeline doing here?" Justin yelled at Riley. I stared at him and his eyes were still furious.

"Dude, we had to bring her."

"No—"

"Scott said it was the only way, man."

"Get Scott on the phone," Justin demanded.

A second later, Scott's body appeared on the digital screen. He was still in his living room, sitting next to Molly, with computer monitors surrounding them.

"Good to see you made it out of there," he said with a grin.

"You had no right—"

"I had to send her," Scott interrupted him, reading his thoughts. "You're worth a lot more to us than Madeline is right now."

"I would have been fine," Justin stated coldly.

"Yes, you are fine," Scott pointed out. "Everyone's fine so let it go. I had to call the shots on this one. You need to trust me."

Justin exhaled a long sigh and started untying his wet shoes.

"What the hell happened back there?" he asked.

"It was a media spoof," Scott said. "They set it up to look like a rally in support of DS. They used a hologram to project about twenty thousand supporters."

Justin pulled his fingers through his hair. "I really hate the news," he said.

"It's their latest ploy to make DS look stronger than ever," Scott said. "Nice timing too, since the nationwide vote's coming up this fall."

"What vote?" I asked.

Justin met my eyes. "People are pushing for DS to be a state-by-state vote, instead of a national law. But the government doesn't want that to happen. Too much control to lose."

He looked back at the screen. "So, that's why they held us hostage?" he asked.

Scott nodded. "They needed to keep you out of the camera's view."

Justin smirked. "That sounds like 'justice and freedom for all.'"

Clare shook her head. "They've never gone this far to brainwash people."

"In some ways it's good news," Molly said. "There must be more people uprising than ever for the media to plan something this elaborate." She looked over at me. "Nice job, Maddie," she said. "Thanks for helping us out." I offered her a single nod. We were never going to be friends, but at least she was starting to see where my loyalties lie.

Riley looked at me through the rearview mirror and demanded a breakdown of what we did. Clare and I laughed as we filled everyone in on the story. I glanced over at Justin a few times but he was less enthused. He stared out the window, his eyes lost in a world of his own thoughts.

❀

By the time we got back to Eden it was late and we were all exhausted. Thomas and Elaine were waiting outside for us when we drove up to the house. I was shocked to see how calm they both were. Thomas didn't even hug Justin, as if he never accepted the idea his son was so close to being arrested. I stared at them and wondered if they truly thought Justin was invincible.

My eyes and my mind were heavy and Elaine and Thomas told us we could catch up in the morning. Elaine squeezed my hand before I went upstairs.

"Thank you so much, Maddie," she said.

"Justin's saved me in more ways than I can count. I owed him," I said.

I pulled my legs up the stairs and threw myself down on the bed with exhaustion. The adrenaline was wearing off and I felt my eyelids drifting closed. A few minutes later, Justin walked into the room and shut the door behind him.

A long yawn escaped from my chest. "Knowing you has definitely made my life interesting," I said, and stretched out on the bed.

He crossed the room and stood by the window. He watched me but he kept his distance. I stuffed a pillow under my head and closed my eyes. I sighed and felt relief hit me to know Justin was here, in my presence. Safe. It was all I needed to feel complete again. Until now, I hadn't realized how unsettled I'd felt the last few weeks.

It was quiet for too long and I opened my eyes to find him still watching me. He slowly walked over to the bed and I scooted over to make room for him.

He lay down on his side and I squirmed closer but he didn't reach out for me. He just stared at me, his eyes liquid brown. I grinned sleepily at him.

"I know why you're mad," I said. He raised a single eyebrow and waited. "You're jealous that I flirted with that security guard."

He frowned at me. "Yep. That's it. I was going to shoot him if you didn't."

I pressed my finger over his warm lips and felt my chest heat up. "Now's not the time to be insecure."

His eyes turned serious and he moved my hand away. "You need to promise me something, Maddie."

"Maybe," I said. He tightened his fingers around mine and pushed me against the bed until he was leaning over me. His chest grazed the top of mine.

"You must never, ever, put yourself in danger to help me again. No matter what happens."

"But—"

"Promise me. You are worth too much to jeopardize yourself, ever. For me. All right?"

He looked so upset it made my voice crack in my throat. "Okay, I promise."

He took a long, defeated breath. Our eyes lingered over each other.

"Did you miss me?" I asked with a grin. I ruffled my fingers through his hair. My smile faded at the intensity of his eyes.

"Miss you?" he repeated. "It's a little stronger than that." He leaned into me and kissed my lips softly. I arched my neck to try to deepen the kiss but he pulled back so he could look at me. He slowly ran his hand up my arm and he winced, like my skin burned his fingers. "You're like fire in a way. You draw me in like fire does." He traced the outline of my jaw with a single finger. "I can feel heat coming off of you."

I nodded because I knew exactly what he meant.

"You're perfect," he told me. He picked up my hand and examined it. "Your fingernails drive me crazy."

"My fingernails?" I asked. I hated my fingernails more than anything.

He nodded. "Isn't that weird? I can't even concentrate when I look at your hands." He kissed each of my fingertips and I stared at him, waiting to wake up from this surreal dream.

"And these," he said as he rubbed his thumb against my lips. "Wow," he said with a shake of his head. "Incredible. Don't even get me started on the rest of you. I don't want to freak you out."

I searched his eyes. "Why are you telling me all this?" I asked.

He shrugged. "Because I want you to know how I feel."

He brushed his hand along my face and down my neck. My voice was stuck in my throat. I hated how every moment I had with Justin felt like it could be my last.

"Then why do I feel like you're always trying to say goodbye?" I asked.

He let out a long sigh. "Because I won't let anything happen to you. I need you to be safe. You're never going to be safe with me."

I needed him to know how I felt so I just kissed him as long as he would let me. I used to think talking was all about words. But you can say so much more with your eyes and your fingers and your touch. Words just make us one-dimensional.

CHAPTER twenty-six

"You shot two cops!" Elaine shouted over the table.

Everyone helped themselves to breakfast the next morning. We sat at the kitchen table and sunshine streamed through the windowpanes and painted streaks of light across the room.

"Three," Clare added.

I took a long, exasperated breath. "For the millionth time, I didn't *shoot* anybody. I *stunned* them. And they were staff security. Appreciate the difference."

"I think you've earned yourself a gunner nickname," Pat told me. "How about Mad Hand Maddie?" I tightened my lips together and glared but it only encouraged him. "Magnum Maddie? Madeline the Barbarian?"

"How about we change the subject?" I suggested. "I'm not exactly proud of what I did."

"I was watching the news this morning," Thomas said. "According to the report, Oregon state will be surveying students this year to get their feedback on digital school."

"It's about time," Justin said.

"Justin," Elaine said, "when are you going to tell Madeline the good news?"

I looked over at Justin and raised my eyebrows. He took a bite of his waffles, obviously in no hurry to tell me anything. Clare tapped her foot on the floor next to me.

"It's almost time. Aren't you going to tell her?" Clare asked.

I looked around at a table of grinning faces. It appeared everyone was in on this *except* me.

I crossed my arms over my chest. "Tell me what?"

A corner of Justin's lips curled up.

"What are you two plotting?" I asked.

"Justin's been working on it for a few weeks," Clare said.

He stood up and motioned for me to follow him. I scooted my chair back and Clare and I both walked through the pantry door and headed downstairs, to the corner of the basement. He picked up a flipscreen off the table and typed something into it.

"What's the surprise?" I asked. Clare sat down on the couch and patted the seat next to her.

"You'll see," she said. I creased my eyebrows and sat down. Clare clasped her hand in mine and her wide eyes focused on the wall screen. Justin pressed a few more buttons on the computer and suddenly the giant screen turned on and cast a blue glow across the room.

"Somebody wants to talk to you," Justin said. He stood up and walked over to the wall screen and pressed a code into a panel on the wall.

"Can you hear me?" he asked, and a voice responded.

"Loud and clear."

Justin nodded and pressed another button and my brother's face filled the screen.

"Joe!" I said. I jumped off the couch until I was kneeling on the floor, in front of the screen.

He smiled back at me. His face was a perfect mix of my mom and dad—he had my dad's dark hair, which he spiked at the top, and he had my mom's light blue eyes and smile.

"Hey, little sister. Or, convict should I say?"

I rolled my eyes and decided to ignore his comment, since he could always beat me at the insult game.

"I can't believe it's you," I said. I hadn't web-chatted him since Christmas. But, no matter how long we went without talking, we naturally bounced back to a joking rhythm.

I studied his spiky hair. "You're so Hollywood now," I said.

"You think?" he asked.

"You look good," I said.

Joe looked down at his shirt and nodded. "I know." He grinned back at me for a second but then his face fell and his eyes turned serious. "How are you holding up?"

"I'm fine," I said, which was my programmed response to everything. It was still taking time to remember I didn't always have to react that way.

"You left quite a big mess for us to clean up," he said.

"Has Dad announced my prison sentence yet?" I asked, not entirely joking.

He shook his head. "You're lucky. Dad's connections always pay off."

"What connections?"

"You might not be as bad off as you think. Since the only people that know you ran off were Paul and Damon, and since they happen to worship Dad like he's a man-god, they're willing to negotiate keeping your escape private."

"What? You mean—"

"You're not off the hook yet." Joe fought a smile. "You broke probation, and then you managed to escape and run away from your parole officer. That's a big no-no. Then you left Paul to get his ass kicked by two hillbillies."

"He pushed me down on the ground," I pointed out.

"You probably had it coming," Joe replied.

I frowned at this. "Sorry I wasn't more submissive about being hauled off to a detention center."

My brother shook his head. A small smile curved on his lips. "I can see the repentance you feel for what you did. Anyway," he continued, "Dad and the Thompsons worked out a deal, probably involving a little money under the table. Conveniently for you, there's a detention center in Los Angeles. Dad and Damon worked it out so you've been reassigned here."

I thought over what he said and frowned. "So, I'm supposed to agree to live in a detention center in L.A.? How is that any better than Iowa? What, will there be celebrities at this one?"

Joe leaned forward. "Just listen. Since when did you get so feisty?"

Since forever, I wanted to say.

"We're only going to make it look like you're at the detention center. You can appear to be anyone, anywhere these days with Dad's contacts. But what's really going to happen is you'll come down to L.A. and live with me. You can finish DS and even look for an internship down here. As far as the law goes, you'll be in L.A. in case they need to track you down. You just won't be in the detention center, exactly."

My mouth fell open. "I'm going to live with you? In Los Angeles?"

"I know, sibling rivalry rears its ugly head. If you'd prefer the detention center, I totally understand."

"Joe, I'd love it. Do you have room?"

He shrugged. "Sure, I have a two-bedroom."

"And you're okay with this?"

"Well." He thought this over and rubbed his chin between his fingers. "You might have to clean my apartment every day and do all my laundry and run all my errands. But I'm willing to let you crash as long as you vow to be my personal slave."

"Done!" I agreed. He raised an eyebrow.

"Maddie, I'm kidding."

I looked over at Justin. He stood against the wall with his arms crossed over his chest watching me.

"You better have a couch for me to crash on," Clare suddenly spoke up.

He nodded at her and looked back at me. "If you can manage to behave until you're eighteen, you're a free woman. Then you can go wherever you want."

My heart was hammering in my chest. "When can I come?"

Joe smiled. "Is tomorrow too soon?"

I clasped my hands over my mouth.

"Tomorrow?"

He nodded. "You're supposed to already be in the detention center, so we can't have you swiping your fingerprint on any public transportation. I'm meeting you halfway to pick you up."

I dropped my hands to the floor. "Joe, thank you so much. I can't believe you arranged all this."

Joe frowned. "I didn't do anything. No offense, but fixing your yearly felony charges isn't my top priority. This was all set up by Mom and Justin. I got a phone call two weeks ago and had to say yes or no."

"What?"

"Justin called Mom the day after you escaped. We always knew you were safe."

"Dad knew where I was?"

Joe shook his head. "He didn't know where. He just knew you were all right. Believe it or not, he does care about you."

"But he was banishing me—"

"Yeah, and he probably would banish you again if you show up at his doorstep. He'd lose his job if he didn't. But Mom and Justin worked out a way around it." Joe's face turned serious again. "Personally, I think Dad's relieved you're not going to a detention center and I swear Mom's proud of you. Even though she'd never admit it. Dad would flip out. Do you ever wonder how they stay married?"

I looked down at the ground and shook my head.

"Joe, I don't know what to say."

"Say I'll see you tomorrow."

I nodded.

"Try and stay out of trouble until then." His eyes flickered over to Justin for a moment and his image disappeared from the screen. Clare joined me on the floor and I wrapped my arms around her. All the heavy thoughts in my head evaporated knowing I'd be with my brother, I'd be safe again, and that there was a chance my parents forgave me. Justin stood against the wall, his arms still crossed. He was staring at the screen, where the image of my brother had been seconds before. Clare looked between the two of us and stood up, making the excuse that she had to call Noah to tell him the news. She went upstairs and left us alone. I stood in front of the couch and stared at Justin.

He finally spoke. "So this sounds okay?" he asked.

"Okay? This is—"

I threw my hands up in the air because it was too good to be true. I was getting a second chance. I was being handed my life back.

"I can't believe you called my mom."

Justin nodded as if I should have expected this. "I wanted your parents to know you were safe."

"And my dad went along with all of this? He doesn't negotiate with anyone."

"Well," Justin said. "Technically your dad can't prove I assisted in your escape. As far as he knows, I'm innocent on that end. He thinks you're the one that came to us that night. And it helps that your mom's the one that did the talking. I never spoke to your dad."

"What about yesterday?"

He shrugged. "I honestly don't think he knew you were at the rally. There were no cameras around the security gates. No one got your picture or scanned your fingerprint. You dropped the gun in the ocean. You're a natural, I guess."

"But your fingerprint was scanned, Justin. My dad's going to find out you were there."

He took a step toward me. "Let me worry about that. I have a few connections of my own. My record will be cleared before people trace anything back to me."

I nodded. "That's right, your dad."

He nodded. "He's a good person to know."

I took a step closer to him but his eyes quickly narrowed with an edge that was too familiar. He was being cautious again.

"I need to do some work, but plan on leaving early tomorrow."

His face was emotionless as he turned away. The shields were back up. I could already feel him distancing himself. Maybe seeing me so happy hurt Justin. Or maybe he was starting to distance himself already, to avoid hurting me.

❀

The rest of the day Justin was nowhere to be seen. I got through the hours in a daze, the idea of moving to L.A. still a dream. I went through the motions of thanking Elaine and Thomas for their hospitality, of saying goodbye to Clare and promising to call her as soon as I got to L.A. But it all felt scripted, as if this wasn't really my life. I went up to my bedroom but it only took a few minutes to pack. I shook my head at what little possessions I had, shocked that what I thought was so necessary only months ago was now a lifetime away. It was the people in my life, the real, physical presence of people that I needed, so much more than material things. I couldn't believe I had settled for so long being satisfied with a partial existence.

When the house quieted down from motion and people and noise, I sat next to the window and looked out at the ocean. I noticed my journal on the bed and stared down at it. I was starting to see it as a friend, like someone I could always open up to without being judged or questioned. I sat down in bed and curled up, turning to a blank page.

August 11, 2060

My life has become consistently inconsistent. And I'm okay with that because my one consistency is how I feel about you. All you need is one safe anchor to keep you grounded when the rest of your life spins out of control.

But are you right? Can love really expand so you can always carry it with you? Because I don't want to leave you behind.

You make me want to get my fingernails dirty. You make me want to see life raw, for what it is, not the digital makeup we paint over life to make it what we want it to be. You make me want to be freezing cold and blazing hot. You make me want to feel.

You make my dangerous ideas sound better than my rational ones. You make me want to think for myself.

You make me want to open myself up and abolish the slavery of wires. You make me want to disengage. You make me want to live.

So what happens now? Without you, I feel like I might trip and fall. I don't want to resurface without you. I've always had fantasies about falling in love. Like castles in the sky that you think are all just a fairy tale. But you helped me tour those castles. Now I want to live inside them.

I'm not safe anymore. I'm no longer hiding in a digital world where I can choose my own ending and never mess up. I know I can't learn anything worthwhile without leaving this safe place. But what does L.A. have in store for me?

Do you have to turn in your old life to start a new one? Is Justin right, that our souls are scattered and life is about searching for all the missing pieces? Is that what makes us whole?

CHAPTER twenty-seven

I tapped my pen on the bedspread and looked at the clock. It was 2:30 a.m. I was miles from sleep. I tossed my journal aside and leaned against the wall. I could feel him on the other side. That's where I wanted to be. On his side. And I was wasting precious time.

I shoved my covers off and tiptoed down the cold hardwood floor in my bare feet. I opened his bedroom door and could feel the energy inside meet my skin like a gust.

I heard Justin move on the bed and as soon as I closed the door behind me I felt a warm hand grab my arm and another hand pulled me down on the sheets. His arms wove their way around me and pulled me against him.

"You've been ignoring me," I whispered.

He shook his head. "I wanted you to get some sleep."

I rubbed my fingertips against the scars I knew were under his T-shirt.

"Are you mad at me?" he said in the darkness. I could feel his eyes studying me.

"Mad isn't the word for how you make me feel," I said honestly.

304

His hand traced the edge of my face.

"I'm sorry," he said.

"For what, exactly?" I asked. "For avoiding me our last night together, or for never calling the last three weeks while you were away?"

He leaned forward until his lips were in my hair and he sighed. "This is exactly why I didn't want to fall for you," he said.

"It's a little late for that."

His dark eyes could smolder even in the dark. "You mean more to me than you realize. Do you know the day I met you how hard it was to keep a level head when I was around you? I'd love to have you in my life every day, but I started something I have to finish. I can't be there for you, Maddie. And you deserve that. You deserve someone that can live for you, every day. But I can never put you first. And I don't want you getting involved in my life. It's too dangerous. What happened in Portland was only a taste."

My mouth tightened stubbornly. "Just so you know, it's okay to invest in yourself once in a while."

He shook his head. "I don't think about myself. It's so hard to explain," he said. "Not many people see life like I do."

I turned on my side and stared at him. "Try me."

He traced his hand slowly up my side. His touch made my skin tingle.

"Think about our bodies. We're a chain of veins and organs and they're all interconnected. If something isn't going right in one area, the whole system can get out of whack. That's the way I see the world. We're all connected. I don't see myself as this separate entity. I see things in a much larger scale. Everything I do directly affects another person, all the way down the chain. Every person I help can help another; we're all connected. Change happens one person at a time. And I want to commit my life to seeing that through."

I studied his profile. "You're the one that says you need to have a balance, that one extreme isn't any better than another. So I'm willing to compromise but you need to open yourself up. You're great at giving yourself, Justin, but let people give themselves to you once in a while. Because someday, when your life slows down, you're going to look around at all the great things you've done and the people you've touched and you might go down as a hero. But no one would have ever wanted your life. Because you'll be alone."

He narrowed his eyes at me. Then a grin slowly played on his face.

"Why are you smiling?"

"Do you think you would have said that before you met me?"

I looked down at his chest and didn't answer him.

"Maybe you're right," Justin said. "Maybe I need more of a balance. But I'm not going to slow down anytime soon. I'm just getting started."

"So am I," I said.

I met his eyes and smiled because I could be just as persistent as him at getting what I wanted.

❖

The next morning Justin woke me as the sun was barely starting to rise. I got dressed and grabbed my duffel bag and quietly followed him outside. We pulled away from the large Victorian home full of dark windows and people inside still asleep. I watched the trees waving in the pink light of the morning sky. I threw the sweatshirt hood over my head and sat back deep in my seat.

We drove along the coastal highway, trains zipping past us every few minutes. We rarely passed a car. My foot tapped anxiously as we inched our way closer to where we were meeting Joe.

"When will I see you again?" I asked.

He hesitated before he answered me. "I don't know for sure. I'll be gone a while. People are starting to fight DS being a national law. Which is really good news, but it's going to be a lot of work."

I stared down at our fingers, interlocked together so I couldn't tell where my skin ended and his began.

"I have to get back to my routine," he added. "It's rare for me to ever be in one place more than a day or two. I told you that."

I took a deep breath. I knew this was a hopeless argument. I loved Justin for how passionate he was, how committed, how loyal. I knew what he did defined him so I could never try to hold him back. I knew his idea of love was trusting people enough to let them go. So I said the only thing I knew for certain.

"I'll miss you."

He looked at me.

"Don't," he said, like it was easy. "I don't want you to waste your time missing me. You're only seventeen. Your life is just starting. If you think too much about the future, about seeing me again, you won't experience anything. You'll just be a slave to time."

I turned and looked out the window. I couldn't make sense of my mind because it was warring with my heart. It was so strange to argue with someone when all I wanted to do was love them.

I watched him closely. "You asked me to join your side."

He nodded. "And that decision is yours to make."

"If I choose you, if I agree to help you out, then can we be together?"

"Don't do that. Don't factor me in to this. It's a larger decision than that. It's not as simple as me versus them. It's your life—it's how you want to live and what impact you want to make."

I felt sadness rise in my chest as I listened to Justin. I was sick of being so frustrated with everyone I tried to love.

We turned off the highway and pulled to a rest stop where another car was waiting. My heart was pulled in two directions to see my brother standing next to his car in the sunshine. When we stopped I jumped out of the car and ran into Joe's arms. I knocked him off balance with surprise.

"Maddie, when did you become such a sap," he joked, and hugged me tightly.

Justin walked up to us and I noticed Joe's back stiffened. He thanked Justin for dropping me off and extended his hand, but his mouth tightened into a straight line. Justin shook his hand and told him it was no problem.

"I'm glad she can stay with you," Justin said.

"Thanks for organizing everything," Joe offered.

Justin nodded and put his hands in his pockets. Joe watched him with a cool edge to his eyes.

"Can you give me a minute?" I asked Joe.

He nodded. "I'll be in the car," he said. He glanced once more at Justin before he turned away. I saw a look pass between them, like a subtle understanding.

We walked back to the car and Justin grabbed my duffel bag out of the back seat. The sun beat down on us in the cloudless sky, but I had never felt more shadows fall around me.

I took the bag from him and felt hot tears pool in my eyes. They slowly streamed down my face and Justin rubbed his thumbs over my cheeks to catch them. He wrapped me in his arms.

"I promise I'll find you," he said. I nodded and let go of him. "Have fun in L.A. Make the most of it."

I turned and looked at my brother's car. The engine was running. I thought about speaking my mind and saying the things I needed to say and what a relief it is to let the heaviest words go. There was a word that sat in my heart like a weight pulling me down. I thought about what I would say right now if I could instantly delete it. Except I didn't want to delete it, I wanted it out there, because that was the good stuff. So, before I could hesitate,

I wrapped my arms around Justin and he leaned down to me. He kissed me and before I let him go I pressed my wet cheek against his warm one.

"I love you," I whispered in his ear. I felt his head nod slowly against mine. I leaned away and fixed my eyes on him. "I'm just being honest." His lips curled up on one side but his eyes were frustrated, like he was still trying to fight this. I wondered how often Justin heard those words. I'd never once heard his parents say they loved him. And he deserved to hear it. We all did.

I took a deep breath and turned forward to face my new life. I slid into the car seat next to Joe and closed the door behind me. My brother looked at my tearstained face.

"Looks like we have a lot to catch up on," he said.

I wiped my eyes. "You have no idea."

"You have no idea how hard it was to rent a car, even in L.A." I laughed through my tears and felt torn, elated to be sitting next to my brother but also a little broken, like a piece of me was falling away.

"You ready for this?" Joe asked. I nodded and held my chin high. My brother turned out of the parking lot and as we entered the highway, I looked out at the western horizon. I saw a seagull in the sky, hovering above the water, and despite everything, I couldn't help but smile. It was a sign something exceptional was going to happen.

Acknowledgments

First, a huge thanks to my agent, Helen Breitwieser, for loving my book and seeing so much potential in my writing. More than anything, thanks for the endless encouragement you gave me along the way—you believed in this book more than anyone. Second, an enormous thanks to Julia Richardson, my editor, for your vision and feedback that helped make this book shine. Thank you to Jennie Bartlemay, my very first editor, for your honest comments and feedback. Thanks to everyone at Houghton Mifflin Harcourt who helped design and market *Awaken.* Thank you to the entire staff of Red Horse Coffee Company for fueling my body with caffeine and my mind with encouragement throughout this entire process, and thanks to Damian Kulp for helping to build and design my author website. I also can't thank my parents enough for all of their love and support through this journey.

Lastly, thanks again and again to Adam. I would not have written this book without you. Thanks for making me leave my comfort zone when I was ready to settle (think of all the experiences we would have missed). Thanks for believing in me more than I believe in myself.